T0146478

IF THE SHOE
KILLS

Books by Lynn Cahoon

If the Shoe Kills
Mission to Murder
Guidebook to Murder

IF THE SHOE
KILLS

LYNN CAHOON

KENSINGTON BOOKS
KENSINGTON PUBLISHING CORP.
www.kensingtonbooks.com

KENSINGTON BOOKS are published by

Kensington Publishing Corp.
119 West 40th Street
New York, NY 10018

All Kensington titles, imprints, and distributed lines are available at special quantity discounts for bulk purchases for sales promotion, premiums, fund-raising, educational, or institutional use.

Special book excerpts or customized printings can also be created to fit specific needs. For details, write or phone the office of the Kensington Special Sales Manager: Kensington Publishing Corp., 119 West 40th Street, New York, NY 10018. Attn. Special Sales Department. Phone: 1-800-221-2647.

Kensington and the K logo Reg. U.S. Pat. & TM Off.

First Electronic Edition: November 2014
eISBN-13: 978-1-60183-240-5
eISBN-10: 1-60183-240-0

First Print Edition: November 2014
ISBN-13: 978-1-60183-306-8
ISBN-10: 1-60183-306-7

Printed in the United States of America

CHAPTER 1

The holidays were supposed to be a time of goodwill, celebration, and community. You couldn't tell it from the glares going around the table as Mayor Baylor talked. Earlier, the leader of our little town had the group eating out of his hand. Then all hell broke loose. Focusing on the uproar going on at the Business-to-Business monthly meeting, I wondered if the shop owners gathered around the mismatched tables had even seen the calendar. As South Cove's council liaison, I volunteered my shop each month for the meeting. I'm Jill Gardner, owner of Coffee, Books, and More, and president of the I-Hate-Mayor-Baylor Club. A red-faced Bill Simmons, chair of the business council and owner of South Cove Bed-and-Breakfast, stood at the front of the table, trying to get the group to quiet down.

Aunt Jackie issued a shrill, earsplitting whistle, two-finger variety. My aunt could make me smile even in the worst situations. She'd been a rock the last year during all the craziness that had been my life. Now I didn't know what I'd do without her help with Coffee, Books, and More. Or without seeing her on a daily basis.

The room finally quieted. I'd been the city council liaison with the business community in our little coastal California tourist town for the last five years. I'd never heard this kind of uproar over a mayor's mandate before. Maybe the Honorable Mayor Baylor was losing a bit of his power over the group.

"Look, I know it's a bad time for many of us to take on a charity project, but think of it this way, you'll have an extra pair of hands for the season." Bill pulled out what he'd thought would be his trump card.

"I don't understand what you're all so upset about. I got you free help for the busiest season of the year." Mayor Baylor glared at me, like their reaction was my fault. "These people want to work. We need to be charitable in our attitude." This time, his scowl was full-on directed at me.

I put on my sweetest smile, the one I saved for the few customers I truly didn't like. "I've already signed up the coffee shop to participate. How about the rest of you?"

"Not all of us have South Cove's finest working part-time in our shops." Darla Taylor, owner of the winery and editor of the local news for the *South Cove Examiner*, sniffed. "I heard he couldn't place these losers anywhere else so Ted paid the mayor to take on these stragglers."

"That is totally unfounded speculation," Mayor Baylor blustered, his face turning a bright shade of scarlet. He turned his stare from me to Darla. "I hope I won't see anything close to that being reported in the *Examiner*."

I turned my head so no one would see my smile widen. As one of the local media, Darla's nose for rumors was spot-on. Ted Hendricks, program director for Bakerstown's welfare-to-work program, Work Today, had come to our tourist town of South Cove with an offer. Ten participants would work for eight weeks with a local business in an intern capacity. South Cove was their last chance.

The mayor's gaze shifted down the table, landing on Josh Thomas, a strong Mayor Baylor supporter. Except even I could see that His Honor wasn't winning any points with his friend today.

"Delinquents. You want me to let a delinquent run wild in my store. Talk to my customers and probably scope out my merchandise so they can rob me blind when I turn my back?" Josh owned Antiques by Thomas, the most recent business to open its doors on Main Street. Today, he pounded a chubby finger on the table.

"Of course, you'd have a problem with this. You don't even know that they are kids, or if they had trouble with the law. Just because someone is down on their luck doesn't mean they are a bad person," Sadie Michaels shot back. Sadie, owner of Pies on the Fly, was my main supplier of desserts for the coffee shop. And a strong advocate for the underdog in any fight.

We'd gone down this path before. Josh and Sadie rarely saw eye to eye on any discussion. For my part, I liked the way she called him on his prejudice and narrow-mindedness. Bill tried again to short-circuit the argument he saw developing. "We don't have time for a political discussion on the topic. This is a done deal. They're coming today for the initial meet-and-greet with a walk through town. Three hours on two weeknights, and six hours on Saturday. Even if you just had them stock shelves, at least they'd be learning about retail and our special niche as a tourist destination."

I jumped into the fray. "We only need three more host businesses. We've already had seven businesses volunteer. The mayor's office is even participating." My friend Amy, who did most of the clerical work for the city as well as served at the city planner, was ecstatic to have a little help, even if it was only for a few hours a week.

Aunt Jackie set a slice of cheesecake in front of Josh. They'd been dating off and on since the summer. He wanted more on, she kept saying she wanted the off. She smoothed his black suit jacket with her hand, brushing lint off the sleeve. "You could use help organizing your store. Just think of what all you could get done with some young elbow grease."

Josh peered up at my aunt and I swear I saw his heart melting, just like the big green monster in the Christmas story. "Fine, I'll take one." He sounded like he was agreeing to foster a shelter animal, rather than a person.

Darla waved her hand. "I've got plenty of work at the winery. But let's try to match me with someone who doesn't have alcohol issues." I wrote her name down. I didn't even care if she was taking on an intern for news fodder, which I suspected. Now I just had to clear the caveat with Ted Hendricks, the program director.

I searched the faces of the group gathered around the table, drinking coffee and, except for a few who had already volunteered, not meeting my eyes. I needed one more placement. Ted would be here in less than thirty minutes to finalize the plans.

Sadie spoke first. "Sorry. I'd take one, but the work with the bakery is first thing in the morning. I wouldn't have anything for them to do on evenings or weekends. That's the time I devote to Nick and the church."

Sadie ran Pies on the Fly out of a remodeled garage behind her house. Calling her business a bakery was a little generous.

Marie Jones, the owner of The Glass Slipper, had her head down, trying to curl up in her seat, apparently hoping I wouldn't see her. I could even see her lips moving in some sort of chant. I watched her closely, wondering if she was a fan of the Serenity Prayer, the favorite of alcoholics everywhere. Finally she glanced up, maybe feeling the weight of the entire table as they turned their attention to her.

"What?" she stammered.

"Could you take an intern?" I liked the term that Ted had used to describe his charges, not typical work-study, but not helper, either. And if they weren't technically interns, no one cared. As long as there wasn't trouble.

"I don't know." Marie's eyes darted from one person to the next. "I have several classes coming up this next month and I don't have time to babysit someone."

"I bet the intern could help you with your classes. Maybe helping slower students or bringing in supplies, or even setting up the room each day." My voice sounded excessively chipper, like I was a game show host, describing what was behind door number two if Marie chose to accept our offer.

"That's a great idea. People love craft projects. Maybe she'll even sit in on the classes herself." Darla smiled at Marie. "You're very generous with your time."

Marie must have known she was being played. I saw her form a response, then she just sank back into her chair, defeated. "I guess."

"Great." I glanced down at my schedule. "Ted's bringing the gang at five. I'm taking the group on a walking tour of town first, then dropping each person off at their assigned store, where you'll have about fifteen minutes to get to know each other. Then I'm hosting a small get-together here at the store. Coffee and cheesecake."

Looking up, I saw Marie's face had gone white. I started to backpedal, thinking that two meetings today must be overwhelming the woman's natural shyness. "You don't have to come, but you're more than welcome."

She took a deep breath, the tension in her body visibly easing a bit. Then she mumbled, "There must be more than one Ted in the world."

"Excuse me?" I frowned, leaning forward.

She looked me straight in the eye. And lied. "I've got a class tonight."

I wasn't going to challenge her, not when I'd just won a spot for our last participant. No use looking for cracks after you've bought the house, my grans always said. Of course, that piece of advice had gotten me stuck in a loveless marriage for too many years.

"Then we're settled. The only other order of business is assigning the chair for the Holiday Festival." Darla waved her hand. The assignment was a formality; everyone knew Darla would be the chair. She'd been in charge of planning the theme and decorating for years before I even moved to South Cove.

"I've got some great ideas this year. I'm thinking a Beach Boys Christmas to play off our successful Beach Boys Summer Fun Festival." She glanced around at the people surrounding the table. "So, is everyone cool with that?"

Bill coughed and then said, "Well, you see, Mrs. Baylor wants to be involved this year."

Darla leaned back in her chair. "I don't understand. Of course she can be part of the committee. We could always use an extra pair of hands."

Bill stacked the papers on the table in front of him. He gazed at the winery owner with genuine sadness in his eyes. "That's the thing—"

Before he could finish his sentence, Mayor Baylor interrupted. "I'm sorry, Darla, Tina's got experience in this type of thing. She used to plan all her sorority parties. I think it's time we brought in a professional. South Cove needs the boost to draw in new visitors."

Darla focused a glare at the portly man. "You're telling me she's chairing the festival? Because putting up college banners around an old sorority house is 'professional experience'?"

The mayor nodded, then glanced at his watch. "Exactly. I knew you would understand."

"Kind of like in an honorary position, right?" Darla wasn't giving in easily. I could feel the tension in the group as they watched the back-and-forth.

"No. Tina's determined to correct all the mistakes of the past and she says the only way to do that is by completely redesigning the project. Or whatever. She'll be contacting each of you for your assignments, and I hope you'll give her your full cooperation." The mayor glowered at me, again.

Taking my cue, I fumbled for words. "I'm sure Tina will do a great job with organizing this year's festival."

That response earned me a dirty look from Darla.

The mayor stood. "I've got a lunch engagement in the city or I'd stay to meet with Ted." He tossed an envelope toward me. "That's the contract for the session. Please make sure he gets it."

Then he strode out of the shop, the bell over the door banging in his wake.

Darla started yelling at Bill before the bell stopped chiming. "Is he freaking kidding? And you let him get away with this?"

"Calm down, Darla. Honestly, it was time for you to let someone else handle the burden of the committee. And we don't know, she might do a good job." Bill glanced around the room. "If there's nothing else, I need to get back to the B&B, we've got a full house this week."

"But I thought we were going to discuss animal control today. I know a bunch of feral cats have taken up in the empty apartment in my building," Josh called after him.

Bill didn't even slow down; he took off out of the shop just like the mayor had, but turned left instead of the other man's right turn.

"This meeting is a joke," Josh muttered, pushing away from the table. "Nothing I want to discuss ever gets on the agenda."

"There's a lot of stuff we have to discuss," I said, feeling guilty. I'd been putting his e-mails in a file. The round file cabinet on my floor called the trash.

He shot me a look that would have melted my face if he'd had a superpower. He nodded to Aunt Jackie and lumbered through the door.

Darla didn't even say good-bye as she left, her fingers twitching around the file she'd brought, probably filled with theme ideas. Darla loved turning the little town into a storyland. Each Christmas season, she'd brought a new look to the street. The first year I'd lived here, the theme had been *A Christmas Carol* and she'd even hired a band of carolers, dressed in era-appropriate costumes. I'd felt like I'd walked back in time, even though the snow was fake.

"She's upset." Sadie stated the obvious as she started collecting paper cups off the tables.

"I think it's more than upset." Aunt Jackie snorted. "The mayor had better watch his back or he'll be found dead on City Hall's steps, dressed up like a holiday turkey."

"Maybe we can talk to him. Ask him to at least add Darla back on the planning committee." I moved a table back to its regular spot. "He had to have noticed how hurt she felt by being cut off."

"He won't care. Men always get what they want." Marie's small voice drew my eyes toward her where she stood near the window, watching the street. "You can't stop them once they make up their mind."

Sadie, Jackie, and I stopped cleaning. I hadn't even known Marie was still in the shop. "That's not always true. Men don't have any more power than women do. It's just he's the mayor." I watched as Marie turned back toward me, tears filling her eyes.

"You're wrong." With that, she fled out of the shop and into the street. I watched her get halfway across before I heard the horn.

CHAPTER 2

Ted Hendricks sat in my office, drinking a second glass of water. "I didn't see her before she was right in front of me. She didn't even look before she darted out from the sidewalk."

I sipped on a cup of coffee even though I didn't need the caffeine after the jolt I'd gotten. "You have quick reflexes, thank God." Marie had missed being squashed by a second. Then, as I'd watched in horror, she'd taken one look at the driver and fled into her shop.

"I guess some people are just lucky." He finished his water, then focused on the page of work sites in front of him. "I've got to get back to town soon, so let's go over these."

With that one statement, the near miss in the street had been dismissed. The guy was cool, maybe even cold. I shook my head; no use labeling people before I knew them. Maybe Ted was just good at compartmentalizing, like most men. I ran down the list and the possible activities each "intern" would be doing at the jobs. When I got to Darla's winery, I paused.

"The owner has asked for a non-drinker." I blushed. "Well, they don't have to be a non-drinker, I meant someone without . . ."

Ted laughed and held up his hand. "I get it. You don't want the guy with the felony DUIs working at the winery. You know, I do think about the placements, even when I'm short on time, like now."

"Of course." I glanced at my watch. Ten more minutes and we'd be done. I could barely keep up a rational conversation with the man. He was drop-dead gorgeous in that I-wanna-be-a-movie-star way. I wondered if he'd been on the actor track when he was younger. So many people moved to California believing their future was on the big screen, then stayed for the laid-back culture and beautiful weather.

Ted tapped his pen on the page. "I didn't realize you had a glass shop here. Stained or blown glass?"

"Actually, I think she does both. Recently she's won prizes for her stained-glass pieces." I thought about Darla and her rant about Marie's refusal to do an interview for the *Examiner*. "The woman who runs the shop is very shy, though." I didn't mention she was also the one that had almost become a hood ornament on Ted's red Mustang convertible earlier today. Marie could tell him that herself.

Ted seemed lost in thought, then glanced at his watch again. "I'm sure we can make these work. I'd hoped for a bit more depth in the assignments, but beggars can't be choosers." He grinned and for a minute, the man resembled a tiger focused on his prey. "At least that's what they say."

He stood, clearly done with the discussion.

"So tonight I thought I'd take them on a tour of the town and then host the participants here for a welcome to South Cove get-together." I stood, too, following him out of the office into the front of the shop.

Ted shook his head. "No need for that. I'll drop them off here with their assignments and you can tell them where to go. They aren't here to socialize."

"I thought it might be nice for them to understand what we do here." I tried again.

This time he turned and all of the handsome had vanished from his face, replaced by barely controlled anger. His words came out low and hard. "Look, do what I tell you, okay?"

I took in the empty coffee shop. Luckily, Toby had arrived early for his shift, allowing me to handle my council liaison duties for the week. I heard his footsteps behind me.

"I get it. No party, just deliver them to the work sites." My voice came out almost as hard as Ted's. I'd worked with bullies before. The type was all sweet and nice as long as things were going their way, but cross them, and you saw the real person.

"Everything okay?" Toby asked, oh so casually. If he'd been at his deputy job instead of working part-time as a barista for me, I'd imagine his hand would have been resting on his gun holster, just in case.

Ted's face changed as he sized up Toby, the friendly mask slipping back on. "Just clearing up a difference of opinion. See you in a week for our follow-up meeting." He nodded to me. "Call me if you have problems."

He turned without waiting for an answer and left the shop.

My shoulders sagged. "Pour me a double with chocolate and whipped cream." I smiled at Toby, who still watched the man through the windows.

"That's a piece of work. You wouldn't believe how many women get caught up with men like that. All pretty on the outside, but inside, he gives our gender a bad name." Toby waited until Ted got into his car and peeled out onto Main Street before he started my coffee.

I slipped onto a bar stool. "He works with vulnerable women all day. I imagine he's got his choice of people to make feel like dirt."

"Well, he's not doing it here. You aren't meeting with him alone again." Toby put the steaming mocha in front of me.

"Thank you, white knight, but I'm fully grown. I can take care of myself." I sipped the creamy delight and murmured my pleasure. "This is amazing."

Toby laughed. "You're too easy. I'm serious about that piece of crap. Make me your assistant for the project. I bet he won't try to bully me." He started a pot of coffee. "Besides, you've got a lot on your plate right now."

"That's an understatement." For some reason, many months ago, I'd promised to host Thanksgiving at my house. As the day neared, I wondered if I'd been drunk at the time. My vision of a small family-like get-together was already up to ten confirmed guests. I'd never hosted ten people, let alone on a holiday. I think I'd overstepped my party comfort level. I focused on my barista. "You decide which of your girls you're bringing to dinner?"

Toby grinned. "Not yet. It's a big step, spending a holiday with someone. Tends to bring out the worst in my dates."

"You mean they think you're actually committing?" I laughed.

The bell chimed and several of Toby's customers from the cosmetology school scurried in. He nodded in their direction. "Something like that."

"I'll be in the back for an hour or two if you need help." I picked up my cup and slipped around the counter for the office-slash-storeroom. I had to review last month's accounting, transfer money, and write up the notes from today's Business-to-Business meeting for the council. I'd rather be reading. Aunt Jackie had taken on most of the administration side of the shop, doing day-to-day orders, bank deposits, and marketing, but she insisted I review her work, sign the checks, and make the big decisions . . . when she let me.

"It's a matter of checks and balances. That way I can't run off with your hard-earned cash," she'd told me when I grumbled.

It was closer to three hours before I finished. Glancing at my watch, I had just enough time to grab a quick dinner at Diamond Lille's before the interns showed up and I needed to escort them to their work assignments. Ted's insistence on no first-day get-together had made my day shorter, at least.

I dialed my cell.

"What trouble are you in now?" Greg King, town detective and my personal boy toy, answered on the second ring.

I rolled my eyes, even if he couldn't appreciate the gesture. "Can't a girl call her beau without him thinking the worst?" Besides, I hadn't called him for help since the drain had stopped up last week.

"Sorry, it's been a slow day." Greg's deep voice warmed me. "I thought you were too busy for me today."

I had whined at dinner Sunday night about my crazy week. I leaned back in my chair. "So now I've got some time. You want to buy me dinner and I can tell you all about my not-slow day?" I grinned then added, "Before Toby rats me off?"

"Oh God, what now?" He chuckled.

"Buy me dinner and I'll tell you." I grabbed my purse. "I'm leaving the shop now. And don't worry, I didn't start anything."

"Now why would I think that?" I heard him mumbling on the other end. "Esmeralda just stepped into the office. I'll be there in ten minutes."

"See ya." I said to the dead line. Esmeralda was the town dispatcher and fortune teller. The woman thought she had a direct connection to the other side and had brought me messages from beyond the grave multiple times. Even without me paying for her advice. Maybe she was like a drug peddler, and the first message was free. Except I'd been given several and still hadn't warmed to her style of advice for my life.

Walking through the shop, I waited for Toby to finish an order. "I'll be back at five, then after I walk the interns around, I'll take over." Toby and I handled the shop by ourselves on Tuesdays so Jackie could have the day off. She'd come in to help serve during the Business-to-Business meeting but had left soon afterward to prepare for a night out in the city.

"No worries, I'm good." He grinned at the shop filled with women who were watching his every move.

"Man whore." I slipped around him and headed to the door. I had to admit, Jackie's hiring Toby had been great for business. Toby seemed to like playing barista. It gave him a softer side than his regular part-time deputy gig where he worked under Greg. Besides, like me and most of the other townies, living in South Cove meant cobbling together enough part-time jobs to keep us financially solvent. I had a nest egg from the inheritance Miss Emily had left me, but I still felt like I needed to keep that separate, just in case.

Before I knew it, I'd walked the two blocks and was in front of Diamond Lille's, the only full-service diner in South Cove. Bill's bed-and-breakfast served, well, breakfast, for his guests. Coffee, Books, and More, my shop, had a good selection of treats to go with your drink order. But if you wanted real food, Lille's was the only option.

To my surprise, Greg leaned against Lille's brick façade waiting for me. I stretched on my toes and kissed him, his soft lips curving into a smile. The man could kiss. Must be why I kept him around. "I half-expected you to call off when you said Esmeralda showed up."

He put his arm around me and led me into the diner and toward the last empty booth. Even early, Lille's was hopping. "His Honor, the mayor, wanted to know if I'd found out anything on his new buddy Ted. I told him again that the police department wasn't his personal private investigation firm."

Slipping into the booth, I frowned. "He's looking into Ted Hendricks? Why?"

Greg shrugged. "Who knows with Marvin? He's always looking for the angle. Seriously, I think the only reason he gets reelected is he has dirt on most of the voters. They're scared not to vote for him."

"Well, he didn't make friends today at the business meeting." I went on to tell him about my morning, only stopping to order. Fish and chips weren't the healthiest option, but I hadn't had lunch, and Emma and I had run early that morning. A run that still wouldn't make up for me being gone late tonight. I'd be paying for my long day in sad, puppy-dog glances all evening.

"Darla must be hot. I swear, she starts planning the holiday festival as soon as the summer one ends." Greg sipped on a soda, scanning the room. A habit that used to annoy me until I realized it was just his cop nature, checking out any possible problems. My ex used to do the same thing, but he was looking for hotter-than-me chicks to ogle. It wasn't that Greg didn't see other women; he just didn't care if they saw him.

"Well, if the mayor winds up dead, I'd knock on her door first."

Carrie, our waitress, slid our plates in front of us. "There you go, guys. Anything else?"

"Nope, I'm good." Greg's mouth almost watered as he took in his plate of chicken tamales. He glanced at me. "You?"

I picked up a French fry, crisp to perfection with just the right amount of salt, and sighed as the taste hit my mouth. Carrie stared and I shook my head, answering Greg's question.

Greg chuckled as she walked away. "You do know how to appreciate food."

"I wish I had Amy's metabolism." Amy, my best friend, could participate in a hot-dog-eating contest, have dessert afterward, and still fit into her surfing bikini. I had to run most days to stay out of my "fat" jeans.

"I like you curvy." Greg's voice dropped and I felt him staring at me. "Amy's built like a stick."

I laughed. "Don't tell her that. She'll find a stick to hit you with." Amy had been a little sensitive around men lately since her breakup with Hank the Loser a few months ago. Greg and I both hoped she realized that Justin, her surfing buddy, was a much better match. We'd gone out with the couple on several double dates since the summer but Amy was still hesitant to give her heart away.

We ate in silence for a few minutes, then Greg paused. "Hey, did you see some kind of accident out in front of your shop today?"

I swallowed and cocked my head toward him. "Not an accident."

"About ten?" Greg pushed his plate away, all business now.

"Ted, the mayor's friend, almost hit Marie Jones as she darted across the street." I held my hand up to stop him from talking. "She ran in front of him and the car stopped in time. So no accident, no need to report. I bet Marie's a little shaken up by the narrow escape. Why? Who told you?"

Greg picked his fork up again. "Small town, who didn't tell me?" He peeked at me sideways, then added, "Oh yeah, my girlfriend."

I pursed my lips together, trying not to smile. "Like I said, no harm, no foul. Besides, Marie was the one who didn't watch for traffic. If anyone had been hurt, I would have called nine-one-one."

"If you say so." He shook his head. "I didn't take you for a blame-the-victim kind of gal."

I felt my eyes widen. "I'm not blaming . . ." Then I saw his body shaking. "You're messing with me, King. And I don't appreciate it." I slapped his shoulder for emphasis.

"You're too easy of a target."

I took a sip of my iced tea and checked the big black cat clock on the diner's wall over the hostess stand. "You're the second man to tell me that today."

This time his eyes widened and I grinned. "Toby said the same thing when I only wanted a mocha after dealing with Ted the Jerk."

"Wait, you didn't tell me you had a run-in with this guy. Maybe I should look into him, for the safety of our citizens."

I grabbed my purse and leaned over the table to give him a kiss. "Slow your roll, big guy. Nothing happened. Besides, Toby already agreed to take over further contact as the liaison from South Cove's business community. I think he wants to take care of the issue. I gotta go."

"Sure, eat and run. Leave me with the check." He tucked a wayward curl behind my ear. "Maybe I'll stop by later?"

"I'll close at nine. You want to drive me home?"

He kissed me. "I'll be the one in the police cruiser."

"Either bring your truck or I'll walk." I paused at the table. Last summer Toby had made me ride in the backseat of his cruiser because the two of them were concerned someone was trying to kill me. Which apparently had been true. Still, silly me, I wasn't a fan of the backseat of a police car.

He grinned. "Just seeing if you were listening."

I turned around and waved over my shoulder. "Don't be late, Detective."

By the time I walked back to the shop, the ten interns had arrived. They had a bus that would bring them to South Cove for each shift and then transport them back to the Work Today office in Bakerstown. I threw my purse in my office, introduced Sasha Smith, our intern, to Toby, and rounded up the other nine to do a quick tour of the town as we dropped people off. First stop, Antiques by Thomas.

Josh was standing guard in his doorway when I introduced him to Kyle. The man almost had a heart attack. Kyle's black leathers and pink spiked hair made him look like the ruffians Josh had railed about in each of the business meetings since he'd arrived. "You can't be serious." Josh pointed a finger at me. "If one thing goes missing . . ."

"Look, man, I'm not a thief. Just unemployed." Kyle held his hands out to his sides. "You can frisk me before I leave each day. I need this placement. And I dig old stuff. My pops put a bunch of this stuff out in the garage before they put him in a home."

Josh's bargain radar went off, and even I could see the wheels turning in his mind. "We'll work something out. Come on in, Kyle."

Amy stood out on the steps of City Hall and welcomed her intern, Cat, with open arms. The small girl who couldn't be much older than nineteen peeked back at me, eyes wide when Amy led her, chattering, into the building. I waved, and a couple of the group members chuckled.

A few more stops, and I had three left. The Glass Slipper, South

Cove Bed-and-Breakfast, and South Cove winery. As we passed by The Glass Slipper, I tried the door. Locked.

Mindy, the woman assigned to the shop, glanced at me. "I can wait here."

"Why don't you walk with us? I'd like the company." I peered into the shop window but couldn't see anyone or any movement. "I'm sure Marie's just running late."

"If you think it will be okay. I don't want to get in trouble." Mindy was the oldest of the group, close to fifty if my guess was correct. I wondered how she'd gotten into the training class. None of my business, I chided myself.

"Come on, I'll talk to Marie if she's upset. You were here on time, she wasn't." I smiled and put my hand on her shoulder. "Besides, it's a nice walk to the winery."

We stopped at South Cove Bed-and-Breakfast, where Bill Simmons along with his wife, Mary, waited on the porch to meet their charge. The young woman whom we dropped off had been greeted like she was returning home from a long trip rather than starting a job. That was the thing I loved about South Cove: most people were warm and welcoming. Maybe it was their nature or they just knew the benefits of being friendly in a tourist town.

The three of us walked up the hill to Darla's. She met us at the barn where she started tours and where on weekends, she usually hosted a band and wine tastings. The woman was still steaming.

"I can't believe Marvin pulled this stunt." She shoved a broom at the man who was her intern. "Go into the barn and sweep out the floor."

"Yes, ma'am." The man's drawl was deeply Southern. I hadn't heard him speak one word on our walking trip. I raised my hand to stop him.

"Hey, Matt? Where are you from?"

He grinned. "Georgia, ma'am. Followed a girl out here to the land of sunshine and never wanted to leave."

Darla watched him walk into the barn. She shrugged. "Could be worse, I guess. At least he's easy on the eyes."

Mindy laughed. "He's the sweetest thing. He had the entire bus rolling during the trip here. He's quite the comedian."

"Well, I could use some humor around here. Today's been kind of a downer." Darla shook her head. "I guess I shouldn't complain, at least she's letting me help. But, Jill, you don't know what she wants to do."

I didn't want to ask. "It's bad?"

"No, it's amazing. I wanted her idea to be horrible, but if she can pull this off, it might be the best festival we've ever had." Darla groaned. A voice called from the barn.

"Ma'am, did you know you had something on the stove?" Matt's deep voice called out from the barn.

"Crap, I have chili warming up." Darla turned and trotted back to the barn, leaving us alone in the driveway.

Mindy and I turned back to the road and the short walk back into town. "I'm making chili and corn bread tomorrow night for my son. He's visiting from Washington."

"How many kids do you have?"

Mindy smiled. "Just the one. His father, well, he wanted a namesake more than he wanted to raise kids. We divorced last year."

"You sound like you would have liked more." I hadn't made up my mind yet on if I wanted kids, not to mention how many.

"Sometimes, what you want isn't what you get." Mindy's words echoed Marie's statement earlier in the day.

When we arrived back at The Glass Slipper, the door was still locked. Several people milled around the door, checking their watches. I knocked hard on the door.

"Don't bother," a short woman said to my left. She held up her phone. "I just got a text from Marie. She's ill and cancelling tonight's class. She says we'll get another week added to the end of the session."

Mindy seemed deflated. I put my hand on her arm. "Why don't you come over and help me in the shop today? I'll sign your time card."

The look she gave me was so filled with gratitude, I almost teared up. "We get a stipend for each night we work. I needed the extra money to buy the groceries for tomorrow."

We walked across the street, and the students from the cancelled class followed us. The woman with the cell phone laughed. "I've wanted to check out the coffee shop for weeks. I guess Marie's cancelling class is the right excuse."

I held the door to the shop open as people filed in, and my eyes caught a movement in the darkened window of The Glass Slipper. A face peered out at us. Marie's face.

CHAPTER 3

Waving at the last few customers, I locked the door and turned the sign from open to closed. I'd needed the extra hands tonight. Sasha handled preparing the coffee, and Mindy dished up desserts and cleaned tables. Tuesdays were typically slow, but with the holiday season approaching and Marie's cancelled class, we had more impulse shoppers tonight.

Turning off the lights, I peered at The Glass Slipper across the street. I knew I'd seen Marie watching us earlier. Had the woman been that nervous about working with Mindy that she'd cancelled her class? Or was the near miss with Ted's Mustang to blame? Either way, I needed to talk to her tomorrow. Mindy deserved a real work experience, with hopefully, a real recommendation when she applied for jobs at the end of the program.

I slipped through my darkened shop and into the back office. Then I grabbed my purse and went through the back door. Greg's truck was parked in Aunt Jackie's regular spot. I locked the door, jiggling the knob to make sure it was secure.

Climbing into the truck, I leaned over, gave Greg a kiss, and held up the box filled with cheesecake pumpkin squares. "You got time for some dessert and coffee?"

Greg pulled the truck out into the road. "My time is yours. I turned everything over to Tim, unless something big happens, of course."

"It must be hell to be so indispensable," I teased.

He didn't even look at me. "If something happened at the shop, you would show up. Nothing different than with my job."

"Except with my job, people don't break laws, get hurt, or die." We passed by Esmeralda's house. Lights blazed out of every window, and a few cars were parked in her driveway. "Is Esmeralda having a séance?"

"I don't think she calls it that, but yes, she's doing a group reading." Greg glanced at the cars in front of his dispatcher's home. "You know she came in to talk to me before dinner."

"I thought she was relaying the mayor's message." I tore my glaze from the window and toward Greg.

He pulled into my driveway and turned off the engine. "Nope. She wants me to tell you that the lady is worried."

"The lady?" I picked up the box and slipped out of the truck. I met him on the other side. "What lady is she talking about?"

"I thought you'd know. That's all she said, then she turned around and went back to the dispatch center. When I walked by to leave, it was like she'd never even spoken to me." Greg held open the front gate, and we walked up the cobblestone walk I'd put in last month. I was still in love with my creation. Next to the path, Miss Emily's fairy circle had returned. If I believed in magic, I'd say my friend was blessing my caretaking of her house.

I unlocked the door and flipped on a light. "Not a clue."

After we'd settled in the kitchen and waited for the coffee to brew, Greg let Emma into the kitchen. My golden retriever had been a housewarming gift from him earlier that year. She still was mostly a puppy and her energy level spiked when she saw both of us in the house. Of course, she gave Greg more attention, teaching me a lesson for working too long of a shift. Normally I was home by noon and the two of us spent the afternoon on the porch reading and napping. Well, I read, and we both napped.

As Emma settled into her bed next to the door and we settled around the table, I tapped my finger on the surface. "Marie Jones stood her intern up this evening. She cancelled her class and everything."

"The same Marie who almost got smashed by a speeding sports car this afternoon? Maybe she was upset and felt she couldn't teach. Near-death experiences affect people differently." Greg sipped his coffee.

"Leave it to you to see the other side of things." I sighed.

Greg shrugged. "It's not always the easy answer, sometimes things just are." He waved a fork at me. "I'd like to give this Ted guy a lecture about safety and speeding in a small town. From what others have told me, the guy was going way too fast."

"I don't know, he said she ran out in front of him. He didn't say he was speeding." I bit into the pumpkin square. Sadie's Pies on the Fly was branching out, and this scrumptious tidbit was one of her successful experiments.

"From what I've heard from the mayor, this guy's a piece of work. He probably thinks everyone should just stay out of his way." Greg finished off one square and grabbed another. "These are great."

"Sadie's." I cocked my head and watched him. "Funny, you didn't let me dog on Marie for playing the disappearing card tonight, yet you have no sympathy for Ted. Did you dig into his history for the mayor?"

His face reddened just a bit. "After we talked, I figured there might be some fire to all this smoke, so yeah. Let's just say, you need to never be alone with the guy. He's got a short fuse when it comes to interactions with women. All kinds of reports filed against him, nothing sticks, though."

I shook my head. It was typical. As a family law attorney, I'd seen it time after time. Abusers tended to get away with it, mostly because they made their victims too scared to report. "I kind of got that vibe today. I thought Toby was going to shoot him."

Greg chuckled. "Wouldn't have been the worst idea." He took my hand and rubbed his thumb over the top. "Just stay clear, and if you do have to meet, stay in the front of the shop. I'll feel better about it."

"Are you telling the mayor what you found?"

"Probably not. Marvin has an underhanded way of using information against people. And I'm not going to be part of his game." Greg stood and took his cup and plate to the sink, rinsed them, and put them into the dishwasher. He then leaned in to give me a quick kiss. "I've got to go. Tomorrow's going to be a long day. Monthly inventory."

"How many times do you have to count rifles and flare guns?" I grumbled as I followed him to the door.

"According to the city charter, once a month." He kissed me again, this time longer, a proper kiss. And one that always made my toes curl.

I watched him stroll to the truck. "Thanks for the ride. And thanks for not bringing the cruiser."

He waved without looking back.

The next morning, I opened the shop and started with the list of things I hadn't finished yesterday due to the business meeting. Sometimes I wondered if the liaison job was worth the effort. At first, it had been a way to prove myself to the more settled townspeople. That I was willing to jump in and work for my new home. Now, besides Bill and Darla, I felt I was pulling the plow by myself. I drafted up the minutes and e-mailed them to Amy for inclusion in next week's council report.

Then, since the coffee run of the morning had slowed, I pulled a new arrival off the mystery shelf and, with a mocha, settled in to read until either Toby showed up for his own shift, or a wandering tourist found my door.

Toby was the first to arrive. I glanced at my watch and as usual, the guy was spot-on time. Not early, not late. Eleven thirty on the dot.

"Hey, boss," he called as he went behind the counter to wash his hands and don an apron. "Slow morning?" He poured a cup of coffee for himself and came to sit by me.

"Perfect morning." I held the book so he could see the cover. "Almost finished."

He leaned back. "You're the only business owner in town I know who enjoys a slow shift."

"There's a reason I take the early shift. I like having time to myself." I grinned. "So what's going on with you? We haven't chatted for days. You got a new love in your life?"

"I'm seeing one of the girls from the cosmetology school. We went to dinner in the city last night after my shift." The boy blushed down to his roots.

I raised an eyebrow. "Just one?"

He nodded. "Yep. Just one. Look, I know I told you I wasn't dating anyone, but Elisa is special. I didn't want you to judge." The bell over the door chimed, and an older couple walked in. Toby jumped up and almost sprinted to the counter. "Duty calls."

Elisa, huh? I wondered if maybe Toby had actually found the one this time. I put a bookmark to keep my place and picked up my empty cup. Time to check in with Marie. The girl and I were going to have a long talk about responsibility, no matter what Greg had said last night.

I stepped out of the shop and crossed the street, checking for traffic. We didn't get many cars during the weekdays, which was probably why Marie hadn't seen Ted yesterday. Most of the tourists parked at the public parking near the end of town, then walked through our small village. My shop was smack-dab in the middle of Main Street, perfect placement for an impulse cup of coffee or frozen treat.

The door of The Glass Slipper stood open. The front of the shop overflowed with small display shelves, each one holding a different type of glass ornament. Currently, Marie had moved the Christmas display closer to the window, but wind chimes and stained-glass pieces held center stage. I stopped to admire a Cinderella-motif stained-glass piece. The large square would be amazing hung over the children's book section at the shop. I was lost in thought when I heard her voice.

"I love how that piece turned out. I'm almost tempted not to sell it." Marie stood next to me, looking at the stained glass.

"I'm considering it for the shop. You can feel the fantasy of the story. It's like walking into the book." I smiled and turned. "You're an amazing artist."

Marie blushed, then shrugged. "I have my moments." She walked back to the counter. "Before you say anything, I'm sorry about last night."

"Mindy's a great person. I think you'll enjoy working with her." I jumped into my sales pitch.

"It wasn't her. I, well, I thought I saw someone I knew." Marie picked up a glass unicorn and started polishing the imaginary dust off the piece. "It upset me. But it couldn't be the same person. I mean, he doesn't even live on this side of the country."

Could she be talking about Ted? I replayed the scene from yesterday in my head. Had Marie been scared from the near miss, or of the driver of the car? "Look, if you want to talk . . ."

My words were interrupted by a group of women flowing through the door. Excited chatter filled the small shop.

Marie set the unicorn down. "Sorry, I've got a lunch class. I'll be ready for Mindy on Thursday, no worries." She glanced at the women already heading to the back of the room. "Did you want anything else?"

Apparently, I'd been dismissed. I shook my head. "I'll think about the piece."

I stepped out into the bright sunshine and wondered what had just happened. One moment, Marie seemed ready to talk about her concerns, the next, a cool professional stood in front of me.

At least she'd agreed to take Mindy on Thursday, and that had been my main objective in the discussion. I wasn't sure the owner of The Glass Slipper would ever be a friend, to me or anyone else in town. But not everyone wanted that kind of relationship. I made a mental note to take her cookies next week. Maybe I needed to reach out more.

The shop was busy when I returned, and I checked in with Toby to make sure he didn't need help before grabbing my purse and walking home. When he laughed, I took that as my cue and grabbed the almost-finished mystery to take back to the house. Research for the bookstore. Friday night was Aunt Jackie's Mystery Readers Group and it was my turn to present the new books for the month. I'd like to say I'd read all of them, but usually, I only had time for a couple each month.

Passing City Hall, I considered stopping in to see Amy, my bestie. A red Mustang sat parked in the one visitor spot in front of the building. Greg's truck sat next to the sports car. Ted must be in visiting with the mayor. I couldn't take the thought of running into one or the other of the men, not even to see Amy. I'd call her when I got home.

Emma stood waiting at the back door when I unlocked the kitchen door. She whined and I knew she wanted to run. "Let me change and we'll go." I unlocked the screen door and grabbed her water dish to fill before we left.

Ten minutes later, we were on the beach. With the waves choppy and the wind cool, we were alone. I unclipped Emma's leash and we took off, the salt in the air cooling my face as I ran. Seagulls cawed and dived at the waves. One came up with a too large fish for his wingspan, and he didn't get far before he was beach-bound, a crowd of gull friends circling his windfall.

We hit our turnaround spot and I slowed, letting Emma play in the surf for a few minutes. She loved the beach run. Although she also loved it when we went inland and ran at the state park just a few miles outside of South Cove. I had to face the fact, my dog was a running junkie.

My cell rang as I watched Emma. I picked up, thinking it had to be Greg or Amy. "Hey."

"Jill? Jill Gardner?" An unfamiliar male voice echoed in my ear. The wind was making it hard to hear.

I cupped my hand around the mouthpiece and talked louder, like that would make it easier for me to hear. "This is Jill."

"You need to stop meddling. If an intern doesn't have work, they don't have work. You can't take on all of the deadbeats." The man continued to ramble. Only now I knew whom I was speaking to: Ted Hendricks.

"Actually, I needed both Mindy and Sasha last night. So it was a blessing that The Glass Slipper had unexpectedly closed." I didn't mention that the overflow came from the store's closure and cancelled class.

The other end of the line was quiet.

"Are you done yelling at me?" I quipped. "Because I have other things to do."

He must have recovered. "You haven't heard me yell, not yet.

Anyway, stop messing with my participants." The line clicked off before I could respond.

If this was the way he treated all his host business owners, no wonder he had trouble placing people even with the enticement of free labor. No one wanted to work with a jerk belittling them for helping out. After this was over, I was finding out who managed the Work Today program and filing a formal complaint about their program director. My voice alone might not be able to make a difference, but maybe I wasn't the first to protest.

Emma had chased away the gulls from the half-eaten fish and was nosing around the corpse, trying to decide if she should claim it for dinner. I called her away. I didn't need my dog smelling like dead fish. Besides, I had a chicken potpie to put in the oven and the rest of the mystery waiting for me at home. Time to check out and relax. I'd leave planning Ted's demise for tomorrow's to-do list.

By five, the book was finished and I'd forgotten to take the pie out of the freezer. I'd written up a cute review for the meeting and I'd done a load of laundry. As I slumped into the couch, I wondered if Greg had eaten. I could surprise him with a basket of Lille's fried chicken and one of Sadie's pies from the freezer. I put a chocolate silk pie on the counter. I'd call Lille's before leaving the house and, by six, we'd be having a romantic dinner in Greg's office.

I let Emma outside and sprinted upstairs, pleased with my impromptu Wednesday date plans.

Carrie helped me pack the woven picnic basket I'd lined with a red-and-white checkered tablecloth. The pie sat at the bottom and I'd slipped in a couple bottles of a locally produced root beer from my stash.

"Greg is going to flip when you come in with this." Carrie grinned as she tucked the box of chicken on top of the pie and added a tub of mashed potatoes and gravy to the side. "You know this is what he orders probably three days a week when he shows up here for lunch."

I frowned, looking down at what I'd thought would be the perfect dinner. "Did he come in today?"

She laughed. "Nope. Esmeralda came in and got sandwiches for him and Tim. But I bet even if he had, he'd still love this." She peered at me as she slipped biscuits into a plastic bag. "Greg's lucky to have you."

I blushed. "We're dating. I'm supposed to do nice things for him."

"Yeah, but you wouldn't believe the way his ex treated him. I mean, when Sherry came in here with him for dinner, you could see her steaming that he hadn't taken her someplace nice. She even ticked Lille off one day, asking for a sparkling water."

I grinned, even though I didn't want to hear Sherry stories. I could see Lille getting upset. "I take it she got tap."

"And Lille slammed the glass down in front of her. I swear, Greg had to hold them off each other before he got the two of them calmed down." Carrie smiled at the memory. She folded up the arms of the basket. "Anyway, you're a peach. Don't forget that."

I paid for the food, waved good-bye to Carrie, and walked out of the diner. The basket was heavy now with all the food, and worse, it smelled divine. My stomach grumbled in protest. "One more block," I whispered. As I came toward City Hall, Greg's truck sat parked right where I'd seen it earlier. The man hadn't even left. Inventory days were brutal.

Then I saw the red Mustang, next to the truck. I had to walk past the front of the building to get to the door leading to the police station on the side. An eight-foot chain link blocked my access from this side. *Just walk fast*, I thought. *Maybe he's still inside with the mayor.*

I sped past the truck, but when I got in front of the Mustang, I snuck a peek toward the car. Ted Hendricks sat in the front seat. "Damn," I muttered, then slipped on a customer service smile and waved with my free hand.

He didn't wave back.

I leaned closer. Ted's head was at an odd angle and there was splatter on the windows. I set the basket down on the sidewalk and took a step closer. I pulled my phone out of my pocket and dialed a number.

"Hey, beautiful." Greg's voice filled my ear, but my eyes wouldn't leave the sight in front of me.

"You need to come out front."

Greg chuckled. "Carrie already told me about the surprise when I called to order dinner. Just come in, the side door is unlocked, and we'll eat in the break room. I don't want to lock up the station."

"Greg, you need to come out front." My voice caught. "Ted Hendricks is out here."

Greg's voice hardened. "Is he bothering you? I swear, that guy is ballsy."

I swallowed. "He's not bothering me. I think he's dead."

CHAPTER 4

I sat in the police station's break room with the cooling basket of food. Greg was out front somewhere, handling the crime scene. I couldn't stop seeing the look on Ted's face, slack and almost peaceful, if not for the blood caking around his flowing blond locks. I shivered and closed my eyes, trying to block the memory.

I had cleaned all the tables, stacked the magazines, shelved the used paperbacks in alphabetical order, and was considering reshelving by genre when Greg came into the break room.

"How you doing, sweetheart?" He took my hand and sat me on the orange plastic couch, pulling me into a hug. "You ready to talk about what you saw?"

My breath hitched. "Can you even question me? Isn't that a conflict of interest or something?" Truth was, I didn't want to talk, not to Greg or anyone, really.

Greg shook his head. "Clearly it's a suicide. The mayor said he'd fought with Ted this afternoon. Marvin told him that he was calling the administrator of the program and getting him kicked off the job."

"Mayor Baylor said that?" I didn't think the guy cared if Ted was a bully, even if the participants going through the program were vulnerable.

"Well, there was also the matter of the kickback Ted was trying to force out of the mayor. Money, it's always about money." Greg stood up and went to the table, opening the basket. He pulled out one of the biscuits. "I'm starving. I can't leave until Doc Ames gets here for the body. I've got Toby out there holding the fort for a few minutes."

"Ted was blackmailing the mayor?" I frowned. Something didn't make sense. "Then how do you know it's suicide? Maybe Mayor Baylor killed him?"

Greg laughed and almost choked on the bite of biscuit he'd just taken. After he'd stopped coughing, he shook his head. "Honey, you always see trouble. Ted put a gun to his head and pulled the trigger. I'm sure Doc Ames will find gunshot residue on his hands as well and confirm the obvious." He pulled out a chicken leg. "You want some?"

My stomach turned. There was no way I could eat, not now. I shook my head. "I don't think I'll be eating anything for a few days."

Greg put the chicken back into the box. "Sorry, I'm being insensitive. I guess after what I've seen on the job, you tend to compartmentalize."

I held my hand up to stop him from stepping back to the couch. "Go ahead, eat. You'll probably be working late, you need the energy."

Greg sank into a chair at the table and unpacked the basket. "This was nice of you."

"Even if Carrie couldn't keep a secret?" I stood and walked over to the table, grabbing one of the bottles of root beer.

"Don't blame her. She thought you were already here, and she'd forgotten to pack something." Greg chuckled as he made a volcano pocket out of his mashed potatoes to hold the gravy.

I thought about my walk to the police station. I'd been happy. Now all I could see was the red Mustang. Not that I cared that Ted was dead. The guy had been a jerk, but no one should die that way. Especially not because of a fight. "So, what do you want to know?" I wanted to leave, to go home, cuddle with Emma on the couch, and watch *Harry Potter* again. Maybe all eight movies.

"Everything you remember from when you left Diamond Lille's to when you called me." Greg started tearing apart the chicken.

"I don't know, I walked. The basket was heavy. I saw your truck in the same spot where it was this afternoon when I walked home. Then I saw Ted's car and wondered if I could walk around the building to avoid running into him or the mayor." I sipped the syrupy drink. "Especially since he'd called and yelled at me during my run."

"The mayor?" Greg paused, holding the chicken halfway to his mouth.

I shook my head. "Nope. Ted. He wasn't happy that Mindy's assignment got changed last minute when Marie cancelled the class."

"Why would he care?" Greg's voice was thoughtful.

"Because he had to be in control of everything." I ripped a biscuit in half and took a bite, but the buttery delight didn't faze my bad mood. "He's a jerk." I stopped and set down the biscuit. "I mean, he was a jerk."

Toby stood at the doorway. "Sorry to bother you, Greg, but the reporter and news crew are here from Bakerstown. Do you want to talk to them, or will the mayor?"

"I'm coming out." Greg wiped his face with a napkin and leaned in to give me a quick kiss. "I'll have Toby run you home."

"I can walk." Suddenly, though, I felt dog-tired. All I wanted was to get home.

"Tough guy." He smiled. "Toby, run your other boss home please."

Toby ushered me to the back of the building, where his personal car, a '69 Chevy Camaro sat. "I don't have to ride in the cruiser?" I glared at him.

"Figured you've had a bad day. Don't want to give the news hounds a false lead, seeing you carted off." Toby grinned and unlocked the car. I sank into the leather seat. "Sorry you had to see that."

I shook my head. "I don't understand why he'd do it. Ted was in love with himself. He wouldn't just end his life."

"You never know what problems people are carrying around. Maybe Ted's past caught up with him and he couldn't go on?" Toby eased the car into the alley and went down to Gull Street, turning out onto Main next to Diamond Lille's and away from the circus at City Hall.

"Secrets," I whispered as I watched the road ahead, thinking about what concerns Ted could have held that would have driven him to such an extreme end.

Emma smelled the fried chicken on my clothes, even though I hadn't eaten anything, and nuzzled my hand. "Sorry, girl, no leftovers." I went over to the stove and turned on the heat under the kettle. A nice cup of tea, a hot bath, then right to bed. Tomorrow was another day. But I wondered when I'd stop thinking about the red Mustang.

Aunt Jackie called after I'd been lying in bed, not sleeping, for an hour. I glanced at the clock. Eight thirty. No wonder my body didn't want to fall asleep.

"Jill, are you all right?" Jackie sounded worried. I heard a party going on behind her words, big band music floating through the speaker.

"I'm fine. A little shaken up, but fine." I pulled on my robe and went downstairs with my cup to warm my tea.

"I'm calling to tell you I'll open the shop tomorrow. My ride is bringing me home in a few minutes." Jackie gushed through the phone. "I was so worried about you."

"Wait, how did you hear?" I got a new tea bag out of the cupboard.

"The bar where the party is being held had the news channel on. Apparently it's a big deal when someone with political ties takes his own life."

"Wait, what?" I couldn't have heard her right. "Who was Ted?"

"The Hendricks family is some shirttail relation to a former president. I guess when the old man was in power, they kind of ruled the Washington scene." I heard Jackie mumble something. "Look, I've got to go. Don't worry about opening, come into the shop or not, Toby and I will cover."

And with that, my aunt clicked the phone off. I set my cup next to my laptop and fired it up. I might as well find out what the scoop was on Ted.

Two hours later, my notebook and my brain were filled with Ted facts. He'd been born into a powerful Washington family. His dad had been an ambassador to more countries than I thought existed. And from the pictures, his mother had been the perfect political wife, beautiful on the arm and her spare time spent on charity work. She mainly focused on child welfare rights, but her name had been associated with some commission on repairing the welfare system twenty years ago.

They had three boys. One had died in a skiing accident as the youngest competitor accepted for the Olympic ski team. One was a lawyer back in DC. And Ted, obviously the slacker of the bunch. The online news outlets said he worked for a local social service agency, following his mother's dream of social equality. From what I'd gleaned over the last few weeks, Ted didn't so much support the ideal of working oneself out of poverty, he just liked pushing people around.

Of course, the sanitized version of his life didn't include his temper. Or probably, the multiple abuse charges that Greg had found in the background check. No, now that the guy was dead, he was an angel.

I was ready to turn off the computer and head back upstairs when I saw the last paragraph of an article. "Ted Hendricks suffered a tremendous loss when his wife, the love of his life and his high school sweetheart, vanished in an apparent kidnapping scheme. Even after the million-dollar ransom had been wired to an offshore account, Katherine Janell Corbet Hendricks was never released. Authorities assumed she'd been killed by the kidnappers." A picture of a young girl in a wedding dress standing alone at the altar ready to take her vows was at the bottom of the page.

The frightened girl in the picture, especially with the expression of fear cloaking her eyes, appeared to be a very young Marie Jones.

Checking the time on my cell, I realized it was already ten thirty. If Greg was done with the investigation, he hadn't called. And if he had been done, he would have called to check in on me. I knew that much. I stared at the picture on the screen. Greg would tell me I was seeing problems where there weren't any. Tell me that Ted had committed suicide.

I glanced at the flyer that still sat on my table. One I'd picked up from the pile Marie had given out at the business meeting, announcing a new Thursday night class. I closed down the computer and put the flyer in my purse. I dialed Amy's number.

"Hey, I just heard. You want me to come over with a bottle of rum and a six-pack of Coke?" Amy didn't even let me say hello. "Or maybe wine? I've got a couple of bottles from the trip Justin and I took last weekend to Napa."

"Neither. I'm fine." I leaned back into my chair. "I do need a favor, though."

"Anything."

"I want you to take a stained-glass class with me."

The line was so quiet, I thought I must have lost her. I pulled the phone away from my ear and glanced at the display; no, it said we were still connected. "Amy?"

"I'm here. Just not what I thought you'd ask." She was quiet again. "Is everything okay? I mean, a stained-glass class? Doesn't seem like your kind of thing."

"I can be crafty," I protested.

And my friend laughed. Not a polite chuckle, but a big, uncontrollable laugh where your eyes tear up and tears roll down your face. If we'd been together, I would have smacked her, just for good measure.

"Ha, ha." I interrupted. "If you're done making fun of me, will you do it? I'd ask Sadie, but with the holidays coming up, she's swamped with baking."

Amy sniffed, and I could imagine her wiping the moisture from her eyes. "You couldn't pay me to stay away."

"Tomorrow night at seven at The Glass Slipper. I'll call Marie and sign us up first thing in the morning." I paused. "Thanks, Amy."

"I don't know what you're looking for, but I'd follow you almost anywhere to help you find it, you know. We're buds."

"And you're totally taking pictures of this, aren't you?"

"Damn right." She clicked off the phone.

Tomorrow I would be a Crafty Cathy and take a stained-glass workshop to make my own Christmas ornaments. And maybe in the process I could prove who Marie Jones really was, one way or the other.

If anyone found out I was taking one of Marie's classes, I'd be laughed out of the room. Everyone knew that I was too klutzy to be crafty. This secret spy thing was hell on my reputation.

CHAPTER 5

The tables were filled with chatting women. Everyone seem to know each other. Except Amy and me. We were at our own table near the back. A woman at the table in front of us turned and stuck out her hand. "I'm Leslie Talman. I don't believe we've met before. Did you just join the class?"

I took her hand and the woman squeezed, causing me to squeak. When she let go, I managed to whimper, "I'm Jill Gardner. I own Coffee, Books, and More across the street." I pointed to the right. "This is my friend, Amy Newman."

Amy smiled and waved, avoiding Leslie's grip. "We're so excited to take Marie's class. Have you taken a glass class before?"

"Tons. I swear, Marie should give me a frequent customer loyalty card. I've even brought her new students from the bank where I work. I don't think there's one teller who hasn't taken the introduction class." Leslie pointed to a woman standing near the coffeepot. "That's Anne, she's a vault teller. The manager's girlfriend is even taking this class."

"Marie must love you." I smiled as Leslie blushed just a bit.

"I can't help it if I'm addicted to the craft. My husband's home watching a football game. Or a rerun." Leslie nodded to the coffee. "You want some coffee before we start?"

"I'm good." I watched as the heavyset woman walked away, her bright yellow T-shirt stretching to cover her midriff. A hand touched my arm, and I turned to see Mindy standing next to me. "How's your night going? You and Marie getting along?"

Mindy grinned and nodded. "She's great. We sat together and she showed me the ornament we're making tonight. Then she had me make one all on my own. I can't believe how patient she was with me. And the angel looks beautiful. Marie says I can keep the projects I make here."

"Sounds like you got the best assignment out of the group," Amy teased. "My intern thinks I'm going to yell at her for asking to go to the bathroom."

"Who's with her tonight?" I'd forgotten that Amy should be working with her charge rather than helping me stalk Marie.

"Esmeralda. She's teaching her dispatch." Amy pulled a strand of blond hair out and checked for split ends. "We're splitting the time between us."

"That sounds fun, too," Mindy said, not convincing us of her honesty.

I was just about to ask about her son when Marie walked into the room and the women quieted like she was the president coming into a White House briefing. I glanced at Amy, who shrugged.

"Good evening, ladies. So glad you took time out of your busy schedules to work on your personal development. Having a hobby isn't being selfish; it's being true to your own development as a child of God." Marie smiled and motioned to Mindy, who scurried up to meet her. "This is my new assistant, who'll be helping me teach tonight."

Mindy shyly waved to the group. "I'm Mindy, I'm glad to be here."

"Hi, Mindy," the group chorused back.

"This feels like an AA meeting," Amy whispered.

I shot my friend a look. "And how would you know that?"

Amy grinned. "Can I plead television?"

"Goofball." I turned back to the front of the room, where Marie was glaring at us. "Sorry," I mouthed. It felt less like a class and more like Sunday services had when I was a kid. My mom used to give me that same look when I'd start to fidget.

Twenty minutes later and we were deep into our project, a heralding angel. I was pleasantly surprised at the fact my effort was beginning to actually look like an angel. At least until I saw Amy's. Her lines were clean, and if mine referenced a female in a Picasso manner, she had the *Mona Lisa* angel. I narrowed my eyes at her.

"My mom wanted her little girl to be an artist, not a city planner. I had classes in all forms of art before I fell in love with architecture." Amy held her ornament up.

"Amy, I didn't know you were so talented." Marie came up behind me and leaned close to examine my friend's foil work. She patted Amy on the arm, then studied my efforts. "I'm sure you'll catch on, Jill. Keep trying."

"I appreciate your support." I tried not to let the envy seep out of my voice. I had to remind myself that we weren't there to learn the craft. I focused on Marie. "Hey, I never asked, how are you feeling? After the near miss in the street? You didn't get hit, did you?"

Marie froze. She glanced around the room. "Time for a break, everyone." Lowering her voice, she answered, "I'm fine. I didn't get hurt, just scared."

"You should have seen Ted after the incident, he was so upset. He kept asking if I thought you were all right. He seemed genuinely concerned."

"Ha." Marie shook her head. "He was probably more concerned that I'd dented his car. He treated that Mustang like it was his baby."

Amy caught my eye. She took the hint and asked, "So, you knew Ted?"

Marie glanced around the room. Most of the students were outside, enjoying the night air and the white Christmas lights twinkling in the trees. "Mindy mentioned that he worried about that car all the time. He had his own parking lot for it. One car in ten spaces. Can you believe that?"

Sounded like Ted, I thought. A few people drifted back into the room. It was now or never, so I jumped to the obvious question. "Marie, were you married to him?"

I swear the blood in her face drained. "Why would you ask that?" She didn't wait for an answer, just put her arm around one of her students and left our table.

"That was a definite reaction." Amy stood closer. "She knew him."

"So, why would she lie?" I whispered.

Amy shrugged. "She didn't lie, she just didn't answer the question."

I focused on finishing the angel during the next hour of the class, wondering how to get Marie to admit that she was Ted's missing wife. Maybe I was seeing something that wasn't there. Thinking about the last time Greg caught me investigating on my own, I decided to hold my opinions until I could take him more than just a feeling and an old newspaper photo. Amy and I stopped to see Aunt Jackie at the shop after class, along with a few other class members.

"So, how was the class?" Jackie asked as she poured our coffee.

"Wonderful," said a woman standing behind me. "Marie makes it seem so easy. I'm all thumbs with most crafts, but my angel turned out beautiful."

I smiled and nodded. "She is something else."

As the women went over to the couch with their drinks, I sat on the stool. "I'm beat."

Jackie patted my hand. "Finding Ted must have been awful."

I shuddered, thinking about the blood covering the car. "I know I didn't know him, but no one should die that way."

Amy glanced around the room toward the women gathered around the couch. "I'm heading over to chat up my new friends from class. Maybe they know more about the mysterious Miss M."

"Spies are us," I joked and Amy gave me a thumbs-up. When she was seated with the group, I turned back to Jackie. "I think she just wants to hang out with the cool kids."

"You mean the crafty kids." Jackie smiled. "You forget I used to get your handmade gifts when you were a kid. I'd tell your mother 'stop sending me that junk,' but she didn't want to hurt your feelings."

"I thought you liked my gifts." I sipped my coffee to hide my smile. I'd known even back then that I wasn't the creative type, but it didn't stop me from trying. "What do you know about the Hendricks family? From what I saw in the news, they were a pretty big deal back in the day."

Jackie tapped her pen on the counter. "It's been a few years. But I think I still have the number of a woman who was tight with the family. I'll give her a jingle tomorrow morning."

"You're the best." I stood and waved at Amy. "I'm heading home. I want to cuddle with Emma and pretend the last few days never happened."

Sasha stood behind my aunt, washing dishes. "You should take care of yourself. My auntie found a dead body last year, she still has nightmares."

I turned to look at the young woman, her dreadlocks pulled back into a pink scarf. "That must have been awful."

"Nah, they expected it. My aunt's a cook at the long-term care facility over in Bakerstown. She took a woman's meal into her room, and the poor woman had gone in the night." Sasha swung a towel over her shoulder, tears filling her eyes.

"Honey, old people die." Jackie patted Sasha's back.

"I know," Sasha sighed. "It just feels so pointless sometimes. I didn't even like Ted and I feel bad for him. Who knew he was that sad?"

Jackie pulled her into a hug. "I know, sweetheart."

As I walked home that night, I thought about what Sasha said. Ted hadn't seemed sad. Maybe there was a reason?

Brenda Morgan, the new manager for The Castle, an old Hollywood glam estate turned museum and tour stop, came into the shop around ten the next day.

"Here's next month's order." Brenda handed me a file with the coffee supplies and books she got from my shop to use in her small gift shop at The Castle. Our partnership had been a recent development after Brenda took over management from her ex-husband. Craig Morgan, a man meaner than a teased rattlesnake, had been killed trying to scam the local motorcycle drug dealer gang. "Pour me a pumpkin latte and dish me up a slice of Sadie's Chocolate Dream pie. Get one for you, too, we're celebrating."

I made up the latte, poured a fresh cup of coffee for me, and plated up the treats. Brenda settled onto the couch looking out of the large picture window onto the street. When I brought the tray over, I glanced around the empty room before settling next to her on the couch. "How do you always time your visits when the shop's empty? I'm glad to take a break, but you're uncannily good at timing."

Brenda shrugged and set down the historical romance she'd been leafing through. She'd taken up kickboxing twice a week in the city and her arms appeared toned. I, on the other hand, hadn't been on a run with Emma since Wednesday, and both of us were starting to be grumpy about the lack of movement. "Just lucky, I guess." She grinned. "So, aren't you going to ask what we're celebrating?"

"Friday?" Brenda didn't need a real reason to celebrate, she just enjoyed life. Especially now.

"That was last week." Brenda grinned.

I took a bite of the pie and almost groaned, it was that good. Deep, dark chocolate with cool vanilla whipped cream on top. Heaven. I opened my eyes and she was watching me. I wiped my mouth with a paper napkin. "What?"

"You're not even going to try to guess?" Brenda leaned back into the couch, her lip stuck out like a five-year-old's.

"I don't know. Sorry." I took a sip of my coffee.

"My sister's coming to visit for Thanksgiving." Brenda squealed and bounced on the couch. "I haven't seen Lori since she moved to New York a few years ago."

"I didn't know you had a sister." I searched for any memory of Brenda talking about siblings. I didn't even remember her mentioning family, well, besides Craig, ever.

"Lori and I weren't close, especially after I married Craig. They didn't get along at all." Brenda finally took a bite of her pie. "According to Craig, I had to choose between him and her. I should have been smart back then and left long before I did."

"We make the best choices we can at the time we make them." I thought about my former life, before I moved to South Cove. "I'm sure she understands."

"Lori's pretty direct, so if she's still mad, I'll know as soon as I pick her up at the airport." Brenda paused. "It's okay if I bring her along to your dinner, right?"

Crap, where would we fit one more person into the house? I was beginning to think Greg's plan of borrowing tables from the Methodist church and setting up out in the backyard was the only way we'd be able to pull off this Thanksgiving dinner. I pasted on a smile and said the only thing I could. "Of course it's okay."

When Greg came over for dinner that night, he regarded me like I'd grown a third head. "You invited someone else for dinner? What does that make, twenty?"

"No, eleven. Stop exaggerating." I'd counted as I'd walked home from the shop. I didn't even own eleven chairs that would fit under a dining room table.

Greg grabbed the steaks I'd set out and went out on the porch to start up the grill. "Stop inviting people."

I followed after him. "I didn't invite Brenda's sister, Brenda invited her. What was I supposed to say, no, now that you have real family coming in, you're not welcome?"

"We don't have any more room." Greg cleaned the grill.

I slipped onto the rocking bench I'd bought last summer. "I'm not inviting anyone else. Not even Bon Jovi. Or Sheryl Crow." I named his favorite singers.

"Now, don't get crazy on me. Of course, if they want to come, we'll find room." Greg came and sat next to me. Emma brought him her ball and he lobbed it out to the end of the yard. I leaned into him and closed my eyes. When he spoke, his voice was so soft, tears filled my eyes. "You okay?"

"I've had better weeks, but yeah, I'm good." Jackie had excused me from tonight's Mystery Readers Group, so I had nowhere to be except here. I nestled into his chest, drinking in the smell of him. My heartbeat slowed, calming me. Just being near him, I felt more at peace with myself.

We sat there together for a while. Greg threw Emma's ball, while I tried to clear my mind of all the images from the last week. The smell of steak grilling brought me back to reality, and I reluctantly straightened. "I guess I'd better get the salad made."

Greg went to the grill and turned the steak. "We've got a few minutes." He paused, then sat back down. "Do you want the bad news now or after dinner?"

My stomach turned. "Now. Then I can have an excuse to just eat apple pie for dinner."

He laughed. "That's my girl, always looking on the bright side." Emma dropped her ball in his lap and he threw it again. We watched her spin around and chase after it. "She's getting big."

Emma was coming up on a year, and the cute puppy had grown into a full-blown retriever. She still acted like a puppy, though, and the legs to my dining room set showed her teething stage. I turned toward Greg, who was still watching Emma. "I think you're stalling. What's the bad news?"

Greg didn't meet my eyes, but he took my hand before he spoke. "It appears Ted didn't commit suicide. Someone murdered him."

CHAPTER 6

Saturday morning I got up with the alarm, put on my running clothes, and jogged to the beach with Emma. After Greg left last night, I'd thought about his warning to stay out of the investigation this time. His words echoed in my head: "Jill, you don't have to be involved with every dead body that washes up in South Cove."

But that was the issue, wasn't it? I was already involved. Once he'd let slip that Ted hadn't done the deed himself, I'd told Greg about the picture of Ted's missing wife, how she looked like Marie. And all I got was a "good to know" and another lecture. I'd made a promise to stay out of the investigation, a promise I didn't think I could keep. I regretted reversing my decision not to talk to Greg before I had hard evidence. I'd kind of slipped into the conversation. He saw things differently than I did. This time, he was a little too different.

Running with the salt air stinging my face, I vowed I'd keep my oath for today. One day at a time, wasn't that the mantra for addicts? That thought made me frown: Was I addicted to the excitement of investigations? Of living out my favorite murder mystery novels?

By the time I'd reached the end of the run, Emma and I were both spent. I showered, got ready for work, and walked into town toward the shop. I had enough to do without adding "find out who killed Ted" to my to-do list. Today would be about the shop. And hosting

Thanksgiving. The big day was three weeks away, and I hadn't even ordered a turkey yet.

After the morning rush of coffee addicts had passed through the shop, I browsed the shelves, looking for a holiday cookbook or how-to guide. Was there a *Host the Perfect Dinner for Dummies* book? My sparse cookbook shelves ran the gamut of Asian, Thai, Southern cooking, and an everything-you-wanted-to-know-about-seafood book. I booted up the laptop and was searching the sales catalog when the bell chimed over the door.

Darla Taylor walked into the shop. She'd started a running/diet program last summer, but from what I'd seen, her progress had slowed, so she still appeared five feet tall and five feet wide. She waved and met me at the coffee bar. "Give me a skinny latte with a vanilla shot, please. I'm treating myself."

"Coming right up." I started making the drink. Avoiding the holiday festival discussion as long as possible, I focused on her new employee. "So, how's Matt working out?"

Her face turned beet red from the top of her fake blond hair to the edge of her neck that showed in her running gear. She shuddered. Her voice shook when she spoke. "Matt?"

Oh God, don't let there be another problem. "Yeah, the intern I dropped off Tuesday night? He did show up Thursday, right? I haven't talked to anyone over at the Work Today place since Ted's"—I paused, then chose the safest word choice—"death."

Darla waved her hand. "Oh no, there's not a problem. He showed up right on time on Thursday and even fixed the door on the shed. He's very handy around the place."

I handed her the drink, and as I rang up her order and gave her change, I wondered about how handy Matt really was. Darla was smitten, that was obvious. I just hoped she wouldn't get her heart broken by this temporary person in her life. "I'm glad. Sasha's been a godsend around here, especially with the increase in evening shopping traffic."

Darla sipped on her drink. She glanced around the empty shop. "You're not very busy for a Saturday."

I shrugged. "It should pick up later, when Toby's on shift. The boy brings in the customers."

She nodded, thoughtfully. "I guess a lot of people are attracted to a handsome man."

"Duh. Wouldn't you be?" I laughed and resumed checking out cookbooks. "You don't know of a good how-to-host-a-holiday-dinner guide, do you?"

Darla chuckled. "The first Thanksgiving is getting to you?"

This time it was my turn to blush. "Is it that obvious? I just don't want to embarrass myself."

"You can't. Holidays are about getting people who care about each other together, not what's actually served on the table. You'll do fine, you have a good heart." Darla smiled. "Although if you want, I can write a series on Thanksgiving disasters for the *Examiner*. Give you some ideas of what not to do."

My jaw set. "Ugh. I'm not sure I want to know about what can go wrong."

"Mostly it's a lot of dumb things. Or people being dumb because of too much alcohol. Each year in the news, there are a lot of fires caused by deep-fried turkeys." Darla laughed. "My stepdad tried that one year when I was a kid, total disaster."

"I promise no deep-fried turkey. I'm going traditional as much as possible." I paused. "So, you like Matt? I mean, as an employee?"

There was that blush again. "He's great. Better than I could have expected. I thought since Ted had been having such problems placing this group, we might have gotten the dregs. But Matt told me a story that explained a lot."

"What story?" I pushed aside the laptop. I'd search later.

Darla squirmed a little in her chair. "I hate to speak ill of the dead, but I'll make an exception for Ted." She leaned forward. "You know he told the mayor he'd had issues placing these ten, so that's not a secret."

I'd wondered about that. Everyone I talked to said how well the placements had turned out, not something I'd expected from Ted's evaluation of the group. "So, what was the secret?"

"Matt said that Ted told him once that he had considered him for an assignment a month ago, but he had placed a girl in that spot instead. He told Matt that she was very, very grateful, if he knew what he meant."

"Wait, you think Ted was involved sexually with his charges?" I sighed. It wasn't uncommon for men who craved power to seek out positions where they held all the cards and others held none.

"I don't think, I know. Apparently there was an incident with a girl a year ago just over legal age. I think Ted's parents bought her silence. I heard she took care of the problem and moved north, probably Oregon." Darla drained the last of her coffee and stood. "So the people working here either were male, too old for Ted's tastes, or had shut him down. I heard Sasha gave him a piece of her mind."

"Now I'm beginning to understand Ted's death a little more." I shook my head.

"I don't. Someone who's that egocentric doesn't commit suicide." Darla studied me, her newshound radar going off. "Greg is saying that Ted committed suicide, right?"

Greg had warned me that the DA didn't want the cause of death released before they had a chance to do some investigation. I tried to blow it off. "As far as I know." I paused. "Did you know about his family ties? Are you working on the story for this week's *Examiner*?"

Darla shook her head. "Tom didn't think it would be good for South Cove's business community to be highlighting a bloody death in a car on Main Street along with the new holiday festival committee chair."

I grimaced. "How are you doing with that? I know you put a lot of your own time into the project each year." I'd wanted to avoid this topic, but it was better than slipping up and mentioning "murder."

"I'm upset, who wouldn't be?" Darla's phone chirped, and she glanced down at the display. "Although the woman doesn't know what she stepped into and she's calling me every hour to ask some other stupid question."

Darla held up her phone to show a picture of Tina Baylor, the mayor's wife. She tossed the phone back into her purse. "She can wait. I told her I'd be glad to take over again and let her shadow me, but that seems like giving up to her. And she said her mother was a Daughters of the American Revolution member and her family never surrendered."

"You can take her call." I watched as a customer entered the store, heading over to the new selections area. "Looks like I need to get back to work anyway."

"Don't worry about it. She'll call back every ten minutes until I answer. I've already tested it up to an hour." Darla grinned as I gasped. "What can I say? Revenge is best served cold, and the girl is getting her share. Although I still don't think she knows why I'm mad."

"I hate to see the festival suffer." I tried to act like the liaison for the city council.

Darla started walking to the door. "Slow your roll, Jill. I won't let South Cove down, even if that's exactly what the town did to me. Maybe if it's a little bit of work, she'll give up and go back to being a housewife and giving huge parties."

I'd forgotten one of Tina's favorite pastimes was entertaining for her husband's political career. "I could ask Tina if she knows of a good guidebook for entertaining."

Darla paused at the door and laughed. "Are you kidding? People like her are born knowing how to set a formal table and what side dishes to serve with what wine. I'm pretty sure that's what she studied in college, not marketing."

I watched Darla disappear through the door. The customer stepped to the counter with three beach reads and ordered a large frozen mocha and a tall black coffee to go.

"My driver loves your coffee. He's been coming by every morning to get our supply, even though I keep telling him the coffee is included in our lodging." She grinned at me. "So I decided I had to meet the woman whom David's been raving about. If I didn't know better, I'd say he's got a bit of a crush on you."

"I'm sure it's the coffee he loves, not me." I mentally reviewed my early customers over the last week and thought I knew whom she was talking about. "I remember him. He's a tall, slender man, likes his coffee very black and dark, and buys young adult. Those must be for you."

The woman laughed and held out her hand. "I'll tell you his dirty secret. He doesn't think I know. He loves tales of teenage angst. And don't get me started on the Greek gods phase. The man reads like he is still in high school." She straightened the Mystery Group flyers on the counter. "I'm more of a literary reader. Although I do allow myself time to enjoy a few genre books when I'm vacationing. I can't tell you the grief I'd get if any one of the members of my book club saw my purchases today. I'm sure I'd lose my chair status."

"I think any reading is good reading, even if it's commercial fiction. A good story well told is worth the time." Jackie had come to the store with the same mind-set. She'd wanted to cut the romance section by half and add a larger classics shelf, but when she saw the figures on the actual sales, she changed her mind, fast. Now I even caught her reading the romance category books we carried. Just for research, she claimed.

"You probably sell a lot of these. When I take the train into town, all I see are people reading romance or mystery or even those kids' books. I can't abide vampires. I guess I'm showing my age." The woman absently touched her face, the skin around her eyes as smooth as a teenager's.

"Everyone has their own taste. I wish I could stock more variety, but as you can see, the shop's limited on shelf space." I put her drinks in front of her on the counter and rang up her purchases.

"Well, today I'm going to just enjoy the story. I've got my camp chair in the trunk and I'm going to the beach outside town and reading until the wind drives me back to the bed-and-breakfast. It might not be summer, but it's a beautiful day." The woman held out her credit card.

"I'm thinking my afternoon's going to involve an hour or two of reading, as well." I glanced at the name on the card—Regina Johnson. "A girl's got to stay up on the newest releases, right?"

"Especially if she runs a bookstore." She signed her charge slip and then walked out toward the street. "I'll see you tomorrow."

Customers like her—smart, funny—were the reason I loved owning a business in a tourist town. You got to know people on their best days. When anything was a possibility. I knew my commuter customers by the mood surrounding them as they ordered. Vacationers were more relaxed, more willing to play. One more reason I loved living and working in South Cove.

Toby arrived right on time, and as I transitioned my barista into his shift, Jackie and Josh walked into the store. Well, Jackie with Josh following her.

"You don't have to explain," Jackie muttered. "A woman knows when there's someone else."

"Jackie," Josh gasped. "How can you even think that? I'm so sorry I forgot to meet you last night. I just got lost researching a new batch of stock I have coming in. Time got away from me."

Jackie stepped around the counter and poured herself a cup of coffee. "Research. Right."

He parked his large frame on a stool by the counter. "I swear. It's pretty interesting. The batch is supposed to be from an apothecary from a central California mining camp. Although I haven't totally verified that yet..." Josh gazed around and apparently noticed Jackie's cold stare causing him to stop talking.

"You're forgetting you live next door in that ratty apartment above your store. You don't think I can see when someone goes up your back stairs. Or did you think I wouldn't recognize her?" Jackie shook her head. "I'm not talking about this ever again."

"Lovers' quarrel?" Toby fake-whispered in my ear.

"Shhh," I said, but it was too late. Jackie and Josh both turned and stared at us.

Josh spoke first, his voice dripping with sarcasm. "Enjoying yourselves?"

"No, I mean, what happened?" I took a step toward the two, hoping I'd be able to turn back if the words started flying my way.

Jackie put her hands on her hips and stared at Josh. She arched her eyebrows, waiting for him to speak.

"I'd asked your aunt to dinner at Lille's last night. But then I forgot. I wasn't even in the apartment until after midnight. No one was there. I swear." Josh had the saddest basset hound look I'd ever seen. "Maybe you saw those darn cats that keep crying in the middle of the night. I didn't remember until this morning, when Kyle asked me how the date went. I came right over to explain."

"And you don't believe him?" I turned to Jackie.

She closed her eyes and took a deep breath. "Not one word. A cat doesn't walk on two feet." She pursed her lips and focused on me. "Don't worry, I'll be here for when my shift starts, but right now, I'm going upstairs."

Josh started to rise.

"Alone." Jackie turned and stomped out the back of the store, where a side staircase led to her apartment.

Toby came by, took Jackie's cup, and put it in the sink. "Man, you've got her hot." He leaned against the counter. "Take it from a multi-chick serial dater, you've got to keep more of a distance between the ladies. Like have one in Bakerstown and one here. You don't ever date two girls in the same town, that's just asking for trouble."

Josh stood, his shoulders sagging. "I don't know how to say this any clearer. I'm not seeing anyone except Jackie. And some days, the way she acts, I wonder if we're even dating."

Josh stormed out of the store.

"That guy has it bad for your aunt." Toby whistled.

I nodded, not trusting my voice. Josh was hurting. I headed upstairs to my old apartment. Knocking on the door, I called out, "It's me."

"What part of 'alone' didn't you hear?" My aunt's voice came through the door.

Leaning against the doorframe, I tried again. "Look, Josh seems like he's telling you the truth. Can't you just give him the benefit of the doubt?"

No answer came from the other side of the door.

"Aunt Jackie? Are you okay?" I wondered if I should grab the office keys. I had a spare apartment key on the ring, just in case.

"I'd be better if I wasn't being yelled at through my door."

My lips twitched. "I wouldn't be yelling if you'd open the door."

Again the hallway was quiet. Finally I heard the television come on.

"Aunt Jackie?" I tried again.

The words weren't louder this time, but they somehow held more power. "Let me be, okay? I need some space."

"Call me if you want to talk. I'm heading home." I pitched my voice higher, hoping she'd hear me over the television. If she did, I didn't know because she didn't answer.

I thought about Josh's statement he'd worked through the night. Could he be lying? But if Josh had been in the shop, whom had

Jackie seen going up to his apartment? I decided to leave the problem alone. My aunt was a big girl. She needed some time to cool off. I took the stairway back down to the office. I tossed my apron into the laundry bin, grabbed my purse, and started power walking home, hoping nothing or no one else would stop me.

One clean kitchen and two loads of laundry later, my phone rang. I glanced at the caller ID, no longer sure I wanted to talk to Jackie and hear about the drama again. "Happy Saturday," Amy's voice was consistently set on loud chipper level. I'd only seen her depressed once, and of course, it was the result of a man in her life.

"You working today?" Amy surfed any time she didn't have to work, so I knew she was probably calling me from her desk at City Hall.

"We're decorating City Hall for Thanksgiving." Amy's voice dropped to a loud whisper. "Tina Baylor is here and we're going all-out. Turkeys, pilgrims, and Indians. It's terrible."

"Sounds like you're her test project for the holiday festival." I grinned. Darla must have struck again, leading Tina in a very bad direction. The girl was evil.

"We're something, all right. In all the years I've worked for the mayor, I've never spoken to Mrs. Baylor more than three times. Today, we're best friends." Amy sighed.

"So I'm being replaced," I teased.

"You couldn't get that lucky." Amy groaned. "She's coming this way, I've got to go. See you tomorrow?"

"Sorry, I'm opening Sunday. Aunt Jackie's had a bad day, and I'd like to give her some time off. How about lunch on Monday?" I took out my notebook and my running list of chores I needed to take care of, including appointments.

"Works for me." Amy's voice changed. "I'm sorry, the office is closed today, but if you'd like to call Monday, I'd be glad to walk you through the building permit paperwork. Thanks for calling."

"She's standing right there, isn't she?"

"You've got that right. Talk to you then." Then the line went dead.

I had to hand it to Tina, she knew how to control her employees, or the people she assumed were her employees. I guess being the mayor's wife gave you certain privileges.

I glanced at the clock. If Greg was going to show up for dinner, he would have called by now. I checked the Internet and saw that if I left now, I'd have plenty of time to get into Bakerstown before the library closed. It was time for some background research on a Mr. Ted Hendricks. And what better place to find it than the local gossip column.

CHAPTER 7

I'd reviewed ten rolls of microfilm before I found even a mention of the man. He'd kept a low profile for the short time he'd been in town. According to an interview in the *Bakerstown Gazette*, Ted had moved there from his hometown of Boston, wanting to experience the more relaxed California way of life. Even in words, the man's arrogance shown through. Some would call it confidence, but I felt the anger behind the words.

At least I knew he'd arrived two years ago. Now I just needed to go deeper into his family tree. Maybe there would be a mention of why he left "the more civilized East," as he referred to his prior home.

My cell rang.

The librarian at the research desk glared at me. I stepped out of the quiet room and took the call. "Hello?"

"Where are you?" Greg asked.

I flushed, even though he couldn't see me. I didn't want to listen to a lecture on staying out of an investigation. "I'm in Bakerstown. I needed to do some research at the library for"—I paused, trying to make up an excuse that he would believe—"our holiday festival decorations. I heard Tina's going for a more traditional theme this year."

"Oh God. The woman came in and had Esmeralda in fits. Esmeralda claims the decorations violate her religion. I've been playing mediator all day. I think she's just balking because it's Tina."

Tina had led the charge to keep Esmeralda off the Methodist church choir years ago and failed. I smiled, thinking about the gypsy fortune teller and the mayor's wife standing toe to toe. "Amy said there were turkeys and pilgrims."

"Well, the mayor's offices are Thanksgiving. For our area, Tina wanted to go with the baby Jesus story. I swear, the woman is bipolar." Greg paused. "When are you heading back?"

"You got plans in mind?" I teased, watching the librarian continue to glare at me through the archway.

He chuckled. "I was hoping you'd pick up a couple of pizzas from Little Godfathers and bring them back. I'll buy the beer and bring a movie. It's been a long week."

"Sounds like a perfect Saturday night date." I'd probably exhausted the resources here anyway. "Call the pizza in and I'll be home in twenty."

"Yes, ma'am." He chuckled and hung up.

I returned to the microfilm reader, printed off the interview with Ted, and returned the rolls to the librarian, who took them without a word. I guess I was on the library Santa bad list for not silencing my cell.

Heading back across town, I passed the building housing the Work Today program. The bus with the South Cove participants was unloading. On a whim, I turned into the parking lot.

Stepping out of the Jeep, I waved at Mindy. "Hey, how'd today go?"

Mindy grinned, hoisting a tote bag with The Glass Slipper logo on the front. "I love my job," she gushed. "Marie let me run the cash register all day, and then when she was teaching a customer how to cut the glass, she had me practice, as well. She said I've got a knack for working with the medium. Me, like a real artist or something."

"I'm so glad." I glanced around the lot. "Your son picking you up?"

Mindy shook her head. "I live in the apartments down the street. It's a short walk."

"I can drop you off. I'm heading to get pizza, then back to South Cove." I pointed to the Jeep.

Mindy shook her head. "I'm fine. I need the exercise." She started to walk away, then stopped, her face showing concern. "We're meeting with the new coordinator next Monday. They didn't take long to replace Ted."

"Is that a problem?"

The woman shrugged. "I just hope the new guy doesn't change up our assignments. I enjoy working for Marie. I'd hate to lose out on the experience."

"I'm sure they won't move you out of a placement that's working out. Marie seems to enjoy working with you."

"Ted did. I've had four placements before The Glass Slipper. Each one, I went for two weeks, then Ted replaced me with another girl." Mindy smiled, but the emotion didn't match her eyes. "A young and pretty girl. I guess I was the test employee. If I liked the work, so would his favorites."

I didn't know what to say. Mindy's story matched Matt's gossip with Darla. I rested my hand on the woman's arm. "Well, it's a good thing Ted isn't making those decisions anymore. Maybe the new guy or gal will be more reliable."

Mindy nodded. "Thanks. I hope I see you next week."

As she walked away, her shoulders hunched and her spirits dragging, I heard her mumble, "And he could be worse."

Matt stood by an old rusted-out F-150 watching us. When I waved, he held up his hand, then climbed in and started the engine, blue smoke filling the parking lot. The rest of the group had already left, so I got into my Jeep and turned down the road to the pizza shop.

Mindy's final comment echoed in my ears. I made a mental note to stop by the work program first thing Monday morning to check out the new director. I was the city council's liaison; it was natural to be curious. At least that was the story I would tell Greg. Hopefully, he'd believe me. The man got cross when he found me messing in his investigations.

By the time I'd arrived back in South Cove, Greg's Dodge sat parked in my driveway and he was on my front porch, my dog lying at his feet in adoration. I waved as I parked and grabbed my purse and the two pizza boxes. Greg hurried to open the gate and then took the boxes, giving me a quick kiss.

"I'm starving." He sniffed the boxes. "These smell amazing."

I unlocked the door and held it open as he followed me into the house. "You have a key, you know." I'd given him a key to the house last month, when he'd house-sat Emma for me when Jackie and I took a weekend trip to the Oregon coast. When Greg had tried to return it, I had waved it off, citing more imaginary trips in the future.

He set the boxes on the table and grabbed plates and a couple of cold beers from the fridge. "I was fine on the porch." He nodded at the table. "Sit down and start. I'll run back and grab the beer off the porch."

"If you'd used your key, the beer could be chilling already," I pointed out. And the man actually sighed. "What's wrong? Am I bugging you?"

He stepped closer and pushed a lock of hair out of my face. "This is your house. I think sometimes, we're together so much here, we tend to forget that. I don't want to overstep." He tapped my nose, then turned and left the kitchen.

I thought about that for a few minutes. As Greg and I had grown closer, we had fallen into a comfort level with each other. Maybe he didn't want to rush into marriage. He'd been divorced only a few years. Could he be wondering if this—we, I amended—was a mistake? I opened the pizza boxes, distracted. Pepperoni and more pepperoni, and a veggie delight, minus olives. I grabbed a slice of the veggie, my hunger tamping down my worry about Greg's feelings.

Greg came up behind me, put the beer into the fridge, and then sat in the chair next to me, grabbing a slice of the pepperoni. "And before you start thinking bad things, no, I'm not rethinking our relationship. I just don't want to assume."

"I wasn't even thinking," I started, but then I saw the grin spreading on his face. "Okay, busted. How do you know when I'm freaking?"

Greg shrugged. "You're always thinking about what something means, or about what someone didn't say. That's why you're so good with researching. You're ten steps ahead of everyone else before the game even starts."

I smiled, ducking my head. The man knew me and how to push my flatter button. I took another bite and almost choked the next moment.

"So, what have you found out about Ted?" Greg reached for a slice of the veggie pizza.

I froze, wondering what had given me away. "I don't know what you mean."

He laughed. "Really? We're playing it that way?" He cocked his head, waiting for me to react.

"Fine, I've been trying to figure out who Ted was, not so much who killed him." I put on the innocent, sweet smile I used on the mayor when he was frustrating me. "That's your job."

Greg burst out laughing. "Since when?"

"Since I want to know what you found out today. Want to swap information?" I gave Emma the crust off my first piece and grabbed a fresh slice.

"You first."

So I told him the little bit I'd discovered, that Ted was from a wealthy, powerful family and must have been the black sheep for his social service-type career.

Greg pushed aside his plate. "That's the feeling I got from the family lawyer. He called on me today, wanting to know when we are releasing the body. They want to ship the body back East to the family plot."

"The lawyer came, not the family?" I put the pizza slice down, my appetite disappearing as fast as it had arrived.

"Sad, huh. I guess his father's at some embassy overseas and the mom, well, she's away. That's all the lawyer would say, away. Probably on some beach somewhere drinking fruity drinks and trying to de-stress."

I gave Emma another bite of crust since she was still staring at me. "They say the rich are different."

"If by different you mean cold, you're right." He nodded to the kitchen door. "Want to go sit on the porch and watch me play fetch with your dog?"

"And some people actually go to movies and concerts on Saturday night." I cleaned off the table, moving the leftovers into one box and shoving it onto the bottom shelf of the fridge. Greg would take the pizza into the station tomorrow for the weekend shift guys. Typically

Greg spent early Sunday morning at the station, then, if I was working at the shop, he'd show up after my shift and we'd drink coffee and read the paper. Our Sunday time was all about Ozzie and Harriet stuff. And yet, I loved our Sunday afternoons together more than the rest of the week. For the rest of the evening, we avoided discussions of murder and family and love and pain. We played ball with Emma and laughed and talked about happy memories as we watched the sunset over the ocean. And when darkness fell, I cuddled up to Greg, my head on his chest, and listened to the beat of his heart.

Sunday morning my alarm went off at five and I felt Emma's cold nose on my cheek, nudging me awake. I reached over and stroked her soft head. "Hey, girl."

I was rewarded with a quiet yip. Stretching, I slipped my feet over the side of the bed and realized I was still dressed in yesterday's clothes. I must have fallen asleep on the swing with Greg. Had he carried me upstairs to the bed? I would have left my sorry butt on the swing. Okay, maybe the sofa. The man was better than me, that I knew.

I let Emma outside while I slipped into my running clothes and got ready for the morning. Coffee had been made and programmed, but I only took a half cup before I clipped Emma's blue leash on her matching collar and we headed out the door. The morning fog was still heavy and we stayed on the footpath running in front of my house all the way to the highway. Traffic was nonexistent as we crossed, then once I could see the parking lot and beach were empty, I unclicked the leash. Then we ran, my footsteps echoing in my mind in rhythm with the waves coming in from the beach.

An hour later, showered and ready for the day, I opened the store and started brewing coffee. Traffic even during the holidays was slow on my early shift, so I knew I'd have time to put in next week's supply order, make a quick breakfast of cranberry scone and juice, and sink down into the couch to start reading a young adult fantasy novel that was coming out as a Christmas season movie. I'd sold so many copies of the book recently, I figured it was time to see what the fuss was about. I'd just started grooving with the story when the bell rang and I put the book away with a smile to greet my first customer.

"Is your aunt here?" Josh Thomas stood in the doorway, peering around the room like Jackie might be crouched hiding behind a chair or under the counter.

"She doesn't work until five. What can I get you, Josh?" I stood and walked back to the counter.

"Large black." When he arrived at the cash register, he shoved an envelope at me. "Give her this."

I glanced at the creamy white linen paper and knew what it held immediately. "You think a Hallmark greeting will get you out of the doghouse?"

Josh blushed, then shrugged. "I'm out of ideas." He hefted his large frame onto one of my bar stools. "You know her. What can I do? I hate it when she's mad at me."

I'd never seen Jackie go back from a slight, but telling him that would only add to his misery. I handed him his coffee. "Give her time. She's never been stood up before."

"I just can't believe she thinks I was with another woman." He stared at the coffee cup like he'd never seen a paper cup with a sleeve on it before.

"Did you find out who had tried to visit that night?" I didn't particularly like Josh, and he and my aunt together just made me shiver when I thought about it, but the man was hurting.

"That's just it. I leave my back door open." He flicked his glance at me. "Don't lecture. I know I'm taking a risk. Sometimes, I forget my keys and I've been locked out too many times late at night when I've left the shop. No one uses that door anyway."

"Well, apparently someone did. Did you notice anything missing? Or out of place?" I frowned. Someone must have thought the antique dealer kept valuables in his apartment and knew he kept the door open.

Josh shook his head. "Nothing was gone. My front window shade was open, but I could have done that and not remembered."

Or someone could have used the apartment's vantage point to watch Main Street. I glanced across the street. The only two open buildings directly across from our side of the street were The Glass Slipper and the liquor/cigar store. A vintage clothing store had bought out the building directly in front of Josh's store, but they weren't scheduled to open until after the first of the year.

Josh noticed my musing. "What?"

I shook my head and smiled. "Nothing, just trying to figure out who would have snuck into your place."

"I know exactly who it was." Josh pounded his finger on the table. "Brenda Morgan."

My eyebrows furrowed. "Why would Brenda break into your home?"

Josh lifted his chin and sighed. "The woman has been after me since Craig died. She's always in my shop, looking at items for The Castle, asking my opinion about purchases. She's trying to woo me."

I barely suppressed my giggle when I realized Josh was dead serious. "Then why would she go to your apartment?"

Josh considered me like I had a third head. "Obviously, she was looking for some late-night entertainment from me." He frowned. "Or she knew I was supposed to be with Jackie that night and was trying to make her jealous. That's probably it. She's probably trying to see if there's a way to combine the two apartments into one when she gets her hooks into me."

I didn't even know how to respond. "Are you sure Brenda's not just trying to learn the antique business from you? You were Craig's expert, maybe she trusts your opinion?"

Josh stood and pulled his wallet out of his pants pocket. He set down two one-dollar bills that were so crisp, I wondered if they'd just come off the press. "I know when a woman is interested, Miss Gardner. Thank you for the coffee and keep the change."

All twenty-two cents. What a big spender. Then I felt bad for being uncharitable. There had to be a better side of Josh that my aunt had uncovered. Although I wasn't sure what it could be. I watched him walk out of the store and then back toward his own business. Brenda stalking Josh? She'd get a laugh out of that.

The door chimed and more customers arrived. I stayed busy up until Toby walked in. As I turned the shop over to him, I thought about the lady from the bed-and-breakfast. I had planned on watching for her driver and asking him how her day of reading at the beach had gone, but for the life of me, I couldn't think of what customer he could have been. Maybe they stayed at the B&B for breakfast today or maybe they just slept in. Sundays were supposed to be a day of rest.

Toby waved me off when I offered to stay longer. "Get out of here. I can handle the shift. If a tour bus shows up, I'll call Jackie down early."

I held up the envelope Josh had left. "When you see her, give her this. Josh is trying to woo her back."

He laughed. "I think Jackie's too smart to be won over by a card. She doesn't seem to be a hearts-and-flowers type of girl."

"True. Josh, on the other hand, thinks that Brenda's in love with him and is trying to break the happy couple up."

Toby didn't hesitate to laugh. When he stopped and wiped his eyes, he cocked his head. "You're serious? Brenda? Does he think she's an idiot? Or a glutton for punishment? Craig's been gone less than six months, and he thinks Brenda's looking for a replacement?"

"That's the story I got this morning from the man." I pulled my purse over my shoulder. "I'd better warn Brenda that Josh is wise to her tricks."

"Keep your phone handy when you tell her, she might keel over with a stroke or something. No one expects that kind of shock to their system." Toby nodded to the customer walking in the door. "See you Tuesday?"

"Have a great day off." I tucked my unfinished book into my purse and headed home, grabbing a copy of the Sunday paper on my way out. Time to spend some quality one-on-one with the main man. I might even bake a pumpkin pie later to thank him for seeing me to bed last night.

Greg's call off began as I was walking home. "Sorry, kiddo, I'm stuck working today. I guess the district attorney wants to go over what we've got on Ted's demise."

"Which is what?" I aimed for casual indifference.

A chuckle came over the line. "Good try. Why don't you call Amy and see if you can do a girl's day?"

"What, you think I can't deal with a Sunday without you? I'll have you know, I already have serious plans."

"You found a new book?"

"Exactly." I paused in front of Diamond Lille's. "Right after I stop and grab some lunch."

A voice sounded from a distance. "Hey, I've got to go, meeting's starting."

I clicked off the phone and slipped it into my purse. So much for quality couple time, I grumbled, but I'd known what I'd been getting into by dating the local police detective. I slipped into a booth and waved down a waitress.

Today definitely deserved a milk shake and something fried. Choices I'd regret later. I'd ordered and had pulled out my book to read when I heard a voice coming from the next booth.

"I don't care what it might look like. The man owes me. It's my right." The woman was insistent. As she stood and threw some money on the table, I realized she was talking on her cell.

She turned away from the booth, and our eyes met. It was Marie Jones.

CHAPTER 8

Marie blanched when she saw me. She nodded a greeting, but I could see in her eyes, she wondered how much of the conversation I'd overheard. The woman nearly knocked the waitress over in her haste to leave. Carrie, holding my vanilla shake, came over to my table.

"Almost wore this. Did you see Marie take out of here like the devil was chasing her?"

I nodded, then with a napkin wiped up the spilt shake that was running down the frosted glass and onto the table. "She seemed upset. You know what about?"

Carrie shook her head, grabbing the napkins off the table where I crumpled them. "No clue, she's been on that phone since she walked into the place. She came in calm and when she left, she'd ratcheted all the way up to ballistic. I've never seen her that way before."

"Me neither."

The cook yelled across the café. "Carrie, your food's dying here, quit yapping and get this to the customers."

Carrie shrugged. "Gotta go. Ed's in a mood. Seems like it's going around."

I sipped on the icy shake, wondering if what I heard would prove Marie was the missing wife. She could have been talking about revealing herself for a part of Ted's inheritance. Had she been declared dead officially, or was she simply missing in the eyes of the law? Something like that would be hard to come back from. And what had happened to the ransom money?

I pulled out my notebook and started writing down my questions and possible places to find the information. I didn't want to get Greg involved, not yet. What if I was putting two and two together and getting five?

When Carrie delivered my chicken strips, I hurried and ate, anxious to get home to my laptop where I could research my questions.

After power walking home, I'd just sat down at the table with a glass of iced tea when a knock sounded at my front door. At least I might have burned off a few of the extra calories from my lunch.

Jackie stood at the doorway, dressed in a dusty blue power suit and heels. A typical Sunday visiting outfit for her. I swung open the door and noticed a Coffee, Books, and More to-go box in her hand. "You don't have to bring something to eat every time you visit."

She air-kissed me, then made a beeline to the kitchen. "I wanted to grab you before you left the shop, but I got caught up in planning my new promotion. I want your approval so I can get the flyers printed tomorrow."

I followed her into the kitchen, where she'd already started making a pot of coffee. "I have iced tea."

She turned and frowned at me. "When have you known me to drink that? You think I'm Southern or something?"

"Plenty of non-Southerners drink iced tea, at least the unsweetened kind." I'd had a visitor at the shop last month who asked if I had sweet tea and when I offered him sugar for his tea, he'd laughed, telling me I didn't have a clue if I thought sugar alone could make it an acceptable substitute.

Jackie grabbed plates and sliced the pumpkin walnut bread that Sadie had begun providing the shop. The bread was moist and flavorful and just the right treat on a not-so-cold fall California day. At least we could pretend we had four seasons instead of two: summer and not summer.

I closed the Google screen I'd been working on, trying different variations of what I suspected was Marie's former name, hoping I'd get more gossip column discussion of the disappearance.

Jackie's eyebrows raised a bit at my action, but she didn't ask, so I didn't have to tell her. Or lie. She pushed a hand-drawn paper in front of me. "I want to do a book drive for the children's center in Bakerstown. Did you know Sasha's daughter goes there?"

I frowned. "I didn't even realize Sasha had a daughter. Isn't she a little young?"

Jackie pursed her lips. "Don't be judgmental. People make mistakes and they learn from them."

I held my hands up in a gesture of mock defense. "I only said I didn't realize Sasha had a child. Don't bite my head off."

"Well, then you need to pay more attention to our young assistant. She's quite a remarkable young lady." Jackie stood and poured herself a cup of the coffee that had just finished brewing. She held out the pot, questioning nonverbally if I wanted a cup, but I shook my head. When she returned to the table, she focused back on the flyer. "Anyway, I thought with us being a bookstore, we could do a children's book drive for the center. Sasha says they don't have many toys or books available for the kids."

"I think it's a great idea. We could talk to the center and see what books they'd want, make up a list, then from what wasn't donated, we could fill in the blanks. I guess we'd have to start with a few on hand to make a display." My mind was racing as I considered the possibilities.

"I already pulled a few of our more popular kids' books earlier." Jackie picked at her bread. "I needed a distraction."

I wondered if Toby had given her Josh's card. I covered her hand with mine. "Do you want to talk about Josh?"

Jackie shuddered, then shook her head. "Not now. I want to talk about the book drive. So I have your permission to get flyers made up tomorrow?"

I tapped her hand, then picked up the flyer. "I love the idea. I wanted to do something for the season, some charity thing, but honestly, I haven't even thought about what. At least not since . . ." I paused, not wanting to bring up finding Ted.

Jackie pointed to the flyer. "I'm going to take a picture of a kid reading a book sitting on the couch in the shop. Toby says his girlfriend has a little girl who would be perfect. They're coming in tonight, about seven, to get pictures taken before the shop closes."

"Wait, Toby's dating a woman with a kid? Elisa, right?" I shook my head. "Is she crazy? Toby's a total player."

"Well, from the way he talked, he's only dating this woman. She kind of laid down the law on him before she'd agree to go out on a first date. Sounds like she has a good head on her shoulders." Jackie took back the flyer. "Now, I need you to go to the Bakerstown Children's Center tomorrow and talk to the manager. Sasha says her name is Mrs. Jenson. Have her pull together a list and send it to me as soon as possible."

"We could just call." I thought longingly about my free Monday.

"If you want to distance yourself from the project, I guess that's fine." Jackie sniffed, letting me know her use of the word "fine" really meant "hell no."

"It just so happens I was planning on going into town tomorrow anyway. I want to meet our new program director for the interns." I opened my notebook and listed off the children's center visit as one of my to dos for tomorrow.

"You want to meet the new guy? Or you just want to find out more about Ted and who would have killed him?" Jackie laughed at my shocked face. "Toby let it slip that the suicide was staged. It's a small town, you think I get all my gossip from you?"

"Make sure you let Greg know I didn't say anything." I shook my head. "He's already taken a more official statement, and for once, I'm not a suspect. I guess Carrie can vouch that I didn't have a gun hidden in my picnic basket as I walked down Main Street."

"You do seem to have the worst luck. I doubt South Cove has had a murder in the last few years that you haven't happened upon or been attached to the victim in some way."

"It's not like I'm looking to be part of these events, they just happen." I thought about the way Ted appeared, slumped in the car. "I'd be happy not to find any more dead bodies." I turned my head skyward. "You listening, God?"

"I think divine intervention doesn't quite work that way. Maybe He has a plan for you." Jackie finished her coffee. "Either way, we need to get this book drive started. I need some good works points in my book before I go and speak to Saint Peter."

"Jackie, you're not leaving this earth that quickly. Besides, I'm sure you're already on the good list." I took her cup. "More?"

Jackie shook her head. "I've done more things I've regretted in my life than you'll ever know. Anyway, I've got to be going. My shift starts in less than an hour and I need to get ready." She kissed me on the cheek. "Thanks for your help with this. When Sasha told me about how little these kids have, it almost broke my heart."

I walked her to the door. "We can't save everyone in the world, but we sure can fix this one problem."

She waved as she got into her car and headed out to the road and the less-than-two-minute drive back to the shop and her apartment. I guess she couldn't have walked the distance in those heels, but sometimes, I wondered about my aunt and her attachment to her car.

I closed the door, bolted the lock, and headed back to the kitchen to continue my search. Instead, I found myself perusing my book supplier's Web site and making a wish list to take with me tomorrow to my meeting with Mrs. Jenson. That way she wouldn't have to make up a list on the spot and she could veto any controversial books.

Although what could be banned for five-year-olds, I had no clue.

The afternoon passed quietly, with a stint out on the back porch with Emma worrying a new bone and me deep into the young adult novel I'd started reading that morning. No wonder adults and kids loved this book. My thoughts were still with the story when I heard the tires of a vehicle spin out in front of the house.

Kids, I thought. Getting one last burst of speed before they entered town and would have their actions reported to their parents sooner than they would arrive home. There were joys of life in a small town, but for the kids growing up here, there were also pitfalls. Everyone felt compelled to watch the kids to make sure no one was causing trouble. That might have been part of life in a tourist town, too; we had an image to uphold. Emma took off for the front yard and started barking.

When she didn't come back when I called, I set the book down on the swing and went around to see what she'd cornered. Probably a rabbit.

She stood at the front door, sniffing a package.

"Hey, girl, what did you find?" I leaned down and realized it was a dead rabbit. But not one my dog had trapped. The body was wrapped in a sheet of paper.

My hands were shaking as I unfolded the paper, setting the body of the rabbit on the edge of the porch rail out of Emma's reach.

"Stop putting your nose in where it doesn't belong," I read aloud. The words chilled my blood even more. Someone wanted me out of the investigation of Ted's murder. The implications of my continued involvement were clear.

I dialed Greg's private line.

An hour later, I was staring at the television, not seeing the movie that Greg had turned on when he arrived, sitting me gently on the couch, Emma at my feet. There'd been more people than him out on the porch, taking pictures and dealing with the deceased bunny. The hair had been so soft, warm still. Yet I'd known as soon as I'd picked it up and it fell limp in my hand that it had been dead.

I heard voices on the porch, then a car drove away. Greg came into the house and slipped onto the couch next to me, turning the volume down on the television.

"You okay?" He rubbed my arm. "You feel cold." He reached over the couch and grabbed the quilt I left, covering the back to lay it gently around me.

I swallowed. "I don't know why this is upsetting me so much. It was just a rabbit."

Greg's voice hardened. "You had a threat on your life. I know you feel bad for the bunny, but maybe you're reacting to the note, not the body?"

"What did you do with it?" I hoped it still didn't sit on my porch.

"Tim took it back to the station. I don't think we could get any evidence off it, but maybe the crime guys can pull a miracle." He pulled me into his arms. "Seriously, are you okay? You're too quiet, you're scaring me."

I shrugged, trying to brush off the terror that I was feeling. My throat was dry and I swallowed, trying to keep the waver out of my voice when I spoke. "I didn't know anyone was watching me. I haven't even found out anything." A vision of Marie's face at Lille's filled my mind. Could she have done this?

"You know Ted was murdered. Why do you mess with things that aren't your business? One of these days, you're going to get into something you can't get out of."

"Like drug dealers trying to kill me in my shop?" I chided him. When Craig had been murdered last year, I'd been targeted by his murderers because of my inability to stay out of things. I laughed, not feeling the humor. "You'd think I'd learn."

This time Greg laughed, too. He squeezed me gently. "Your heart's in the right place. I guess I am just going to have to keep you closer to me when trouble visits South Cove."

"Being close to you isn't a hardship, you know." I laid my head on his chest. "Thanks for putting me to bed the other night."

"I was on a Boy Scout mission, to help a woman in distress." He put up three fingers. "I didn't even steal a kiss."

I leaned back and stared at him. "You let me fall asleep without a kiss?"

"Okay, so that part I lied about." He chuckled and put his hand on my head, laying it back down on his chest. "What do you say I take you to dinner? You feel up to heading down to Lille's?"

Lille's. I sat up and pushed the quilt aside. "I need to tell you something."

When I added the conversation I overheard at Lille's to the list of evidence that had me, at least, convinced Marie Jones was the missing wife, he narrowed his eyes. When he didn't say anything, I couldn't stand it and burst out with "Well?"

He glanced at me. "Possible. At least it's a lead. This case is dryer than the Mojave." He tapped my leg. "You ready to get dinner?"

I nodded, stunned. I thought I'd been giving him a viable lead and yet he couldn't be bothered with checking Marie out to see if she was the one throwing threats at my front door? It had to be her, there was no one else.

I figured I was dressed good enough for a dinner in town so I put Emma out the back door with a bowl of water, more food, and her bone. I grabbed my book off the swing and set it on the kitchen table after locking the door. Greg picked it up, glancing at the back.

"Not your typical reading material."

I swung my purse on my shoulder and stood waiting. "I wanted to see what the fuss was about. I've sold more copies of that one book than anything else in the last three months. And next month, they're releasing a movie based on the books."

"I've heard about this." He set the book down and put his hand on my back. As he led me out my front door, I glanced at the place where I'd dropped the note. The porch was empty.

Lille's was quiet for a Sunday night, but as soon as we'd ordered, Mayor Baylor and his wife made an entrance. As soon as Tina saw us, she dragged Marvin through the tables and stood in front of our booth. "Jill, I'm so sorry about your little mishap. I hope you're doing better."

It took me a few seconds to realize she was talking about my finding Ted's body not the rabbit. "It was quite a shock, but I'm fine now. Thanks for asking."

She leaned closer. "We'll have to talk soon. I want all the details." Tina glanced at Greg. "Especially since your boyfriend refuses to tell me anything."

Mayor Baylor cleared his throat. "Now, Tina, you know Greg can't talk about an open investigation. It would be"—he paused and glared at me—"unethical."

Greg turned his pizza-and-a-game smile on Tina. "That's why I've been staying away while you decorate. You know I have trouble telling you no."

I almost gagged as I listened to him flirt with the woman. Greg was much better at this politicking game than I'd realized. Tina was still talking and now they were looking at me.

"So I'll be over Tuesday morning to discuss your business's contribution to the festival." Tina arched an eyebrow. "Around ten?"

"Sounds good. I'm excited to see what you've come up with for a theme." I felt a tad bit guilty for not standing up for Darla, but if Greg could be nice to the meanest couple in South Cove, I could give it a try.

"It's not just decorations, you know. We'll have to do a town charity project." Tina glanced around the almost empty dining room. "I'm sure we could find some family who's poverty-stricken to support this year. The Good Book says we're supposed to take care of our neighbors."

"Jackie's doing, well, the shop is doing a children's book drive for the Bakerstown Children's Center. The entire town could help us with that, if you'd like." Jackie would love the idea, well, once she got over the fact that Tina would bulldoze her out of being in charge. Maybe I should have kept my mouth shut.

Tina exchanged a look with her husband that clearly said, Can you believe this woman? Then she turned back to me, and in a calm voice like I was a child, said, "That won't do at all. I mean, I'm sure it's a fine project for your little store, but we're going to do something that will change lives. Not just entertain a bunch of kids."

"Studies show kids who learn to read early are less likely to drop out of school and later stay out of jail or prison or worse." I felt my back stiffen as my words sounded more and more clipped.

"Why, yes, I've read those sad stories, too, but if a family needs food and shelter and heat, giving them a book is just rubbing their noses in their inability to care for the family's basic needs." She focused her attention on Greg. "Don't you agree?"

Before Greg could answer, the ringtone version of "My Heart Will Go On" filled the café. I wondered if she realized how appropriate a sinking ship theme song was for her personal ringtone. I didn't get a chance to ask as she answered the phone. "Tina Baylor," she crooned into the mouthpiece as she motioned for her husband to follow her. They sat in a booth on the other side of the dining room, the mayor studying the menu like he hadn't eaten here two or three times a week for the last ten years.

"I guess we're dismissed." I took a sip of the soda Carrie had brought over before the visitors had arrived at our table. "Boy, she has you wrapped around her little finger."

"I'm used to the game." Greg shrugged. "She's always been like that. She didn't even know my name the first three years I worked for South Cove. Now that I'm divorced and available for her to try to set me up with her friends, suddenly I'm interesting."

"Available, huh?" My blood was beginning to heat. I hadn't liked Tina before; now I wanted to strangle her. "Why would she think you were available?"

He grinned and put his hand over mine. "Well, I was interesting before I started dating you. Now I just think she's confused."

Our food was delivered and for the next hour, we talked about anything but the case. He recounted Amy and Esmeralda's day with the steamroller that was Tina Baylor. I told him about Aunt Jackie's book drive and, because I knew he loved gossip as much as I did, about her fight with Josh.

"The guy needs to learn to shut up when he's ahead. Jackie will calm down, but not if he keeps making himself a target." Greg pushed away his plate, empty except for the crumbs of the bacon big burger and one last French fry, which he grabbed and popped into his mouth.

"Is that how you deal with me when we fight? Stay out of reach?" I took the last bite of my enchilada, eyeing the dessert menu.

"You've discovered my evil plan." Greg grinned. "Sherry wouldn't let me stay away. If she wanted to fight, she'd come down to the station or wherever I was to get it done and over with. You, on the other hand, you steam for a while, then the issue works itself out."

"I'm going to be very upset if you don't order the Brownie Surprise and two spoons." I pointed at the picture on the table flyer standing in the salt and pepper holder.

Greg waved over Carrie to give her the order. "And that's the other thing; you can be plied with food into a good mood. Sherry wanted jewelry or later, in our marriage, cold hard cash."

"Well, maybe we should invite her over for Thanksgiving and I can learn a few things from her," I teased. Jim had tried to push an invite for Sherry and her new banker boyfriend.

"If you do, she can have my place. I already told Jim that she wouldn't be on the guest list." He nodded to the dessert Carrie had just set on the table between us. "Be good or I won't let you have a bite."

CHAPTER 9

One in three people dread Monday. They've done studies. It's a day filled with sleep deprived commuters, grumpy receptionists, and annoyed customers. Problems that any other day would be handled quickly with a smile seemed to take forever to complete. It was that way when I worked for the law office. The group I hung with typically gathered at the little tavern next to the office building every Monday evening, throwing out war stories, trying to best the story told by the last guy.

Now I loved Mondays. It was my day off. Typically when the tourist seasons were slow, the shop was closed on both Sunday and Monday, but the holiday season traffic demanded the doors stay open during the weekend. I slept in that morning, only rousing when Emma gave me a slurpy kiss. Sunshine filled the room and I threw off the covers, padding downstairs to let her outside.

Last night, Greg had dropped me off at my door close to nine, giving me a quick good-night kiss as he returned to the station to pore over the files and notes from the investigation. I threw a load into the washer, grabbed a bottle of water, and took my book upstairs to continue exploring the fantasy world. It was almost one when I'd finished the book and turned off the light, visions of elves and talking mushrooms taking over my dreams.

After I'd brushed my teeth and pulled my hair into a scrunchy, I started the coffee and opened my notebook-slash-day-planner. During the week, I'd write off all the housekeeping jobs I'd put onto Monday's schedule as well as any errands I needed to run. Like visiting the Work Today program and meeting the new program director. Time to find out who'd I'd be working with for the next eight weeks. And find out if Ted had left any hints of why he'd moved so far west from his family's influence. I was sure I wasn't going to be able to walk in and search his desk, but maybe there'd be something.

Emma barked at the door. She eyed the hook where I hung her running leash, then looked back at me, gauging my interest.

"We'll go, just give me some time to do a few things." I patted her golden head. She gave me a lick on the hand in response, then grabbed her teddy bear and headed to her kitchen bed to try to tear the stuffed animal to pieces.

I sipped my coffee as I wrote Ted's name on the top of a page in my notebook, then wrote Marie's name at the bottom. Would Marie stoop to threatening me because of the conversation I overheard? It didn't seem her style, but really, what did I know about the woman? I had paid for one more class with her next Thursday. Maybe I'd have a chance to ask her about her phone conversation then.

I wrote the name *Katherine Janell Corbet Hendricks* in the middle of the page, and opening my laptop, I started working on finding out anything and everything on Ted's missing wife. Like had she studied glass design. At nine, I closed my web browser and frowned at the paper. I hadn't added anything to the page except the name of the college where Katherine and Ted had met. I'd pulled up the college's Web site, and besides the fact the library was named for the Hendricks family, there wasn't a clue that Ted had even graduated. I'd sent a quick e-mail to the address listed for the alumni committee saying I was putting together a story about Ted and Katherine for our local newspaper. I even threw in the part of feeling connected since I'd found the body. Maybe if the recipient was just a little nosy, she'd respond to find out more about Ted's death.

When I stood to put my cup in the sink, Emma watched me, hope filling her face. If I was going to get a run in before my Bakerstown trip, it was time to go. "Let me get changed and we'll go."

Emma's tail beat on the floor in happy response.

Just over an hour later, I was showered and on the road, my note-book in my purse. I would stop by the work program, make a detour to the children's center, then I planned on a quick lunch at the new café that had opened last month. From what Aunt Jackie had re-ported, the food was amazing. Then a quick stop at the grocery store, and home to South Cove. I should be back in the house and curled up with a book by three.

I turned into the nearly empty parking lot. Maybe the place was closed on Mondays, too?

I walked into the deserted lobby. Folding chairs lined one wall. On the other, five antique computers sat side by side, the large, bulky monitors dark. A printer sat on another table, a bulletin board hung above the table. Flyers were tacked to the board, most yellowed with age. In one corner of the room, a play area had been built up kind of like a sandbox, with a few broken and partial toys on the floor. I walked toward the back and a young girl burst from the hallway, a box in her hands.

"Oh, I'm sorry. How long have you been waiting? I didn't hear anyone come in." The girl set the box on the desk. She pushed it to-ward me. "I wasn't expecting you for another couple of hours."

"What?" I wasn't sure I'd heard her correctly.

The phone rang. "Bakerstown Work Today, may I help you?" The girl twisted her hair as she grinned at me. "Hold on a second, I'll find out."

She put the call on hold and pointed to the box. "There's most of Ted's stuff, but I've got a few more things to bring out." Then she dis-appeared toward the back.

"Wait," I called after her. I glanced at the box, my curiosity get-ting the best of me. I looked in the direction the girl had disappeared, then started digging through the box, just in case there was anything there. I found an old wedding picture of Ted and Katherine, his smile bright, hers more tentative. I turned over the picture and saw the back coming loose, a piece of paper hanging out. When I twisted the hold-ers on the back, a folded sheet of paper fell into my hand.

A voice called out from down the hall and I stepped away from the box and the desk, shoving the paper that had somehow stayed in my hand into my purse. This time when the girl returned, an older woman followed. She smiled and greeted me. "So you knew Ted?"

I nodded, but quickly added, "I think there's been a mistake. I'm not here to pick up his things. Actually, I'm Jill Gardner, the business consultant for South Cove's council. I worked with Ted on the placements he made recently in our community."

The woman narrowed her eyes at the young girl, who shrugged. "I figured she was the person who called earlier."

"Alice means well," the older woman said to me as if the girl wasn't sitting three feet away from us. "She just makes assumptions."

I smiled at Alice, silently thanking her for leaving me alone to rifle through Ted's things. I might have found a clue because of her mistake. "No worries." I held out my hand. "We haven't been introduced. I take it you're the new program director?"

The woman laughed. "New, old, just depends on your perspective. Bakerstown was my assignment before Ted came and replaced me. I got moved into the city. I have to say, I'm glad I'm back home." She shook my hand. "Candy Peterson. I've heard good things about you from all the South Cove placements, especially Sasha."

"She's a sweet girl." I glanced around the lobby. "Seems quiet for a Monday. Don't people look for work at the first of the week?"

"We're in between sessions. In fact, the South Cove group is our last one until January rolls in. Of course, all of our participants, past and current, are welcome to use the facility, but it's hard to get them to come in, especially when they can search the web at home without driving or walking someplace to do it."

"What kind of placement rate do you have?" I'd worked with a program in the city as part of my community service work required of first-year hires in my office. I'd wanted to stay on, but making billable hours for the partners became more and more difficult, especially with the family law I enjoyed practicing. Something had to give, and since I was still trying to keep my failing marriage alive, charity work fell off my to-do list.

"For the last three years, it's been one hundred percent placement rate." She paused, waiting for a reaction.

My eyes widened. "That's amazing. I worked with a center a few years ago and they typically never made it past sixty."

"Most centers average sixty to seventy, depending on the location." She threw a dark look to the box. "Let's just say I'm hesitant to stand behind the validity of our numbers."

Matt had told Darla that Ted had been playing with the placements for his personal gain. Could he also have been fudging the numbers? He seemed like the type who would want to win at all costs. I pointedly viewed my watch. "I didn't mean to take up so much of your time. I hope the next time you're in South Cove you stop by and have a cup of coffee on me. We can talk more."

Candy walked me to the door. "I'm planning on visiting the placement sites next week, just to clean up the files a bit. I'll be sure to stop by."

I paused. "Who's coming for Ted's things? I didn't think his family had arrived." Actually, I didn't think his family was even coming.

"I'm not sure. Alice said it was an older woman who called, but I think anyone over twenty-five, she considers ancient." She straightened the open sign on the door. "I feel bad that I'm benefiting from such a tragedy. Who knew Ted had such deep feelings that he could have been drawn to this end? Between you and me, I always thought he didn't have it in him. Ted was not someone with real emotions."

"He did have strong opinions." I paused, my hand on the door handle. "Thank you for making the transition so easy. I look forward to working with you on this placement and maybe others."

Candy acted like I'd promised her the cake batter bowl. "I'll bring some pamphlets when I come by next week."

We said our good-byes, and I wondered about how upset Candy had been to be transferred out of an assignment she considered home. As I turned the Jeep out of the Work Today parking lot, a dark Lincoln Town Car turned into the lot. I'd almost talked myself out of listing Candy as a suspect when I'd arrived in front of the children's center. Someone had painted a mural of sea animals cavorting in the ocean that covered the entire south side of the building. It was beautiful and a bit disturbing at the same time. The deep blue of the ocean scene made me dizzy as I stared into the fake depths.

I located the front door and slipped into the ice cool of the air-conditioned building. The sounds of the fans echoed through the open foyer, lined with tiny lockers, all with combination locks built into the doors. The lockers had been painted primary colors and seemed to be set in sections of red, blue, and yellow.

I heard noises down the hall, and when I walked into the main room, I noticed the same division of colors in the carpet. The large gym had been painted the three colors too, and now I could see that blue held infants; yellow, the toddlers; and finally red were the older children almost ready to be sent off to public school.

A woman sat at a metal desk to the left of the door. "May I help you?" she asked, without much enthusiasm.

I pulled out a bundle of children's books I'd pulled from the store's shelves as an introductory gift and handed them to the receptionist. "I'm here to help you. One of your customers, Sasha Smith, has a child here. She's temping at our store for the season, and we'd like to run a book drive for your center."

The woman stood, her energy level changing immediately. "Let me get you to Diane. She's the program manager. I'm sure they'd love to have you sponsor." She held on to the small pile of books like it was a check for an unspeakable value. "Come with me."

She led me through the blue area to a small office in the wall, a window looking out into the larger room. I could see a woman at the desk who was on the phone, but when she heard the knock, she waved us in and quickly terminated the call.

The woman appeared to be in her late forties or early fifties, but she stood and held out her hand. "I'm Diane Jenson, I take it you're here to enroll your child?"

My head snapped back in unconcealed horror. "Uh, no. I don't have kids." I almost added "yet," but that would have been looking into a future that might or might not happen.

The receptionist bubbled, "She's Sasha's new boss. They want to run a book drive for us." She gently set the books on the worn wooden desk in front of her manager. "Isn't that wonderful news?"

Diane leafed through the books I'd carefully chosen off the shelf, tapping her finger on one before she moved on. "These are lovely. Thank you for the donation."

"I don't think you understand. We're doing a holiday drive at Coffee, Books, and More in South Cove. Those are just the books I brought you today. We haven't even started collecting yet." I rushed to explain our plan. I handed her mine and Jackie's business cards ending with, "My aunt is the force behind this project. She'll be in touch, but I wanted to stop in and get your blessing before we started advertising."

"How nice. Many of our children don't have access to books at home." She sighed, looking out the window. "I suspect some of the kids are actually on the street when they leave here. Story time is the most popular time of day. Could I give you a wish list from the staff?"

"We thought you might want input." I tapped Jackie's card. "You can call my aunt or just fax over a list when you get one together. We'll make certain your Santa list is filled." I'd order the books myself, even if we didn't get donations. I had a bit of money set aside I liked to call the Miss Emily Fund. This would be a perfect use of some of my inheritance from my old friend.

Diane forced a tired smile and offered me a tour of the facility. Glancing at my watch for real this time, I reluctantly begged off. If I was going to get anything done today, I needed to get moving. Leaving the center, I blessed my parents for instilling a love of books in me. When my day wasn't going as planned, or life just continued to kick me in the gut, I knew I could escape into a world where happily-ever-afters were a given and problems were overcome. One of my patrons loved her true crime stories. I'd read one, the Ted Bundy story, and swore the genre off my reading list. I knew evil existed in the real world; I didn't want to be reminded as I read for pleasure.

A longer-than-expected trip to the grocery store and finally I was back on the road to South Cove. I'd had to trade my leisurely lunch at the new café for a drive-through bag. Munching on the fries as I steered my Jeep down the coastal highway, glimpsing the ocean at times, low mountains at others, I felt content. Everything would work out. Jackie and Josh would stop sniping, Greg would find Ted's killer, and the store would get so many donations for books, we'd be able to gift each child their own small library. Hope sprang eternal for about three minutes until I arrived back at the house to an unexpected visitor.

Jackie sat on my porch, tapping her Jimmy Choo heels when I arrived at the house. I waved as I climbed out of the Jeep, opening the back hatch and grabbing an armload of grocery sacks.

When I reached the porch, she took my keys from my hand and

unlocked the door. As she power walked into the kitchen, she waved at the sacks. "Put those down and go get the rest. I'll start putting things away."

"Thanks." I set my purse down and hurried to grab the final few sacks. I'd bring in the soda later, not wanting my aunt to see how many twelve-packs I'd bought. The stuff had been on a crazy good sale, so I'd have drinks covered for weeks, maybe months.

By the time I'd brought the final load sans most of the soda into the kitchen, Jackie had everything else put away. She glanced into the remaining sack. "You should shop at a warehouse store. We could save a lot of money by buying in bulk and sharing the cost."

I hadn't thought of that. I'd been tempted to get the store a membership, but my suppliers were all local and loyal and I didn't want to cut their deliveries. And just buying for me and the occasional Greg's dinner visit, didn't warrant a lot of groceries. I'd always seen warehouse stores as being more effective for people with big families. But maybe I could get Amy into the buying club, as well.

"That's a great idea." I grabbed a soda out of the fridge and sat at the table. Jackie had already started a pot of coffee in between unloading sacks. The woman was an efficiency machine. "Come sit down. I want to tell you about visiting the center."

My aunt sank into a chair and groaned while looking at the oversized clock on the wall. "I knew I was forgetting something. I never got to the printers."

"Oh, I thought that was why you were here." I took in my aunt's appearance. She wore her usual suit and heels, but the buttons on the jacket were off-kilter, and glancing at her face, I saw she'd put eye shadow on one side, but not the other. Not the typical polished Jackie look. "Are you okay? You look . . . off."

She gave me a look that if I'd taken it seriously, would have frozen me in my chair. "I don't know what you mean."

I dug in my purse. "Well, for one thing, your jacket is buttoned wrong."

Jackie glanced down and straightened her buttons, letting out a short sigh as she did. "I'm perfectly fine. I just got dressed in a hurry this morning."

I found my compact, a holdout so I could at least pretend I wore makeup most days. I flipped the small circle open and dusted off the mirror before I handed it to her. "Check your eyes."

"They aren't red, are they?" Jackie glanced at one, then the other, and when she turned back toward me, I knew she hadn't even seen what was missing.

"Why would they be red? Have you been crying?"

Jackie shook her head quickly, a little too quickly in my opinion.

I nodded to the mirror. "Look again, you see something missing?"

She frowned but then checked a second time, horror filling her face. "Oh. My. God. And I've been out and about for hours like this. Why didn't someone tell me I'd forgotten an entire eye?" She pulled out a small makeup bag from her purse with a mini mascara, eyeliner, and shadow. She set out her lipstick, as well. "Might as well refresh everything."

"Do you want to tell me what's going on?" I leaned back and watched her correct her glamour mistake from that morning.

She ignored me, focusing on the compact. "Are you telling me this is the only makeup you carry with you?"

"Heavens, no." I grinned as my aunt's face filled with relief. "I also have a tube of cherry ChapStick at all times."

She groaned as she finished up with her corrections. "I taught you better than that. No wonder Greg hasn't taken the next step and put a ring on that finger. You're not trying hard enough."

I sipped my soda, feeling pleasure at the slight burn as the cola slipped down my throat. "No, you're wrong. I'm not trying at all. If Greg and I do take this to the next level, it's because he loves me, not some ideal version of me."

Jackie tucked the makeup away into her case and handed me the compact. "Studies show that women who wear makeup are more confident than women who don't. It's not a matter of showing an un-real persona. It's showing your best version."

"Can we just disagree and you can tell me what's bothering you?" I ignored the compact on the table.

She stood and poured herself a cup of coffee. Her head turned away, and she sighed. "That man. He left me a card."

"Josh, you mean." I didn't want to say I knew about the card and get a lecture about taking his side in this fight.

She didn't turn around, just stood at the counter after putting the pot back on the coffeemaker. "He says he loves me."

I was stunned. I knew Josh had it bad for my aunt, but I'd never considered them a real couple. I didn't know what to say, so I went with the obvious. "Do you love him?"

She came back to the table and sipped her coffee before she answered. "The man is infuriating. I don't know how I feel, except I'm mad at him most of the time. If he's not insulting you or the shop, he's complaining about the town. Seriously, I have no idea why he even moved here, except his profits are three times higher here than in the city."

"So you don't love him," I prodded.

She didn't meet my eyes. "Honestly, Jill, I don't know." She glanced at the clock again and stood, taking one last sip of coffee before dumping most of the contents down the drain. "I've got to run if I'm going to make it to the printers before they close. We'll talk Wednesday. I'm going to stay in the city tonight and relax."

"Shopping?" I grinned. Usually "relax" was her code word for "I need a Michael Kors fix." This time my aunt shook her head.

"I don't think so. The stores will be packed with holiday shoppers. There's a movie I want to see and I might walk through the museum. I'll be at the hotel if you need me." She air-kissed me and reached down to pet Emma, who adored my aunt.

And then she was gone. I turned my attention back to my to-do list, crossing off the things I'd completed and adding things I'd forgotten. As I was putting the compact back into my purse, my hand brushed against the folded paper from Ted's picture frame.

I pulled it out and saw it was a bill from a company named Elite Investigations in the amount of two thousand dollars. The one-word descriptor for services made my heartbeat speed up: *retainer*. Ted had hired a private investigator. *When?* I wondered. I checked the date of the bill. Exactly three years ago, before he'd moved west. But the office listed on the top of the page was San Francisco. Elite Investigations was the same company that my law firm had on retainer for the less-than-clean research that needed to be done at times.

Definitely a clue. One that seemed to suggest that Ted had tracked his missing wife down to California before he'd left his comfortable surroundings in Boston for the sunny coast. But was it enough? I wondered who had worked his account. I grabbed my old day planner from my law career out of the desk drawer in my office. I paged through until I'd found the name, Rachel at Elite. I dialed the number. While the phone was ringing, I brought up my e-mail, looking to see if the alumni contact had responded. Nothing.

Rachel wasn't in so I left a long voice mail, hoping *she'd* actually talk to me, especially since the client was deceased. I'd give the note to Greg and let him pursue the lead if Rachel gave me the privilege spiel. *You should give the note to Greg anyway*, the angel on my shoulder nudged. *I would—I will*, I corrected myself. It might be a total dead end. Besides, I'd already let him know about my suspicions about Marie, it wasn't my fault this information had just fallen into my lap.

I could almost hear the sigh from my good side. I ignored it.

CHAPTER 10

By the time I'd turned down the sheets and crawled into bed with a book, I still hadn't heard from Rachel. The good news was I hadn't heard from Greg, either. I could go to sleep with a clear conscience, knowing I hadn't lied to him even by omission. Of course, I had stolen a piece of evidence from Ted's belongings, but apparently the police had already been in his office and had considered the box clear to hand off to family. Greg would thank me for allowing the paper to slip into my hand and then into my purse. The little bit of guilt I did feel didn't keep me from getting engrossed in the second book of the young adult series I'd started last week. I could get accustomed to the fast-paced and fun stories.

I woke early Tuesday, running with Emma on the beach before going in to the shop to open. This was my long day as I worked mine and Jackie's shifts, with Toby spelling me in the middle. I remembered halfway through my shower, Tina Baylor was coming over to discuss festival ideas with me. Oh joy. At ten that morning, I'd be stuck playing nice with the mayor's wife..

My first customers were the daily commuters who stopped by on their way into the city. Some even dropped off the highway on their way from Bakerstown to the city to make a special trip to my shop, even though they passed at least one chain coffee shop on their trip.

I'd talked to Jackie about making up cards that gave a free dessert for every ten cups of coffee, but she told me we'd implement that after the first of the year when sales dropped off. Give the people trying to save money an incentive for stopping in to get their morning jolt.

The morning rush over, I was surprised when the bell chimed at about eight thirty. A tall man dressed in a suit entered the room and went straight for the young adult section. After perusing the shelves, he picked up the first book in the series I'd just started. He laid the book on the counter, and in a deep voice ordered two large coffees and a carrot cake muffin to go. I quickly poured the coffee, setting the cups into a carrier with a small bag containing the muffin. I slipped the book into a larger bag, tapping the bag with my hand.

"I read that last week. I loved the author's way with words." I rang up the purchases and gave him a total. "I just started book two and I love that one just as much. I won't say more, I don't want to spoil the story for you."

He smiled. "My brother gives me crap for reading kid stuff, but ever since I read the Harry Potter books, I've been hooked. I ran through all of the Percy Jackson books, but frankly I was a bit disappointed in the movie." He sighed and gave me a credit card for the purchase.

"Until this week, I hadn't read any young adult since the Potter books. I've been lost in catching up with historical romance." I ran his card, glancing down at the name. "David. There's just too many books and not enough time."

He grinned as he filed his card into his wallet. "Ain't that the truth."

As I watched him leave the shop, he held the door open for a woman entering. Tina. I groaned on the inside, wondering why some people could make you feel good about yourself with just a few words, and some could make you feel horrible with just a look. I pasted on a smile, wondering why she was so early.

"Can I get you something to drink?" I pointed to the menu board. "On the house, of course."

"Spiced coffee would be lovely. We can pretend it's a chilly fall day out there at least. You should visit New England in the fall, Jill, it's quite lovely. I've told Marvin for years that we need to move somewhere with four seasons, but he won't even talk about retiring." Tina glanced around the room, putting her large tote on a four-seater table. "I guess we can set up here."

I set cups down on the table and turned back to the counter. "I'll get a notebook and a calendar. I like to take notes so I don't forget."

"Great idea," she mumbled, then picked up a call on her chiming phone. "Oh hey, honey. No, I didn't mean to sneak out . . ."

I left her talking to the obviously put-out Mr. Baylor, who had apparently expected a little marital comforting this morning. The image made me shudder. I guess there was someone for everyone. But the thought still made me cringe.

I took my time grabbing my notebook and paused at the door until I heard her say good-bye. Then I went back into the front.

"My, that took long enough," she chided. "What were you doing? Making a personal call?"

I swallowed the first ten things that came to mind to say, nodding at her phone. "I wanted to give you some privacy for your personal call." I tried extremely hard to keep the emphasis off the word *personal*. Then I added my best customers-suck smile and somehow, she bought my sarcasm as not.

"So, about our charity project." Tina ignored my slanted apology.

I held my hand up to stop her. "We've already committed to the Bakerstown Children's Center. The lady who runs the place is overjoyed at the idea. I don't think we could do more than a token support for a South Cove–wide project."

Tina's eyes narrowed. "I specifically told you that your store was expected to work with my project. Don't you listen at all? No wonder Greg hasn't married you."

This time I didn't bite back my words. "Don't bring my personal life into our discussions. It's unprofessional and honestly, quite rude. If you want my help with South Cove's festival, you can keep a civil tongue."

Tina's eyes widened at my outburst, and as her face started to harden, I'd realized my mistake. I'd made her the enemy. The only person who had more power over the council and the business community than the mayor was the person who kept him happy in the sack. And I'd just ticked her off.

Tina threw her papers back into her briefcase and stood, shaking the table hard enough that her coffee sloshed on the surface. "Well, I guess we're done here."

I sighed, trying to take back my words. "Look, I didn't mean to be so bitchy. I'm just tired of people questioning my relationship with Greg. It's no one's business besides ours."

Tina's face stayed as smooth as marble. "Understandable. However, I've just realized I have another pressing engagement."

I blocked her as she stepped toward the door. "I'd love to hear about your festival plans."

Tina sniffed, then stepped around me. "Some other time maybe."

As she walked out the door, I knew the day wasn't going to be pleasant. Maybe she'd force Mayor Baylor to kick me out of my liaison position. Wait, that could be a good thing. I cleaned off the table and went back to my list of must dos for the morning. I'd just finished the first page of reminders when the door chimed again. This time, two women wearing dresses so tight you could see the Spanx underneath clicked their way into the store. The height of their hair rivaled the heels on their stilettos. The blonde was focused on her phone, her thumbs texting away. The other rushed to the counter. "Two skinny, no-fat lattes to go."

"What size?" The blonde kept glancing around the shop, then texting something. If she'd been a teenager, I would have wondered if the place was being scouted for a late-night break-in. But there was no way these women were anything but trophy wives. They probably didn't have a minute to spare what with running to the gym for Pilates and their spa treatments.

The brunette rolled her eyes. "Large, I said that."

Again I had to bite back the words. What was wrong with me? I mused as I prepared the Kardashian wannabes' drinks. I slipped sleeves on the cups, then started ringing up the purchase. "Anything else? We have a special on pumpkin pie with real whipped cream this week."

The brunette handed me her credit card, shaking her head. "The coffee will be fine, thanks." But her gaze did drift over to the display case, and I thought I saw a flicker of desire for the treats.

I swiped the card. "Remember, the women on the *Titanic* who skipped dessert were sorry later."

She glared at me as she signed the receipt, crossing out the tip line. "That's a rumor." She walked over to the other woman and shoved a cup in her hand. "Here, are you done yet?"

The blonde nodded, watching me closely.

The morning was turning into a *Twilight Zone* episode. I watched the two walk out of the door, turn left, and all of a sudden the blonde fell out of sight. I ran to the door and, throwing it open, saw her sprawled on the brick sidewalk cradling her ankle.

"Sherry, are you okay?" the brunette cried out.

The blonde, Sherry, held out her shoe, the heel broken off. "Not hardly. My Christian Louboutins are ruined."

"Oh dear." The woman helped Sherry up off the ground, dusting off her dress. "At least your Vera looks untorn."

Sherry focused her blue-eyed glare at me, slipping off the other shoe. "I expect you to replace these."

"Excuse me?" Now I knew I must be dreaming. No morning could actually go this bad.

Sherry shook the shoe at me. "You heard me, these were two hundred dollars on sale and your lack of maintenance on this sidewalk ruined my shoes. I should sue you for pain and suffering, too, but I'm not a total bitch."

My anger bubbled inside. "Look, I'm sorry you tripped. And I'll give you a new coffee, free of charge. But I am not responsible for the sidewalk maintenance. If you have issues with that, please report them to City Hall."

"Don't think I won't." Sherry stepped closer, pointing her finger at me. "I can't even imagine what he sees in you."

"Sherry," the other woman hissed. "Let's get out of here." Sherry shot me a die-bitch-die look and started to follow her friend down the street.

"If you need directions to City Hall, I'll be glad to tell you where to go," I said.

At this she turned and smiled. A really mean-looking smile. "Believe me, honey, I know exactly where City Hall is."

And then she turned and whispered something to her friend, who laughed as she snuck a glance at me over her shoulder.

Weirder and weirder.

By the time Toby had arrived, I'd scrubbed clean the spilled latte off the sidewalk, and emptied and cleaned the display case and the entire back counter area. I'd just started taking the books off the shelf to dust and restock when he sauntered in. He stopped at the sight of me with a pile of books in my arms heading to a table.

"Did I miss the fall cleaning memo?" He walked over and started reshelving the books out of my arms.

"It's been that kind of morning, and staying busy helps me not kill someone." I sighed as he took the last book out of my hand, and sank into one of the large reading chairs. "I'm so glad you're here. I need a run. Or a drink."

"Don't you run before work?" Toby leaned on the table watching me, concern filling his eyes.

"I do, and I did. I just need a second one."

His eyes widened. "Man, it must have been some day."

I told him about my slip with Tina, then went on to tell him about the falling Sherry who wanted me to buy her shoes. He frowned when I mentioned she knew the way to City Hall. "Blonde, lots of makeup, tight clothes, probably early thirties? Was her friend's name Pat?"

I thought about the credit card, had it said Pat? I nodded. "Don't tell me these are a couple of your old girlfriends."

Toby laughed. "Nope, not mine, but I think that Sherry might be Greg's ex-wife. Haven't you met her yet?"

My stomach rolled. "No." I stared at Toby. "Seriously? Could that have been her?"

As if in answer to my question, my cell rang. Amy.

"Hey, lunch?" I asked, wondering what was going on that she wanted to meet on Tuesday rather than our normal Wednesday.

"You need to get down here. Mayor Baylor is steaming." Amy's voice was quiet.

I sighed. "Look, I didn't mean to upset Tina. I'll smooth things over tomorrow. Right now I need some alone time before I have to be back here for the late shift."

"No. Now. It's not just Tina. Greg's ex is here, throwing a pitch fit and saying you sent her to have the mayor buy her new shoes."

Toby raised his eyebrows in a "told ya so" manner since he could hear Amy talking over the speaker.

"You sure she's Greg's ex?" My shoulders sagged. No way would I get out of an apology for this one, even though the woman had been totally in the wrong.

"The mayor called him in to the office to calm her down. Now she and Tina are making plans to burn you at a bonfire for the witch you are. And then throw a party." Amy paused. "Are you coming or not? I don't want to be the only one defending you in the room."

"I'm coming. Wait, Greg's not defending me?" I stood, pausing and waiting for an answer.

"He's playing good cop, trying to get the women to calm down. He's not on their side. At least not totally," Amy said. "Crap, the voices just got louder. Get down here."

The phone went dead and I slipped it into my pocket. "I'm heading to City Hall," I repeated, even though Toby had heard the entire conversation. "If I'm not back here by five to relieve you, they've either arrested me or killed me. So just lock up when you leave."

"Drama queen." Toby put his arm around me as we walked back to the counter so I could collect my purse. "Greg won't let them shoot you."

"At least one of my worries is without merit then." I smiled. "I am so looking forward to this day being over."

By the time I reached City Hall, the lobby area was quiet. Amy sat at her desk working on her computer.

She considered the door to the mayor's office. "They're all in there, including Greg. The voices got lower a few minutes ago, so I guess he calmed them down."

"Seriously, this is out of hand. Tina was being an ultra-freak, and Sherry, I don't even know why she was in my shop. She doesn't seem the treat and latte type." I rolled my eyes.

"According to her friend, who just left to get her a new pair of shoes to wear, they were checking out Greg's new girlfriend." Amy pushed back her straight blonde hair. "Of course, Pat, my new bestie, is a horrible gossip. Apparently Sherry didn't understand why Greg wasn't hanging around her anymore."

"He's been done with her since the divorce." I shook my head. "Some women just don't give up."

Amy arched an eyebrow. "Not according to Pat. She thought Sherry and Greg were working on getting back together, to hear Sherry tell the story."

"That's not true," I protested. "Greg said . . ."

She held out a hand to quiet me, glancing backward at the door. "I'm not saying it's true, I'm just reporting what Sherry has been telling her friends."

"Greg wouldn't do that to me." Today was just getting better and better. Not.

Amy put her hand on my shoulder. "Forewarned is forearmed. So she won't be able to attack you with that weapon. This woman is everything we hate in our sex. She's manipulative, conniving, and knows how to work her assets. You should have seen the mayor drooling until Tina almost knocked him off his chair."

That image brought a smile to my face.

Amy hugged me. "That's my girl. Now, go slay the dragons."

I felt her hand on my back pushing me toward the closed door. I reached out for the doorknob and stepped into a firestorm.

CHAPTER 11

"Miss Gardner, you do realize that knocking on a door is the appropriate way to enter a private office, right?" Mayor Baylor stared at me.

I glanced around the room. Greg was sitting on the couch in the middle between Sherry and Tina. I'd never seen him look that uncomfortable. He bolted to his feet when our gazes met. He stepped to my side. "I'm sure Jill was alerted to the issues and felt she needed to tell her side of the story. It's been a little one-sided so far."

He actually put his arm around my shoulder then. I didn't know whether to kiss him or ram my elbow into his side. My fist tightened as I started to lean in. "Thanks, Greg. I'm kind of lost here, what's the problem?"

Voices erupted, both Tina and Sherry trying to get their list of complaints against me on the table. The mayor stood and bellowed at the two women. "Stop."

They both quieted and sank back into the couch. He glared at me.

"Did you tell my wife you didn't want to be part of South Cove's festival planning?" He paused, waiting for my answer.

"No."

Tina stood up. "The hell you didn't."

Mayor Baylor interrupted his wife. "Tina, sit down and shut up."

Greg nodded at me. "Go ahead."

"What I said was Coffee, Books, and More was doing their own charity drive for Bakerstown Children's Center, therefore we couldn't play a major role in whatever Tina has developed for the town's sponsored program." I sighed. "Look, you got me upset and I said stuff I didn't mean. Can't we just get past this?"

Tina's death stare was the only answer I got.

Mayor Baylor pointed to Sherry. "Now, this woman tells me that you ignored her pleas for assistance and told her to sue the city."

Sherry smiled, her eyes glinting evil. "That's correct, Marvin."

At the coo of her husband's name, Tina refocused her death stare from me to Sherry.

Greg cleared his throat. "Is that correct, Jill?"

I saw Sherry's eyes narrow as he used my name, which, heaven help me, made me want to kiss him again. "No. I heard her scream and went running out, but all she kept saying was I was going to pay for her broken shoe. I explained that the sidewalks weren't part of the store and said she might want to talk to someone at City Hall."

"Whatever." Sherry dismissed me and Greg. "Marvin, what are you going to do about my shoes? Will the city replace them?"

"Yes, Marvin," Tina drawled out his name. "What is the city going to do about Sherry's poor little shoe?"

I bit my lip to keep from smiling. For the first time, I wanted to be a fly on the wall at the mayor's home tonight. He was in trouble. Big trouble. And everyone in the room, except apparently Sherry, knew it. But maybe she did, too, as I saw her sneak a sideways gloating look at Tina.

"Mrs. King, you can file a claim with Amy, but it has to be approved by the council. And honestly, things are kind of tight in the budget right now." Mayor Baylor focused on his wife next. "Tina, it doesn't sound like Miss Gardner was being totally unreasonable. I'm sure she'll work extra hard on the decorating committee since she's unable to help with the fund-raising."

I sighed inwardly. Like I had the time to be Tina's slave. But I put on a smile, hoping it would seem at least a little genuine. I doubted my acting ability. "Of course, whatever I can do."

"See now, everything is back to normal. And if you don't mind, I've got a few phone calls to make before the end of the day."

I glanced at the large grandfather clock in the corner, two thirty. My midday break was almost over. Greg and I turned back to the door.

"Greg, dear," Sherry called out. "Would you please help me out to the car? My ankle hurts."

I stood still, wondering what Greg's answer would be. As he turned, I knew he couldn't step away without helping. It wasn't in his Boy Scout nature. It was just like helping an old lady across the street. An old lady who looked like a beauty queen and whom he'd been married to and slept with.

He rolled his eyes, then kissed me on the cheek. "Let me walk Sherry and Pat back to her car, then I'll stop by the house. Have you eaten?"

I shook my head, not trusting my voice. I went over to Amy's desk and slumped into her visitor chair. We didn't talk until we saw Greg and Sherry leave through the front door. She clung to him like they were teenagers on a first date.

"I can't believe that woman," I hissed at my friend. "You would think they were still married by the way she was all over him. The mayor even called her Mrs. King."

Amy handed me a tissue. "Well, she is technically Mrs. King until she remarries, right?"

"No." I took the tissue and started tearing it in pieces. "Well, maybe. I don't know. Can't we look it up on the Internet or something?"

"What and then tell the mayor he can't use the term anymore?" Amy tried to sound reasonable. "Calm down, Jill. Greg divorced her because he knows all her games. He's with you now."

"Well, he's dating me now."

Amy raised her eyebrows. "Like there's a big difference in Greg's mind."

She had a point. I said my good-byes and started walking home, wondering what else the day could bring. At least I'd finally met Greg's ex-wife—and I was dressed in jeans and an old Bon Jovi T-shirt that I'd gotten at one of his concerts. A far cry from Sherry's polished appearance. *Greg likes me this way*, I chided myself. But then I wondered.

Had I let our comfort level get too lax? Should I be dressing up more for our dates? Taking more time with my hair?

I'd worked myself into a funk by the time I'd reached home. Emma's over-the-top welcome did nothing to refresh my mood. I sat at the table spinning a banana.

I stood and shook off the negativity. Greg would be here in a few minutes with lunch from Lille's. I had probably ten minutes before he'd arrive, so I ran upstairs, took a quick shower, and dressed in a light blue cotton shift, not too fancy, but not jeans and a tee.

Thirty minutes later, he finally arrived, food sacks in hand.

He buzzed my cheek as he walked past me. "Sorry, Sherry kept me longer than I wanted. Man, that girl can talk."

I followed him back into the kitchen. "About what?" I tried to sound casual.

Greg shrugged, pulling out burgers and fries and, God bless him, milk shakes. "Absolutely nothing. She blabs on and on about people we used to know, friends who were always more her people than mine, and all the good old days. I think she forgot she hated being married and has told me over and over how I made her life miserable."

I sat and dipped a fry into Lille's special sauce. Ketchup and Miracle Whip. "Maybe she realizes she made a mistake by letting you go."

"Her mistake, not mine." He took a bite of his burger. Cocking his head, he smiled at me, a drop of cheese on his lip. "You're not worried about Sherry, are you?"

I reached out and wiped the corner of his mouth. "Why would I be worried? You just spent time with a woman who looks more like a supermodel than a real person." I put on a stronger smile than I felt.

"You don't want to know how much she spends on those stupid shoes of hers." Greg kept his eyes cast downward, but his lips twitched. "I like the dress, by the way. Maybe Sherry should come rile you up more often?"

I slapped his arm. "Jerk. Don't think I dressed up for you." I smoothed the blue skirt of the sundress. "I'm heading back to work after lunch."

"Yeah, and that's what you typically wear for a shift at the coffee shop." He shrugged. "Whatever you need to tell yourself. You know you're crazy about me."

I needed to change the subject and not toward the mess of a situation we'd just left at the mayor's office. Tina and Sherry weren't going to ruin the rest of my day. "Did I mention that I met the new program director who took Ted's job? Or I should say, took her job back after Ted had forced her out?"

"Is that where you disappeared to on Monday?" Greg finished off his burger. "I stopped by early, but you'd already left."

"I had some errands to run." I polished off my fries and cut my burger in half. "Her name's Candy Peterson."

"Whose name?" Greg pinched one of my fries.

I moved the container farther away from him. Lille made to-die-for steak fries. "The new program director."

"Oh, her." He popped the fry into his mouth. "She seems nice."

I glared at him. "You already knew about her?"

"Honey, what do you think I do for a living? I'm the one who's supposed to be investigating Ted's murder, not you." Greg stood and let Emma out the back door. "I arrived there ten minutes after you left."

"So you know Ted forced her out of her position when he came into town." I wrapped up the leftovers and tossed everything into the paper bag. I threw the bag into the kitchen trash and slapped my hands together. "Dishes done."

"My little Suzie Homemaker." He leaned back in his chair. "What else did you find out?"

I pulled the sheet out of my jeans pocket. "I think Ted was still looking for the wife who disappeared ten years ago." Greg glanced over the receipt. "It's for a private investigator."

Greg rolled his eyes. "I can read, you know." He slipped the page into a plastic bag he'd pulled out of one of the kitchen cabinets. "As far as leads go, it feels like a dead end."

"But . . ."

"I didn't say I wouldn't check it out." He kissed me on the top of my head. "Gotta get back to work."

I followed him to the door. "I'll be right behind you. I'm just closing up the house, then back to the shop to relieve Toby."

"Your aunt and Josh make up yet?" Greg leaned against the doorway, watching me, and his gaze made my blood heat.

"Not yet. She's sure he's seeing someone else. Even swears she saw the girl sneaking up the back stairs."

Greg laughed as he walked down the stairs. "I just can't see Josh as a player."

"Me neither." I watched him drive away and then glanced at my watch. I had better get moving before my barista started thinking with the cop side of his brain and assumed something bad had happened.

I walked into the shop with ten minutes to spare. The women from the cosmetology school, or Toby's girls as Jackie called them, had all but disappeared. The only customer was a young woman reading the latest novel from a popular romance novelist turned mystery writer. A cup of tea sat in front of her as well as what appeared to be part of a brownie. Toby was cleaning the back sink when I approached the coffee bar.

He turned and a wide smile filled his face. "Hey, boss. How was your break?"

"Besides getting yelled at in the mayor's office and having Greg's ex-wife look at me like I had just been rescued from the woods where I'd bonded with bears." I came around the counter and poured a cup of coffee, chocolate-flavored.

Toby poured his own cup and, glancing at the lone customer, nodded at the counter. "Come tell me all about it."

"You're not a psychiatrist or even a counselor." I crawled up on a stool and sipped my cup, wondering if Toby's ability to listen was what drew women to him. And yet I started talking about the crazy meeting in the mayor's office, finishing with the one thing that irked me more than anything else. "Then your other boss decides he has to walk his old flame back to her car and leave me hanging."

Toby laughed. Not quite the response I'd been looking for.

"Men, they all stick together."

He shook his head. "You don't get it. Greg hates Sherry. It must have driven him crazy to have to be nice to her."

"He didn't seem to mind." I thought about the way Greg had acted with Sherry hanging all over him. Maybe Toby was right and I in my jealousy could only see their past, not the reality of the present.

Toby shrugged. "Greg does a lot of things that you'd never guess drive him crazy. You should have seen him being nice to Tina when she came over to decorate the jail. He tried to tell her that the jail wasn't supposed to be bright and cheery, even at Christmas. In true Tina style, she totally ignored his request for her to leave. Face it, around women your boy toy's kind of a wuss."

"Most men are," a female voice agreed. Toby and I glanced away from each other and the window. The young customer reading by the window had abandoned her book and was standing in front of Toby and me. Her face was drawn and thin, apparently from a lack of regular meals. Her jeans and T-shirt looked like she'd been wearing them for a week. She couldn't have been old enough to be on her own. This was the type of person who needed to be protected. "Sorry, didn't mean to intrude. Can I get another tea?"

I stood and walked around the counter. "No problem. How's the book?"

"Okay, I guess. My boyfriend was always reading crap like this. I wanted to figure out what the big deal was." She glanced out the window toward the street.

I pointed to a display book, another young adult vampire knock-off. "I could suggest some books you might enjoy."

The girl didn't even look at me before she answered. "Don't know if I'll be around for much longer this time. No need to be nice to me."

The pain in her voice twisted my heart a bit. "I'm not being nice. Part of my job is to suggest books you might not know about. I sell books as well as coffee." I nodded over to the row of bookcases that lined the dining room. "Do you want to talk about books you've read and liked in the past? I bet I could list off five great authors for you to try after talking to you for ten minutes."

The girl shrugged again. "Maybe tomorrow. I just want my tea now."

I'd forgotten I was working on her drink. I doused the tea bag with a blast of hot water to get the brewing process started, then filled the cup. Handing it to the girl, I waved away the dollar bills in her hand. "No charge for refills."

She glared at Toby, then stomped back to her book.

"Great, now I'm the bad guy for charging her a quarter for each of the three refills she's already had." Toby stood and pulled off his apron. "I'm beat. I've got tonight off from the other job and I'm heading home for a quick nap."

I pulled out my own book and took a seat at the table. "See you tomorrow."

Toby leaned against the counter. "You know, Jackie usually checks the receipts before I leave."

I snorted. "I trust you. Besides, if you're dipping into the till, who am I going to tell? If you're stealing from me, who do I report it to?"

"I'm just telling you, we have a routine. She snips about how low the sales were, and I tell her she's an old grump and I can outsell her any day of the week." Toby tapped his fingers on the counter. "I hope she gets over being mad at Josh. I think they make a cute couple."

After Toby left, the girl at the window finished her tea in two long gulps and followed him out the door. She zipped her Oregon Ducks hoodie up against a chill and swung her backpack over her shoulder. A flash of greasy blond hair peeked out near her neck, but she pushed it away. I watched her walk out the door and for a moment, our gaze met. Anger flared out of that look, making me turn my head and drop my hand that had been starting to lift in a friendly wave.

When I glanced back out the window, she'd disappeared. Street kid, I guessed. Probably a runaway using the café as a break from being outdoors. A real chair to sit in rather than the park bench. I sent good thoughts into the universe to ease her way and returned to reading my book.

For the next two hours, I had three customers, if you counted the mother looking for a bathroom for her daughter. But Jackie's display of children's books caught the woman's attention and before she left, she'd purchased three books for her daughter and matched the three for the center. My last customer before I shut down for the night was Matt, stopping for a large coffee on his way to Darla's winery.

"I didn't expect any of the crew until tomorrow." Sasha worked the evening shift with Jackie, giving my aunt plenty of time to think up new projects and marketing ideas for the store. Eight weeks, well, seven now, would go by fast. Not for the first time, I wondered if the business could afford to bring Sasha on for anything close to full-time.

Matt blushed. "Darla needs help redoing a section of her patio before the rain sets in, so I thought I'd come over and get a start on it tonight."

"Have you met Candy over at Work Today?" I wondered what the program director would say if she knew her charge was putting in extra hours. Were they even allowed to do that?

Matt shook his head. "We've got a meet-and-greet tomorrow afternoon before they bus us over. You'd think they wanted us to look for work rather than waste our time with social teas."

"It's all about the networking and who you know," I said, mostly as a joke.

Matt's jaw clenched. "You can say that again." He handed me two dollars for the coffee and walked toward the door. He stopped with the door half-open. "Although for all his connections, it didn't save Ted from being a jerk and getting killed."

CHAPTER 12

Jackie came down from the apartment during my morning shift the next day. She pulled a batch of flyers out of a box and shoved them toward me. "Standard drill, give everyone who buys a drink one with their cup, and if they get something from the dessert case, shove one in their bag."

The flyers were sectioned off into fifty-page bundles, the better to monitor the distribution in Jackie's mind. I unclipped the binder and held one up. Pictures of the center and one of a little girl sitting alone with a book on her lap in front of the shop's bookshelves told the story with quiet elegance. The plea went way past just buying a book for a needy child. Jackie had almost promised world peace with an end to the theory of Mutually Assured Destruction finishing with ending childhood hunger. A typical Jackie overdo. "Nice," I said and meant it. "We can slip them into the books we sell as a bookmark."

Jackie stared at me, her eyes narrowing and her lips pursing.

"Or not," I faltered.

She shook her head. "No. It's a terrific idea. I'm just wondering when you started thinking marketing rather than spending your free time reading all day."

Busted. I guess I had used most of the evening shift to get caught up on my favorite owner duties, researching the new releases. How could I recommend a book I hadn't read? The door chime kept me from having to explain my lack of measurable work yesterday.

Regina Johnson waved. She didn't come right up to the counter. Instead, she wandered over to the bookshelves, running her finger across the books and stopping occasionally to pull one out. David, her driver, stood behind her, and as she took books from the shelves, she handed them to him. By the time they walked up to the counter, the man held ten books, ranging from classics to several modern authors.

She waved him to set the books down and tipped her head upward to read the menu board. "Two large mochas and a random dozen of your treats over there. David's got some reading to catch up on."

"You don't have to buy me these books. I can afford them." His face was turning beet red.

I started the mochas and smiled at Regina. "Trying to get him to branch out from his reading rut?"

She picked up one of the books and glanced lovingly at the cover. "When I realized he'd never read anything from Mark Twain or any of the classics, I knew I had to correct that error with his literary education. Besides, I'm paying him for his time. He can at least try to read what I ask him to read."

David mumbled something so low, I couldn't even hear him. Regina ignored the comment, but I jumped in with both feet.

"What?"

He blushed, then straightening his shoulders, said in a clear voice, "I like my books."

Regina laughed. "You sound just like my son did growing up. Petulant and stubborn." She patted David on the arm. "Relax, you might even like some of the books I bought for you. What did you do in high school? Some of these must have been on your English reading lists."

He grinned. "I restored my teacher's '69 Duster. I was in auto shop and didn't have a car of my own to work on, so Mr. Higgins let me restore his. I guess maybe I didn't do all the English homework and he didn't care."

Regina pursed her lips. "Our education system at work. This is why we need standardized testing to pass from grade to grade. My son spent so much time in the garage with his dad working on that hot rod of his, I'm pretty sure he schmoozed his way through some of his classes. The boy was class president all four years of high school." She paused. "He was a charmer."

Something in Regina's words made me wonder if her son wasn't in her life anymore. Before I could answer, David put his hand on her arm and she turned to him, brightening.

"Right, we're not talking about the old days." She smiled at me. "I've made it my mission to try to widen David's reading choices. He'll love these stories."

He didn't answer aloud, but I could read his answer on his face. Fat chance. I bit my bottom lip to keep from smiling and changed the subject. "I'm sure I gave my mom grief about her summer reading list." I handed a cup to Regina. "Let me ring this up for you."

She picked up a flyer on the counter. "A book drive, how sweet. Remind me to write you a check for the cause before I leave."

I frowned, confused. "Today?"

"No. I meant before I end my stay at your quaint little town." She paused, looking wistful, like she'd lost something and she didn't know where to start searching. "I guess I have to go back to the real world someday."

"Reality is overrated." Jackie's voice jarred me. I'd forgotten she was in the shop she'd been so quiet.

Regina turned her head and considered Jackie's comment, her face solemn. "I think you're right about that. Unfortunately, I have commitments to keep. Ones that won't go away just because I'm feeling blue."

"I'm sure you've heard the adage about putting your oxygen mask on first in case of a crash. Just tell the people hassling you that you need some Regina time." I handed her the charge slip with her credit card.

She signed the credit card slip and picked up her packages. "I'm sure that works in some alternate universe, but not in my world." Regina smiled, but the light didn't reach her eyes. "Thanks for listening to the meanderings of a doddering old lady."

"You're not old," David chided her, his voice growing soft at the end. The man seemed to care for his boss, maybe a little too much, in my opinion. But as I watched them walk out of the shop together, I knew Regina had at least one person watching her back. Sometimes, one was all you needed.

"That woman is deeply depressed." Jackie straightened the flyers by the register.

I kept watching the two as they walked toward the bed-and-breakfast. "I wonder what brought her to South Cove?"

"Probably a cheating husband. Married couples around her age, they all go off the reservation at least once."

"That's pretty cynical." I watched my aunt as she ignored my gaze.

"Just being realistic." Jackie filled her travel cup and grabbed a chocolate pastry. "I'm heading upstairs for some me time before my shift. Let me know if you need anything."

I wondered if there had been problems in the perfect marriage she had with Uncle Ted. *Not my business*, I thought as I took the box of flyers to the storeroom in the back. Wednesday mornings were slow, so after I'd gotten the work area supplied for the day, I grabbed a slice of Sadie's pumpkin pie, topped off my coffee, and sat down to read. Today I chose one of the books Regina had purchased for David, a love story with two ill-fated souls, coming back to the world, over and over, and still missing each other. Not recognizing their soul mate until it was too late. I'd heard good reviews of the story, but had avoided reading it, mostly because I'm impatient with my happily-ever-afters. I don't want to wade through years, let alone lifetimes, for two people to make it work.

I'd gotten halfway through the book when Toby arrived for his shift. I wiped tears from my eyes and put a bookmark into the paperback. I'd finish it tonight at home . . . where I could sob in private.

"Good book?" Toby slipped behind the counter and tossed his jacket into the back room. It probably landed on my desk. The one covered with boxes of books and other shop supplies. I did most of my bookwork for the shop at home.

"There's a coatrack back there, you know." I cleaned up my plate and cup from my breakfast, depositing them into the sink on my way to the back room.

Toby slipped on his apron and turned on the water to wash his hands. "I know. I just don't want to walk that far."

I grabbed my purse from the top of the desk, hung up Toby's light-weight jacket, and returned to the front of the shop. "You expect people to take care of you."

He shrugged. "You hung up my jacket when you went to the back. So I guess I'm not wrong in my assumption."

"You drive me crazy sometimes." I checked the time. I was meeting Amy for lunch in fifteen minutes. "So, Elisa has a kid?"

Toby nodded. "Isabella. She's five. Looks like a little princess but loves playing in the dirt with the neighbor boy's Tonka trucks. I think she's going to be a race car driver when she grows up."

I grabbed one of the flyers. "I forgot. Jackie said you were bringing her in for pictures." I studied the little girl so focused on the book in her lap. "Is this her?"

Toby grinned. "Yep. She was a wild thing most of the time, then we sat down for some coffee and to look over the pictures we'd already shot. After we stopped paying attention to her, she sat down and started reading. That's when Elisa snapped that photo."

"She reads?" I didn't know much about five-year-olds.

He shrugged. "She knows a lot of words. I read to her after dinner on nights I visit. She's pretty smart, that one."

"Sounds like it." I patted Toby's arm as I passed by. "She clearly has your number."

As I walked down the still-undecorated streets, I thought about the look of pride that had shown on Toby's face as he talked about Isabella. I hoped Elisa turned out to be the one, because if this relationship went sour it might just break Toby's heart this time. The boy was invested in the two of them. The man, I corrected myself. And for the first time when I thought of my barista, I thought the word might just describe him.

Amy had already claimed our favorite booth when I arrived at Diamond Lille's. I watched her tapping keys on her phone, texting someone. She bit her bottom lip as she texted, not a normal Amy gesture. I slid into the opposite bench, tucking my purse onto the seat next to me. I waited for her to finish before I spoke. "Happy Camel Day."

She smiled, but not very wide. "I've been looking forward to our lunch since Justin dropped me off last night. I would have called you, but it was so late."

"Wait, what's going on?" I pushed away the menu I'd been studying even though we'd eaten at Lille's at least once a week since I'd move to South Cove five years ago. Last summer, I'd worried that Lille might ban me from the only restaurant other than my coffee shop within ten miles. She'd believed I had been trying to steal away her loser boyfriend. Luckily, his arrest and my almost demise allowed her to tolerate me coming into the diner. A forgiveness that made me happy, especially on Wednesdays when the daily soup was a loaded potato bowl of heaven.

Carrie stood by the table, snapping a piece of gum. I'd heard through the grapevine that the waitress was two weeks into her third try to give up smoking. The last two attempts had ended badly when a customer had gotten on her last nerve, pushing her out to the sidewalk. She'd confronted the first tourist who even looked like they could be harboring a cigarette pack in their coat pocket. Carrie narrowed her eyes on Amy's phone. "You guys ready to order or you got more phone calls to make?"

Amy pushed the phone toward the wall. "I'm ready. I'll have a cheeseburger with onion rings. Add in a caramel chocolate shake."

Carrie scribbled on her order sheet. She shot a look at me.

"Bowl of potato soup and a dinner salad, bleu cheese on the side." I waited for a split second, then decided against the lower calorie choice. "And a Cherry Coke."

Carrie harrumphed and walked back to the kitchen, grabbing empty plates on her way. I breathed a sigh of relief when she slipped behind the counter and into the kitchen.

I leaned over the table. "I like her better when she smokes."

Amy waved the comment away. "Wait a few weeks and she'll be back to normal, one way or the other."

"I'm not sure if we can survive a few days, let alone weeks." I sipped water waiting for my real drink to arrive. A few minutes later, another waitress dropped off our drinks. As I took a sip of the sweet syrupy soda, the caffeine hit made me shiver. I focused back on my friend. Justin was a history professor by day and a cool surfer dude at night and weekends. He was perfect for her. "So, you and Justin fighting about where the best waves hit?"

Amy narrowed her eyes. "We aren't fighting."

Confused, I asked the follow-up: "Then why did you need to talk to me so bad? Something with work?"

She shook her head. "It's Justin."

My head was spinning like on my favorite ride at the carnivals, the Tilt-a-Whirl. "Wait, you just said you weren't fighting."

"We aren't." Amy sniffed and grabbed a handful of thin paper napkins from the silver holder on the table. She blew her nose, loudly.

"Then what's wrong with Justin?" I prayed he wasn't sick, or dying, or secretly married. No, that would be a fight, I was sure.

Amy's eyes widened. "He wants me to go to Missouri for Christmas."

I tried to think of anything good to say about Missouri, but honestly, I'd never even been to the state, so I said the first thing that came into my mind. "St. Louis is in Missouri."

"It's not St. Louis. He's taking me to a little town in the middle of nowhere." She took a sip of her milk shake, then calmed, said the offending words again. "No. Where."

"I don't understand, just tell him you don't want to go to Missouri for Christmas. Maybe he thinks it's a good vacation, but what about Cancun? Now, that would be one amazing Christmas. Tell him Mexico would be better."

"You don't get it. He's from Missouri." Amy waited for a second, then when she was convinced I still didn't understand her words, added. "He wants to take me home for Christmas. To meet his parents."

"Oh." My words dried up as I considered her dilemma. Meeting the parents was a big deal. Especially when the parents lived halfway across the country. Amy looked lost and afraid, sitting across from me, her short blond hair and thin body giving her a waifish look. And the way she was downing that milk shake completed the package. "I didn't realize you guys were already that serious."

"Exactly. I didn't, either. I mean, we have fun. We like the same activities. He's funny, charming, intelligent." Amy slowed.

"I can see why you're upset. Justin sounds like the perfect catch. Who wouldn't be scared to meet his folks? There has to be something wrong with the guy. Maybe it's the family bonds." And then, just because I couldn't help myself, I added, "You never know what skeletons are in someone's family tree."

"You mean, real bodies?" Amy leaned forward, fascinated by my words. "Oh God."

Laughing, I tapped the table. "Earth to Amy. This is sweet Justin we're talking about. I was kidding."

Amy stirred her shake with her straw, focusing on the milk swirl she was creating. "I still don't want to meet them. It's too soon." She caught my gaze. "Have you met Greg's parents yet?"

"No, I haven't."

"See. It's creepy, right?" Amy slumped back into her seat, the milk shake decimated.

I shook my head. "Actually, it's sweet. I haven't met Greg's parents because they've passed away."

Carrie dropped our plates in front of us. "Need anything else?"

I shook my head. Amy didn't even try to make eye contact.

"You two are sure in a snit today." Carrie spun around and headed back to the kitchen, ignoring a man at a nearby table trying to get her attention.

I bit back a smile. "So, back to the Justin problem. I think you should say yes. You might enjoy the trip."

Amy bit into her cheeseburger, ignoring my comment. Finally, when she came up for air, she waved a French fry at me. "You know what happens when I meet parents. They never like me."

"One set of parents, one time. And he was as crazy as his mother. You dodged the bullet on that one. You should send that woman a thank-you note for keeping you away from her Norman Bates–reincarnated son." I lifted a spoonful of the soup to my mouth. Creamy sauce, potatoes, cheese, sour cream, crunchy bacon bits: heaven.

I'd talked Amy out of running away to live in an undisclosed European castle before lunch was over, but I had to agree, getting away from the hustle of the holidays sounded like a reasonable plan to me. Especially with Tina on my butt for not serving as her right-hand man for this entire festival. Honestly, Darla had been the best choice for years because she lived to do this kind of crap.

As we left the diner, Amy hugged me. "Thanks for being there for me." She turned toward City Hall, then stopped. "I almost forgot. The mayor asked me to give this to you. I guess it's Tina's list of festival requirements for shop owners. Just wait until you read number twelve. You are going to die laughing."

"Somehow, I doubt that." I shoved the envelope into my purse. I'd open it tomorrow during my morning shift. When I was working. Right now, I was heading home, grabbing a bottle of wine and a book, and heading upstairs to my bathtub to soak, pre-nap time. And if I slept all evening, who cared.

I almost skipped home, I felt so giddy about my planned afternoon. As I walked up the sidewalk to my house, I noticed a person sitting on the porch in my white rocker swing. My pace slowed as I tried to see who it was. Opening the gate to the house, the person regarded me as I walked up the sidewalk.

Marie Jones stood to greet me. "We need to talk."

CHAPTER 13

A few minutes later, we were sitting at the kitchen table, sipping on cinnamon apple tea and still making polite small talk. Emma sat outside on the porch, looking in the glass screen door wanting to be let in so she could either curl up on her bed or slather wet dog kisses on the visitor. I worried about the latter, so I kept her outside. As I watched, she finally made three circles and laid down, her head between her front paws, clearly annoyed with me.

"Pretty dog," Marie said, nodding at Emma's now-prone shape. "I had a golden as a child. Or I guess my dad did. He hunted."

"You've never mentioned your folks. Do they live close?" I was curious, mostly because I knew she wouldn't tell me.

Marie lips twitched. She took a sip of the tea, then set the cup down. "We both know I haven't seen my family in a long, long time." She focused on me, cocking her head quizzically. "I just don't know how you found out."

So we were talking about the Ted connection. I leaned forward. "When the media ran the stories on Ted's death, most also mentioned the sad tale about his wife disappearing. The picture they ran was a dead ringer for a younger you. I kept digging."

"I didn't kill him," Marie said flatly. "Not that I hadn't thought about it, especially after he showed up here. Seriously, what were the chances of him just happening to be in the same town clear across the county? The only luck I've ever had was bad. And Ted's appearance was the worst thing that could have happened."

I considered keeping quiet, but I couldn't stop myself from admitting this one tidbit. "Ted hired a private investigator to find you. He must have been still looking after all these years."

Marie uttered a short, tired laugh. "The man was a bulldog about things he considered his property. Like toys, money, and me."

"He must have been mad you took the money?"

She shook her head. "I didn't ask for the ransom. All I wanted was out. Ted must have figured out a way to get part of his inheritance early."

I felt bad for the woman, hiding all these years in plain sight. "Why did you leave? I mean, all those years ago."

"Same story as a lot of women. He liked to hit me. Apologized, bought me gifts, then when he'd get angry about some slight caused by anyone, including the doorman at our apartment, he would hit me again. I got tired of the cycle." She studied me, gauging my level of belief. "I know, you're thinking he's from a good family, we were wealthy, it couldn't be true."

"Spousal abuse happens in all families." I knew this to be true. As a family law attorney, I'd seen my share of abused wives. Ones who tried to escape, only to be sucked back in by the heartfelt apologies. Once I'd even suspected an estranged husband of killing his wife who'd been to see me for divorce papers the day before. Of course, no one could prove a thing, so the police let him go.

"My mother told me I'd made my bed and to go home and lie in it." Marie pursed her lips. "I never said another word to her. When I'd made my plan, disappearing seemed to be the only alternative. I left so I could live."

"You need to tell Greg." I sipped my tea and watched her face.

She twisted her lips, "I know. I'm on my way there now. I just wanted to let you know. I came off a little rude the other night at class."

"I was treading on your secret. You had a right to shut me down."

Actually, I was surprised she had even showed up here now. Then the reason for her visit became clear. "You want to know how much I've told Greg so you can protect yourself."

Red spots appeared on Marie's cheeks. "Wouldn't you want to know? I mean, if you were me? So, yeah, I'm curious. How much of your pillow talk with our town detective was about me and my possible motives to kill my ex-husband?"

"Did I tell him my theories? Yes. Did I tell him what I heard at Lille's? Of course. But only because someone threw a dead rabbit on my porch with a note to stop snooping." I tapped the table with my finger. "That was totally uncool."

Marie's eyes widened. "I didn't threaten you. I would never sink to any level of hostility. That's part of the reason I moved to California. I lived in a New Age commune for years before I started the shop. I'm very anti-violence."

I'd seen the way she bent metal at the shop. I wasn't totally convinced of Marie's innocence, but I wasn't going to argue the point as she sat in my kitchen. "Look, I've got things to get done. Did you need something else?"

She stood and glanced around the kitchen. "You've done a nice job with the remodeling. I visited Miss Emily a few times before she passed."

The shock of that hit me. "You knew Miss Emily?"

Marie smiled, this time with her eyes as well as the rest of her face. "You didn't think you were her only project now, did you? She helped me when I first moved into South Cove. I was scared living on my own. She convinced me that Ted would never find me here." She stood and picked up her purse, hanging the strap over her shoulder. "I guess she was wrong."

As I watched Marie walk back to the road, I wondered how many other lives Miss Emily had changed through the years. Trying to get someone to believe in themselves or in their personal power wasn't easy. I know how long it took me to understand my own worth. Now Marie was free from the source of the fear. Ted couldn't hurt her anymore. So, why did she still look like she expected someone to run her down in the street?

I didn't need Greg's tests to prove that Marie wasn't behind the threat. I could see it in her demeanor. But if Marie hadn't left the dead rabbit on my doorstep, who had?

Grabbing my book, a glass, and the bottle of wine, I headed upstairs to start my mini at-home spa treatment. Mostly soak and sip, but some women paid big bucks for sessions that weren't half as effective. I poured a jasmine bubble bath into the steaming water, making Emma sneeze.

"You know you're not getting in the tub with me, right?" I rubbed under her chin as she stared at me. She wasn't in love with baths, but she loved swimming in the ocean when we went on runs. A habit requiring I give her more frequent baths to keep Emma from smelling like salt water. Sometimes life was a vicious circle. The things we love can draw us nearer to the things we hate. I slipped out of my clothes, filled my glass, and slid into the almost too hot water. I closed my eyes and enjoyed the perfect feeling.

Emma whined and then I heard her lie down on the bathroom tile. Scooting up, I opened the book and got lost in the story.

When the water cooled, I climbed out, wrapped up in a terry-cloth robe, and took my reading party to the bed. Covering myself with my quilt, I refilled my wineglass and tapped the empty side of the bed for Emma to come and cuddle.

After a few more chapters, my stomach growled, and I realized the light in the room had dimmed. The bedside clock read ten after seven. I tended to eat early most nights, wanting to get the chore of cooking and cleaning over quickly to give me more time to indulge in my guilty pleasure, reading. Emma watched me for signs of movement. "Ready to go outside?"

Emma barked and jumped off the bed, waiting for me at the door. I slipped on a pair of jeans and a tank. By the time I arrived in the kitchen, Emma sat at the back door waiting. I let her outside and went to stand in front of the fridge, waiting for inspiration to hit me.

Finally, I grabbed the makings for a salad, took a piece of cod from the freezer, and went outside to start up the grill. Back in the kitchen, I wrapped a couple of frozen rolls in foil, greased a second piece of the foil, and seasoned the frozen fish. Then I chopped lettuce, tomatoes, and cucumbers, filling a large serving bowl. I set the filled bowl aside and took the fish and rolls outside to the grill, grabbing a bottle of water.

Emma chased a squirrel out of the yard as I opened the door. Once she'd made the back yard safe for her human, she trotted back to the porch and lay by my feet. I felt a little tipsy from the wine, but my mind kept spinning back to Marie and her apology. I wanted to believe her, but something about what she'd said just sounded off. I couldn't put my finger on the problem though, so the nagging feeling that I'd missed something continued to plague me.

I finished grilling my dinner, and ate my salad in front of the television, where I found a rerun of an old romantic comedy about a man who could read women's minds. Of course, just like in real life, he used his superpower for evil, not good, at least not until he found himself in love with the heroine. I curled up on the couch, wishing I could read minds. Then I'd know who killed Ted and who wanted me to keep my nose out of things that didn't concern me. I fell into a dreamless sleep.

The next morning, I woke to Emma's nose in my hair, pushing my head to try to wake me. "Stop that," I said, but without much determination, causing Emma to change her tactic from nudging me to licking my ear.

I sat up, my head only pounding a little from the one too many glasses of wine last night. I clicked the remote to the guide to check the time and leaned back on my couch. Five thirty. Too late to get a run in, but I had plenty of time for a shower and some coffee before I walked into town to open the shop promptly at six. Or I would if I got a move on.

Walking to the kitchen, I let Emma out and started my day. Thursdays were pretty busy at the shop, so I needed to wake up, sooner than later. I put a dark roast into the pot to brew and headed upstairs for a quick, hot shower. By the time I got back downstairs, the coffee was ready. I fed Emma and locked up the house, pouring coffee into a to-go cup. I could walk and drink.

The morning flew by, customers already waiting outside the door when I arrived. Between coffee and adrenaline, I worked as quickly as possible, handing out flyers for Jackie's book drive and even taking several cash donations for the project. I grabbed an old biscotti glass jar, taped a flyer to the front, and slipped the money into it. After that, most of my customers dropped their change into the jar. I should have done this days ago. Marketing maven Jackie move over, Jill Gardner had her own moves.

By the time Toby had come in for his shift, the effect of the caffeine was wearing off. I took a piece of chocolate cheesecake out of the display case and slipped onto one of the bar stools, watching Toby prepare for his shift. We all had our odd habits. I liked my supplies to the left of the espresso machine, Toby liked the cups there. So they moved. Jackie must agree with me, because by the time I came in the next day, they were back in their correct places. I took a bite of the chocolate heaven and sighed.

"Long night?" Toby leaned over the counter, grinning.

I nodded, finishing the bite before I responded. "Do I look that bad?"

Toby shrugged. "I'm too smart to fall for a loaded question like that. I have dated a few women in my time."

"I've had a bad week." I polished off the cheesecake. "Is Greg any closer to figuring out who killed Ted? Or is it all confidential now? He didn't even call last night."

Toby straightened and threw a clean towel over his shoulder. "Honestly, I don't know. Greg's looking into something, but he's being pretty tight-lipped about the whole case. Maybe he's worried we talk too much."

"Everyone's worried about my close relationships with South Cove's finest. Between dating Greg and hiring you, I'm supposed to be connected." I laughed. "Unfortunately both of you hold your cards close to your chest. Especially when the stakes are high."

The door to the shop opened, and Greg in his tan police dress shirt and slim Wrangler jeans walked into the shop.

Toby grinned. "I swear, the guy has superhuman hearing. He's always showing up when his name's mentioned." He waved to Greg. "Hey, boss, want coffee?"

Greg nodded. "Please. That crap Esmeralda is brewing lately is making me think about giving up coffee."

"That's because she's been doing green tea in the office pot instead of coffee." Toby shook his head. "Why do you think I've been bringing my own carafe when I show up for my shift? She's great at dispatch, but she's sure into that woo-woo stuff."

"Green tea isn't that unusual," I muttered, pouring Greg's coffee and getting him a brownie out of the case, as well. "Maybe she thinks you need to cut your caffeine?"

"Not her decision." Greg bit into the brownie and groaned. "One of Sadie's?"

I nodded and grinned. If Sadie Michaels had been in the market for a husband before Greg and I had started dating, her mad baking skills would have won the battle for the man's heart. "What brings you out of the station? I haven't seen you in days."

Greg pulled me close. "That's what brings me out. We need some time together. How about I take you to dinner, then over to the winery for a couple of drinks and some live music? Darla's got an eighties cover band playing starting tonight."

Toby stepped away from the counter. "I'm going in the back to grab some more flyers and to-go boxes. Yell if a customer comes in before I get back."

"I can watch the front." I ran my fingers through Greg's hair, finger-combing it back into place after his walk from City Hall.

Toby chuckled. "I'm giving you guys some time alone, why would I want you to work the counter?"

I heard the door to the back open and then Greg pulled me into a kiss. He paused just before leaning in. "I thought he'd never leave," he whispered and then his lips covered my own. He tasted like a mix of the chocolate and coffee.

A few minutes later, Toby reappeared and Greg sipped his coffee, rubbing his thumb against the back of my hand. He finished his brownie and focused on me. "So, we on for tonight?"

"I guess. I mean, I was going to wash my hair again, but I could be persuaded to spend some time with you." I thought about Marie's visit. Dinner would give me some time to get his take on her declaration of innocence.

"Glad you could move me up on your list of chores." He stood and held out his cup to Toby. "Top that off for me, would you? I've got a stack of reports to get through before I call it a day."

Toby took the cup, dumped the coffee out into the sink, then filled up a new cup with fresh coffee. "I saw the stack of files. You'll need this."

I touched Greg's arm. "Hold on a second, I'll walk with you." I hurried to the back and got my purse, checking my hair in the mirror Jackie had hung on the wall next to the door. The curly mess actually leaned toward cute today, not just messy.

When I returned to the front, Greg and Toby had been talking in low voices. When they heard the door, both stood straighter, leaning away from each other, and the silence seemed to echo. I glanced back and forth. "Something I should know?"

"Work stuff." Greg took my elbow and guided me to the door. "Later, Toby."

"Call me if you need help," I called back. "Or at least before three. After that, I'm getting ready for a hot date."

"TMI, boss, TMI." Toby chuckled as Greg and I left the shop.

We headed down the street toward the end of town and my house. We walked in silence for a while, the fall air feeling a little chilly but the sunshine warming my back. The streets still hadn't been decorated. I guess Tina wasn't ready to commit to a theme yet. Typically by the week before Thanksgiving, we were knee-deep in Christmas cheer. Not this year. Darla must be going crazy. I'd have to talk to her tonight when Greg and I visited the winery.

"Tina's in over her head," Greg said, seeming to read my thoughts.

"I feel sorry for Darla. She lived for the festivals."

Greg leaned closer. "I hear she's living for someone else nowadays."

Laughing, I squeezed his hand. "You're a gossip, you know that?"

He shrugged. "I didn't say who told me. Or what they said."

"It's Matt. He's the one people are talking about, right?" We came up to the front of City Hall and stopped. "Darla deserves some happiness."

"Well, I hope he's not just being nice. Darla could use some good news in her life." Greg glanced at the building.

He kissed me on the forehead. "Gotta get back to the investigation. See you at five?"

I turned and headed home, throwing good thoughts into the air for Darla and the new man in her life. By the time I got home, I'd decided that the run I'd considered for the morning would happen that afternoon. When we got to the beach, Emma chased seagulls out of the waves to her heart's content, and after we'd made our rounds, I sat on the sand watching her.

Ted's unfortunate demise circled around my thoughts. Well, not unfortunate for Marie or anyone else who actually had to work with him. I considered Candy Peterson. Was she upset enough about losing her position to kill? That didn't make a bit of sense unless she had a really, really long game. Ted had ousted her years ago. But then again, Ted had still been looking for a missing wife after decades. Maybe people held grudges longer than I could imagine.

I knew one thing, Marie had been scared. I'd seen it in her face the night I'd asked her about Ted at the stained-glass class. And if he scared her that badly after so many years, who else had been afraid of Ted and why?

CHAPTER 14

The winery grounds were lit up with tiny white lights. The barn where the stage was set had been decorated in a not quite full-out Christmas theme but more of a holiday party with touches of fall and winter mixed together. Tables were filled with couples and groups both inside the structure and flowing out onto the patio, where a few gas heaters had been set up for the more adventuresome patrons.

Greg escorted me toward a small table in a corner of the barn, one where he could watch the entire show. Once a cop, always a cop, I guessed. But I didn't mind. Greg took his job seriously, and I appreciated him for his dedication, even when he was on my time.

Scanning the room for Darla, I noticed her at the bar with Matt, their heads tipped together as he whispered something in her ear. Even at this distance, I could see the blush on Darla's cheeks deepen. Yep, the girl had it bad.

I moved my attention away from the couple. Somehow it felt like I was eavesdropping on a private conversation even without hearing the words. Many of the town regulars were here tonight. Lille, the owner of the diner, sat at a table with a man I didn't recognize. Her last boyfriend was still in prison on a drug charge. This man appeared a tad more respectable than her usual type, his jeans and T-shirt clean, and he wasn't sporting biker colors. Maybe she'd changed her ways.

Greg brought me a glass of white zinfandel along with a bottle of his favorite brew. He slipped into the chair next to me. "Crowd watching?"

"Do you know who's with Lille?" I inclined my head toward their table.

Greg followed my gaze and narrowed his eyes. "I don't. Want me to find out? You interested?"

I slapped his arm. "I was just wondering if she was dating again. She's been kind of grumpy since Ray went up the ocean."

He laughed. "I think the term is 'up the river'. And yes, she has been a bit of a . . ." He paused, seeking out an appropriate word.

"Pain. Witch. Nightmare. Take your choice." I giggled. Lille was one of those women who lived the old motto, if Mama ain't happy, no one is. I sipped my wine, relaxing into my chair. The band was playing an old ballad, one I'd grown up loving. Couples sprinkled around the dance floor, not worried about who might be watching. A man dipped his partner, sparking a laugh from the woman. The ballroom couple was David and Regina. The two floated around the room like they'd been dancing together for years. No matter what the official story was, the man adored his boss. You could see it in his eyes as he focused only on her.

Greg caught my focus on the dancing couple. He nodded toward them. "You want to dance?"

I shook my head. "Not yet. I'm still watching."

He scanned the couples again, looking confused. "Who?"

Leaning closer so that I wouldn't be overheard, I whispered, "The woman in the fuchsia top and way-too-expensive jeans and the tall man who can't take his eyes off her."

Greg studied them for a while. "Tourists?"

"Yeah. They've been in the shop a lot this week. He's her driver." I watched Greg's face. When he didn't show any reaction, I added, "He works for her."

"And, so?" Greg turned his gaze back to me. "He works for her and they are dancing. In public. No hip grinding in sight. People can do that without being in a relationship."

"Sometimes for an investigator, you can be kind of clueless." I sipped my wine, pleased at the slightly sweet taste. I lowered my voice just a touch more. "You should see the way he looks at her. It's like she's a princess or something."

"Okay, so maybe he has a thing for his boss. She's attractive. Why not?" Greg took a pull off his bottle.

"I'm pretty sure she's married from the rock on her finger."

"Then she's married and her driver has a crush on her. Even if they are engaging in extracurricular hanky-panky, that's not our business. I'm sure she's not the first wife to stray." Greg started to take a sip out of the bottle, then paused, holding it halfway up to his lips. "No, make that, I'm *certain* she's not the first wife to stray."

We didn't talk about Sherry much, but when we did, Greg never had good things to say about his ex-wife. It wasn't like he was mean about it, though. I got the impression he was more hurt than angry. During the last year, even the hurt had started to ease from his voice. Now, he seemed to find the entire marriage ancient history of the worst kind. I held up a finger, but he shook his head at me.

"Not our business, sweetheart. Let's talk about something else. How's the book drive going? Tina seems to think you'll fall flat on your pretty little butt on this one."

"She does? That woman is a bad seed. She couldn't pull together a community festival to raise money for baby seals. No one likes her." I stopped talking when I saw Greg grinning. "You tricked me out of talking about Regina and David, didn't you?"

"I know your buttons, darling, what can I say?" He finished off his beer and glanced at my wineglass. "Ready for another? Then we can take a few spins on the floor? I'll even let you pretend you're my boss." He waggled his eyebrows.

"So you'll call me Mayor Baylor?" I deadpanned.

Greg stood. "Man, you know exactly what to say to kill a mood, don't you?"

I watched him make his way through the tables, stopping to talk to one person, then the next. He could be a politician the way he smoothed through people. When I'd asked him about a political office being in his future, he'd shut me down saying he didn't want the pressure. "Yeah, like being a lead detective on a murder case isn't pressure," I whispered to Greg's retreating form.

Matt walked across Greg's path, zigzagging through the tables to avoid meeting up with him. Then someone blocked Matt's path. It was the girl from the coffee shop. I watched the two of them exchange a few words, then Matt grabbed her elbow and dragged her toward the doorway. He glanced around the room as they walked out, and our gazes met for a brief second. Then he disappeared out of the door.

"Damn," I muttered, under my breath. I'd hoped Matt had actually been able to look past the physical and actually like Darla. I guess I'd been too caught up in the romance to actually see the obvious. Matt must be dating the woman who had been hanging out in the coffee shop. Although she seemed way too young for him. And that, of course, led me to my next utterance, "Men are pigs."

"Uh-oh. What did Greg do now?" Darla put her hand on my shoulder and scooted up a chair to the table.

"What—no, Greg didn't do anything. I was just making a statement about most men." I glanced around the almost full room and tried to change the subject. "You've got almost a full house."

Darla followed my gaze. "It's the holiday coming up. People know they're going to be stuck in the house with distant relatives in a couple of weeks and they want to have one last hurrah before the madness begins."

"The place looks amazing. You've got such a flare for design, I'm surprised you opened the winery instead of an interior design shop."

Darla blushed again. That was twice tonight I'd seen her face this red. "Honestly, I didn't have the right degree. My folks insisted I get a straight business degree, and well, they started the winery years ago. So I was expected to keep it going." She paused, deep in thought. Then she shook her head like she was coming out of a dream. "Not that I don't love running the winery. Pipe dreams are just that, puffs of smoke about what could have been."

"I spent ten years as a lawyer before I woke up and realized I wasn't cut out to do the suit and court thing." I motioned toward my jeans and silk tank. "Now I only get dressed up for dates."

"Hey, I should have brought another glass." Greg set my wine in front of me and kissed Darla on the cheek. "Nice turnout tonight. You must be happy."

She shrugged. "It's a good band. Matt knows the lead guitarist. He's very handy. I'm not sure what I did without him."

Greg shot me a look and I knew what he was thinking, but I let that comment slide. "Too bad the guys will be gone at the first of the year. Aunt Jackie's gotten pretty attached to Sasha. I think she likes training someone as much as she likes running the business."

"Your aunt likes telling people what to do. Me included." Greg laughed.

Darla looked at me, then at Greg. "Is she pushing you guys to set a date?"

"No." The word came out a little too emphatic. "I mean, Greg and I haven't even talked about anything like that."

Greg watched me, amusement tickling his eyes and his lips twitching. "I can see even the thought has you freaking out. I guess I'll have to take the ring back to the jewelers." He nudged Darla. "Unless you might have use for it."

Darla slapped his arm. "Stop teasing. I know the rumors flying around. Matt and I are just friends. Besides if you had bought her a ring, everyone in town would already know. Except Jill, of course."

"He's just kidding you, Darla." I put my hand on her arm. "Wait, why wouldn't I know?"

"Because, dear, you don't gossip." Darla stood and squeezed my shoulder. "You two have fun. I've got to go check in with the bar. And find Matt. He was fixing a heater out on the patio, but if it's taking this long, the darn thing's probably done. He never gives up."

I thought about the girl Matt had ushered out of the winery. Darla would be crushed, no matter that she'd just declared she and Matt were only friends. "Hold on, I'll go with you."

Greg stood, but I motioned him down. "Save our table, I'll be right back. I want to see if Matt talked to the new program director yet."

"Her name is Candy," Greg amended.

I raised my brows. "And that exactly is what I'm having trouble with. What kind of woman goes by the name of Candy after forty? She's definitely not a stripper."

Greg snorted. "You forget, I've met the lady in question. Sometimes you take this women's lib thing too far. I think Candy's a sweet name."

"Very funny, big man." I put my hand on Darla's back and we wove our way through the tables. At least this way if Matt was still talking to that girl, I'd be able to keep Darla from killing him. Or at least try. Maybe I should have let Greg come, too. He could have helped hold her back, giving Matt a chance to run away.

Matt stood at the end of the patio, working on a heater. My shoulders dropped an inch before I saw who was standing next to him, holding a screwdriver. The girl from the coffee shop. When I glanced at Darla, her face told me she'd already seen the two and come up with the same conclusion. Her voice hitched a bit when she said, "He's still working on the heater. I'm probably going to have to break down and head into Bakerstown and buy new ones."

We kept walking, but now it felt as if our feet were sinking into concrete. Matt turned toward us, a smile growing on his face. "Hey, Darla." He nodded up at the sputtering heater. "It's not completely up, but it's starting to put out some heat. I need to clean out all the grates tomorrow before we light them up in the evening."

Darla didn't respond. As the silence grew, Matt's grin faded and he tipped his head, examining her face.

"What's wrong?" He put his tools on the table and put his hand on her arm. Still Darla didn't say a word. He studied me. "Seriously, you guys are scaring me. What's going on?"

I glanced at Darla. This wasn't my story to tell. But at least I could get her some information. I focused on the girl who had started to move backward, away from the gathering. "Hey, you're the tea drinker from the shop. I thought you were just passing through?"

The girl's eyes widened, surprised I'd talked to her or remembered her, I wasn't sure which. She glanced at Matt. "I'm visiting friends."

"I never did get your name." I reached out my hand. "I'm Jill Gardner. This is Darla Taylor. She owns the winery. And apparently you know Matt."

"Becky was part of the job crew a few years ago. When Ted ran the program." When Matt said his name, Becky cringed. "She's pretty upset over his death."

Darla glanced back and forth from Matt to Becky. "Oh, you were, I mean, oh." She paused, then leaned toward me and whispered, "Ted had favorites."

Becky's eyes narrowed. She stepped away from the group, this time with a purpose. "I've got to go. I'll see you before I leave." She didn't look at Matt, but it was clear who she was addressing.

"You don't have to leave. Do you want a drink? Or a sandwich?" Darla called after her, but Becky kept walking. She put her hand in the air and waved Darla's words away.

"Wow." I hadn't ever met someone that angry at the world, especially someone so young.

Matt rubbed his hand over his face. "She's messed up. Ted did a complete number on her. She thought they were in love."

"But she's just a kid. He must have had twenty years on her." Darla shook her head. "Where was her mother?"

"Hell, where were the police?" Matt sank into a chair. "You realize she was underage when she and Ted first hooked up. But as usual, nothing stuck with that creep."

"Sounds like you didn't like him very much." I watched as Becky stomped down the road to Main Street. I wondered if she truly was staying with friends or if she had made friends with the homeless who liked to hang out at the public beach.

"No one liked Ted. At least no one who knew the creep. I'm glad he's dead. He can't ruin another girl's life this way." Matt leaned back in his chair and his face froze. I turned to see Greg standing there, his beer in one hand and my wineglass in the other.

"Being glad someone's dead doesn't mean you killed them." Darla sat in the chair next to Matt. She shook a finger at Greg. "And don't you be trying to blame Matt for being honest about how he felt about the guy."

Greg's lips curved. "If I arrested people for saying they were glad someone died, my jail would be filled constantly." He smiled at me. "And this one would be a repeat customer."

"You're always trying to get me behind bars, Detective. I think you may have a fetish or something."

Darla put her hands over her ears. "La la la, TMI. You two should be more careful about what you say in public."

Darla's words haunted me throughout the evening. Matt had come close to saying the world was a better place without Ted in it, a sentiment that Becky didn't agree with at all from the look on her face.

As Greg and I walked back into the building, I glanced down the road to see if I could catch a glimpse of where Becky was heading. But she'd disappeared. Greg's hand moved on my back and I turned to look at him.

"Everything isn't a problem to be solved, you know." Greg's voice was warm and comforting, but it also held a twinge of humor.

Chuckling, I leaned into his shoulder. "Am I that transparent?"

"Practically invisible." He squeezed me closer. "I'll see what I can find out about the girl. Will that make you happy?"

"I just wish I knew she was sleeping indoors tonight." As bad as my own childhood had been, I'd never been homeless. Although sometimes I wondered if I would have been stronger if I'd taken a chance as a teenager, leaving the constricting house my mother called a home. But the world, like the ocean I could see sparkling in the moonlight, was filled with sharks who preyed on the young and naïve. Traits Becky shared with the younger version of me. "Hey, I need to tell you about Marie's visit today."

"That can wait." Greg kissed me on the forehead and moved toward a table. He set our drinks down and put out his arms. "To everything there is a season. Time to stop worrying for the evening and time to dance."

"I'm not sure that's how the Byrds wrote the song." I followed him out to the parquet floor.

He pulled me close into his arms, matching our steps to the soft ballad playing. "The Byrds didn't write that—it's Ecclesiastes, from the Bible."

"Oh." I felt my face heat. Attending church hadn't been a house rule, so I hadn't gone very often. My mother had stopped going once my dad passed, worried that those people would look down on a single woman raising her only daughter. And in a way, she was probably right. Not because of being a single parent, but her use of alcohol to get through the day would have been an issue. "I didn't know that."

Greg pulled me closer. "If you'd spent your childhood attending St. Catherine's Academy, you would know all the popular songs they stole from the Bible. According to Sister Mary Francis, the musicians, their groupies, their production crew, and anyone who had ever listened to the songs were damned to eternal suffering." He spun me around the floor. "Of course, I think it was mostly because no one asked her to her own prom in high school. The nun could hold a grudge forever."

I giggled and snuggled into his chest. Yes, the wine was doing its magic. Maybe tonight would be all right after all. Darla hadn't killed Matt for talking to Becky. Regina and David had left earlier. They hadn't even stopped by the table to say good-bye. But maybe she hadn't seen me as clearly as I'd watched the couple on the dance floor.

And I was dancing with my own personal white knight. Although his faithful steed was parked at the house, and we'd walked from my house to Lille's, then from dinner to the winery. When I had questioned Greg earlier, he chuckled. "I plan on having more than one beer tonight, and no way am I giving Toby a reason to pull me over. The kid would have me breathalized and sitting in the drunk tank at the office before I could say, 'Did I do something wrong, Officer?' "

"He's got a high level of integrity." I smiled as I thought about Toby.

Greg shook his head. "Nope, the kid would snap pictures and blackmail me with the evidence."

That had made me chuckle over dinner, and now, thinking about Toby hunting drunk drivers made me pause. I turned my attention to Greg, who was humming along with the song. "Did you know Toby was dating a real person? With a kid and a job?"

"I'm sure he's dated real people before, love." Greg continued humming.

I put my hand on Greg's chest. "Yeah, but this time he's monogamous. He's only dating one woman."

Now Greg's brows raised and I had his complete attention. "So, the boy's getting serious, is he?"

"That's what I'm asking. Has he talked to you about this girl at all?"

Greg shook his head. "Not a word. But we had a deal tonight. You were going to stop trying to save the world and I would ask you to dance. Now one of us has kept their side of the bargain."

I leaned my head back down on Greg's chest, listening for his heartbeat. "Sorry, I forgot about the contract."

"You realize there are substantial penalties for breaking the terms. You'll probably have to give me several advantages next time we play the Xbox." He leaned in and kissed me quickly, our lips barely touching. "And maybe there's something more in the fine print."

"You're smooth, Detective King. Very smooth." I smiled and let the music transport me.

I heard Greg whisper in my ear, "Just trying to keep it interesting."

CHAPTER 15

Greg's phone buzzed. We were dancing so close, I felt the vibration on my leg. He pulled the offending cell out of his jeans and, glancing at the display, frowned. Greg led me off the dance floor and sat me down at our table. "It's Toby, I've got to take this."

I watched him walk out of the building, answering the call in motion. Damn that kid, he knew just how to ruin a perfect evening. I finished my glass of wine, knowing that as soon as Greg came back to the table we'd be leaving. I was dating Mr. Dependable. Besides, I knew Toby. He wouldn't have called if he didn't need his boss.

I was knee-deep into my pity party when Greg sat back down next to me. "You've kind of figured out what I was going to say, huh?" He wiped a stray tear from my cheek.

Sniffing, I nodded. "Toby wouldn't call unless there was a problem. So, what's going on?"

Greg tapped his phone absently. "Honestly, I'm not exactly sure, but Toby says someone's broken the front window in The Glass Slipper."

"No! Any other damage on the street?" Coffee, Books, and More sat across from Marie's shop. "Was it a riot?"

He laughed and took my hand. "No riot. Toby says your shop is fine. He's on his way here to pick us up. He'll drop you off at the house before taking me to the crime scene."

"Great, another drop-off in a police cruiser. If I had any neighbors besides Esmeralda, I'd sure be giving them gossip fodder."

"Why do you think Esmeralda works at the station? She's the biggest gossip in South Cove." He put his arm around my shoulders and walked me out to the patio to wait for our ride.

Toby had the lights of the cruiser flashing but he didn't have the sirens going. At least until he spotted us sitting at an outdoor table. People sitting around us jumped, glancing around to see who was in trouble. When Greg led me out to the cruiser, I heard the whispers. Great, by this time tomorrow I'd be arrested, convicted, and on my way to the California Penitentiary for Wayward and Wanton Women, at least in the South Cove gossip mill.

Greg sat me in the backseat. I blocked the door with my arm.

"Seriously? Not again. I call shotgun." I started to stand, but he gently pushed me back into the seat. He closed the door quickly this time.

Toby was laughing, I could tell from the shake of his shoulders and the crinkle in his eyes as he glanced into the rearview window. "You okay back there?"

Greg climbed into the passenger side and turned his head toward me. "Toby, didn't anyone tell you never to poke a caged bear?"

"Sorry, boss." Toby swung the car back out onto the street.

I leaned my head back on the bench seat, then jerked upright. I'd drunk just enough wine that the movement of the car was starting to feel like a roller coaster. "I'm not sure if I'm more upset about the bear comment or being stuck in the back, again."

"Well, make up your mind soon, sweetheart, we're almost at your house." Greg flipped through the electric file that had been created when the 911 call had been placed. "Marie called in the vandalism?"

"She wasn't on site when I arrived. It was her intern, Mindy." Toby pulled the cruiser into my driveway.

"Mindy saw who did this?" I leaned forward, trying to see what Greg was looking at on his tablet.

"No, she was in the building cleaning up after the last class. Mindy said Marie had left instructions for her to lock up after she was done and ..."

"That's enough, Toby. Jill needs to stay out of the investigation." Greg pointed his finger at his deputy. "You're just feeding her addiction, you know that, right?"

"I'm not addicted to sleuthing. I'm good at it." I pouted as Greg came around to open the back door.

He pulled me out of the car and kissed me. "Go inside and go to bed. I'll call you in the morning."

"Find Marie. I'm worried about her." I leaned into him as we walked to my front porch. "She might be in danger."

Greg took my keys and unlocked my front door. "And you might just read too many mysteries. I'm sure Marie's home in her apartment. I'll make sure to check though, just for you."

I kissed him quickly. "I'm serious, I'm worried. I signed up for the class tonight. Maybe if I'd been there ..."

"Jill, stop. The class was already over before the incident happened. There was nothing you could have done."

"I feel guilty skipping."

His slow, sexy smile gave me pause. "I know you do. I'll make sure she's okay. Just make sure you lock up tonight."

"No one's going to try to hurt me." But Greg had already turned and stepped off the porch.

"Let's keep it that way, okay?" he called back. When he reached the car and I was still standing in the doorway, he motioned me into the house with both hands. I nodded and closed the door, engaging the dead bolt along with the one in the doorknob. And then I went to the kitchen to let in Emma.

I glanced at the clock on the stove, ten thirty. My night out had lasted longer than most of our impromptu dinners, especially in the middle of the week. I wondered if Sherry had felt lonely when he'd chosen work over time with her. I knew Greg had to be available twenty-four/seven. But, of course, so did I. My afterhours emergencies so far this year had added up to exactly one trip down to the shop to let Aunt Jackie in because she'd locked her keys in the apartment upstairs. When I asked her where the spare was, she had nodded to the locked shop.

"At least it was secure," I told Emma, who wagged her tail like she knew exactly what I was saying. I grabbed my notebook and a pen. Time to sketch out a possible motive for Ted's murder and update all the possible suspects. I grabbed the laptop, as well, and settled into the couch. I threw a blanket over my legs against the chill and started writing down names.

An hour later, I found a mention of Becky and Ted. Apparently a gossip columnist had seen them on an alleged date at the boardwalk carnival. The woman had known Ted's family history and apparently played up the fact that Becky "might" be underage. I moved down to the next entry from the search listing. A full retraction of the column as well as a mention of how the author had been let go. The newspaper regretted their inaccurate portrayal of an upstanding member of the community.

I didn't think they were referencing Becky.

I bookmarked the web pages and wrote the links in my notebook just in case. I closed down the laptop and glanced at Emma, who slept curled up on the couch next to me. "Time for bed?"

She jumped up and went to the bottom of the stairs and waited. I turned off the lights and glanced out the window toward town, wondering what had happened on Main Street tonight and praying that Marie was all right.

Friday morning came without the alarm going off, since Toby and Jackie worked all the shifts, giving me a full day off. Jackie liked having Monday and Tuesday off. And Toby just liked working. I wondered how long that would be the case once he had a family to go home to. It sounded like that time was closer than I'd imagined.

After Emma and I ran, I puttered around the house, throwing in laundry, considered a grocery run, and then found myself curled up on the couch with a book. When the cell chimed, I considered letting it go to voice mail, but saw the shop's number on the display. "Hey, how are things this morning?"

"Peachy." Aunt Jackie's voice sounded pleased with herself, like she'd just won a salesmanship prize. "Did you know Marie's shop was vandalized last night?"

"Good morning to you, too." I absently petted Emma's head. "Have you seen her? Is she all right?"

"She's fine. Madder than a wet cat, but fine. She came over and bought coffee for the work crew that's replacing her window. Does Greg know who did it yet?"

I pursed my lips. I hadn't even thought about calling to see what he'd found out. Maybe I was losing my touch on this sleuthing thing. Last night Darla had called me basically clueless and now I hadn't even called my one reliable source. "If he does, he hasn't told me." I sat forward on the couch. "Maybe I should come down and talk to Marie."

"Don't bother. She drove into Bakerstown to pick up Mindy. She's giving her some real work for the next week."

The line quieted and I'd thought I'd lost the connection.

"You know, if we all gave up a few hours, we could bring Sasha on full-time after the first of the year. It would give her time to get up and running before tourist season hits full force. And we always need extra help during whale-watching season."

My aunt had made the pitch I'd been thinking about for a week. "We'll see. I'll talk to Toby first. I don't want to short him hours to bring on someone new."

"I'm sure he'd be on board with the program." Jackie paused. "By the way, we're having a little party next Saturday."

"Who's 'we'?" I wasn't sure I wanted to know.

"Coffee, Books, and More. We're doing a book drive promotion and bringing all the kids into the shop to meet Santa and give him their wish list. I'm sure I mentioned this to you when we set up the program."

"I'm pretty sure I would have remembered a party." I walked into the kitchen and pulled out a notebook, needing to start writing down all the things that needed to be done in a week. "I don't have a lot of time to pull this off."

"No worries, Sasha and I are handling everything." Jackie sniffed.

"Besides, the mayor's wife flat-out told us we couldn't have a Santa because it didn't fit with her festival plans. She thinks the New Age parents will be insulted."

"Wait, so you're not having Santa?"

Jackie laughed. "You're kidding, right? I told the witch to go ruin someone else's holiday. That we've got plans and won't be participating in her watered-down holiday festival. I hear she wanted a black and silver theme. Who does black and silver for Christmas? I swear, the woman is crazy."

"When did you talk to Tina?" I groaned. The mayor would be calling me into his office for once again failing to support his wife's mission. I was beginning to hate Christmas.

"This morning. She came in looking for you with a list of dos and don'ts three pages long. I threw it away."

"Aunt Jackie, did it ever occur to you to play nice? The woman is in charge of the town's festival program this year. Maybe we should at least read the material she's presenting." I heard the door chime to the shop.

"Fine. I'll pull the Nazi woman's list out of the trash and put it on your desk. But you aren't telling me no on the kid's Santa party. I think this could become a CBM tradition." Jackie called out a greeting to the customer. "Look, I'm busy. We'll talk tomorrow." Then the line went dead.

I flipped through my call history, just to make sure I hadn't missed a call from City Hall today. But no, the call from Jackie had been my first of the day. Not unusual in quiet times, but I knew Tina wouldn't let Jackie's refusal stay unpunished. I would be getting a reprimand.

I started a list of items that needed to be completed before next week's party. I checked my pre-planning list for Thanksgiving. Nothing I needed to do this weekend, but next weekend was chock-full of must-dos. I highlighted a few chores and moved them up a week.

Greg found me out in the shed at four, still in sweats, my hair pulled into a ponytail. I had gone through most of the boxes and still hadn't found the gravy boat in Miss Emily's good china pattern I knew I'd seen. I had found a glass turkey centerpiece vase for the table; all I had to do was purchase a potted plant to set inside the brown glass feathered body.

He kissed the top of my head as he surveyed the mess. "You looking for something?"

"Thank you, Captain Obvious." I glared at him. "The rose-patterned gravy boat that goes with the good china."

"The one in the china cabinet in the living room?" Greg appeared puzzled.

I groaned. "It isn't in there, is it?" I'd spent the last four hours digging through the boxes of china and other miscellaneous stuff. I'd meant to get an antique dealer in from Bakerstown to appraise the lot and sell what I didn't want. I just couldn't bring myself to part with my friend's stuff, not quite yet.

"Remember, we came out and found the missing serving pieces last month when you were freaking out about Thanksgiving?" He pulled me into a hug. "What's got you going today?"

"Jackie's decided to host a party with Santa at the shop next week for the center kids. It threw off all my plans; now I have to move things around." I stepped away from Greg and closed a box and pushed it to the side, dusting off my hands. I surveyed the piles of boxes. "I need to do something with these."

"You will, when you're ready. No need to push the process."

I watched him, standing in the gloom of the shed as the daylight drained from the one dirty window. "You're pretty good at this boyfriend thing, you know?"

His grin flashed. "Better than you realize sometimes. Now, let's go in. I thought we'd have an early dinner since I didn't have lunch, and if I'm right, you forgot to eat."

My stomach growled in answer. "I've been busy." I waved my hands around the shed. "Looking for something that apparently I'd already found."

Greg put his arm around me and we walked together toward the house. "Life's a lot like that, sweetheart."

The smell of chicken Alfredo and garlic bread hit me as soon as we walked into the kitchen door. I kissed Greg on the cheek. "You cooked."

He laughed as I dug through the cabinet for plates and silverware. "I ordered. We may not be able to have the whole evening to ourselves, but we can carve out an hour or so." He disappeared into the living room, returning with the gravy boat. He set it down on the table with a low bow. "Tada!"

"Total waste of an afternoon." I slid half the noodles onto each plate, topping the brimming plates off with fresh parmesan and a couple of slices of garlic bread.

Greg picked up the glass turkey centerpiece. "I wouldn't say it was a waste. This is interesting."

I held up a soda out of the fridge and cocked my head in an unspoken question to Greg. He nodded so I grabbed two. "You say 'interesting' like it's ugly."

He took a bite of the Alfredo. "I suppose someone liked it enough to buy the thing in the first place. Unless she made it in one of those classes Marie gives."

"Oh God, I forgot about Marie." I ignored Greg's jab at the centerpiece. I liked it. Miss Emily had liked it. So it was going on the table. "How is she? Jackie said she was steaming mad when she saw her."

Greg laughed. "Last night she ranted against the kids hanging around town so hard she made Josh look like a Boy Scout leader. She was certain some misguided youth was to blame."

"You think it was one of our kids?" We'd gone through a perceived youth problem the past summer with Josh Thomas spewing hateful jibes at what he called "the loitering mass of the unwashed." Actually we'd had problems with one kid, and that kid had been more attached to a gone-bad motorcycle gang than her fellow teenagers.

"I don't think so. But who knows? She did mention the two of you had talked. Is that what you wanted to tell me last night?"

I nodded, my mouth too full of pasta to talk.

"I still don't buy her as a killer." Greg chewed a bite from the slice of garlic bread, his look troubled. "What I did find out today was interesting, though."

"Interesting in a good way or an ugly way, like the centerpiece?" I took a bite of the creamy fettuccini noodles and almost groaned, it was so good.

"I don't hate the centerpiece," Greg countered.

I swallowed and pointed my fork at him. "And you didn't answer my question, either."

He wiped his mouth on a paper napkin and teepeed his fingers together, watching me. Finally he spoke. "The fingerprints on the brick that was thrown through Marie's window matched the ones we found on the paper from the threat left on your porch."

CHAPTER 16

After Greg left, I cleaned up the kitchen and wandered through the house. He'd returned to the station to meet with the district attorney. "Just a routine update session," Greg had said, trying to assuage my fears. But no matter how positive a picture he'd tried to paint on the evidence, he was worried.

Besides, I knew one thing. Whoever had killed Ted was still in town, trying to scare off anyone who might be close to solving the murder. Marie had declared that she was going after the estate for money she felt owed. Me, I had just been the unlucky person to find the body. *And you have a history of solving murders*, my rational side added.

Whatever was going on, I needed to figure out who wanted Ted dead and fast. Marie's name was still on my top-ten list, but honestly, even I didn't believe she had the guts to shoot someone. Up close and personal? That took passion and heat. Marie was scared of Ted still, but not angry.

I stood at my front window gazing out on the ocean view that I could see if I stood on my tiptoes. I wanted to slip into my running clothes and take Emma down to the beach, but I'd promised Greg I'd stay close to the house tonight. My gaze dropped down to the flower bed along the front porch. Gardening I could do, at least until the sun dropped below the horizon.

I grabbed my gloves, a trash sack, and a carryall that held a small shovel, a trowel, and a mini hoe. I called Emma and we headed out front, my cell in my pocket just in case. She wandered through the front yard as I pulled weeds and dug up the beds in preparation for bulbs I'd buy on Monday.

As I worked, my mind wandered through the facts I'd known about Ted. For a guy I'd only met a few weeks ago, there was surprisingly a lot of material already in neat lists in my project notebook. I'd thought about calling it an investigation manual, but thought Greg might not find the humor. Besides, if it said "project" on the front, he wouldn't be tempted to look inside, especially if he thought it could mean a weekend remodeling my upstairs bath. (That item was totally on the to-do list. As soon as this investigation was over.)

Starting at the beginning, I listed out my facts. Ted had lived most his life in Boston. Had married and scared away one wife, Marie. Then, out of nowhere, he decided to move across the country three years ago to work at a program director position that probably paid less than what he'd paid for housing back in Beantown. That had to be because the private investigator had found Marie. But why wait three years before approaching her? Or trying to run her down in the street on his first visit to South Cove? Now that made no sense at all.

"You're troubled," a soothing voice said.

I sighed. "Darn right, I am. The whole thing doesn't make sense."

Emma barked from her favorite napping spot on the porch and ran to the fence. Crap, that voice hadn't been in my head. I had a visitor. I pulled off my gloves and stood, brushing the dirt off my knees. Turning, I saw my neighbor petting and whispering to my dog. Esmeralda had come to call. I steeled myself, squaring my shoulders, and walked to the fence.

"Esmeralda, so nice of you to drop by." I glanced over at her house, ablaze with light. "I assumed you'd have clients coming in tonight."

"I do. The sitting doesn't start for another thirty minutes or so. But as I was preparing myself in my reading room, I was told to come to see if you were all right." She straightened from petting Emma. "Your dog is an old soul."

I smiled and Emma licked my hand softly. "Now that I believe. She's been a blessing. No puppy terrors for her. Now, if I could get her to stop chewing."

"Emma's worried about you. She says that there are dark forces surrounding the house." Esmeralda scanned the area. "I can't believe I didn't notice them before. You need to be careful."

I laughed and Esmeralda's eyes widened. "You're always saying that. Both you and Greg are sounding like broken records. Don't get involved. Stop investigating. Be careful, the dark forces are out to get you."

"People do care about you." My neighbor sniffed, her eyes narrowing.

A heat of shame crept through me. She was only trying to be nice. In a crazy gypsy fortune-teller way, but nice. "Sorry. I'm a little on edge tonight. That's why I came out to work in the flower beds. Idle hands, you know."

"I don't think that's funny, Jill. You don't want to even use that word until things are cleaned up around here." Esmeralda glanced back at her house, where a black Town Car had pulled into the driveway. She started to walk away from the fence.

I frowned. "I don't understand, what word?"

She turned back toward me. "The devil. We had a devil killed in town. Now his murderer is still running free, jacked up with stolen power."

I watched as she hurried across the road and greeted her guest. I squinted to watch the woman who climbed out of the back of the car. I recognized her. Glancing up at the man who stood dressed in a black suit holding the door open, there was no doubt in my mind. David stood there. Regina was Esmeralda's client. I wondered who from the spirit world would be visiting through the fortune teller's glass ball. Maybe Regina's husband wasn't in a big city making money while she and David played by the seashore. I could have read that all wrong. If Regina was a widow, that would explain the ring and the trip to Esmeralda's.

Emma whined next to me.

I reached down and patted her head. "Ready for dinner?"

She bounded toward the porch, and when she reached the front door, she turned and barked.

"I'm coming. Hold on." I grabbed my gardening kit from the lawn and set it on the front porch so I could finish the bed preparation tomorrow after work. Then Emma and I went into the house. As I locked the front door, my gaze caught Esmeralda's house. The place appeared welcoming, even inviting in the dusky light. I hoped Regina would find peace with the information Esmeralda told her. If I'd known it was Regina, I would have put a bug in the fortune teller's ear about a new love from an old friendship or some crap like that.

But maybe Esmeralda was perceptive enough to pick up on David's longing for his boss all on her own.

After filling Emma's bowl, I grabbed my own and filled it with ice cream. Then I turned on the television and found a sappy old movie. So much for an exciting Friday night. I kept looking out the window to see when Regina and David left, but when the movie ended, I walked over to peer out and the Town Car was still there. Emma nudged my leg.

"Yep, bedtime." She trotted over to the kitchen door and sat waiting for me to follow. I double-checked the locks on the front door, then grabbed my empty bowl and went to the kitchen to let Emma out. I rinsed my bowl and set it in the half-filled dishwasher. During the next week or so, I'd hand-wash the good china, getting everything ready for the big day. Desserts I'd already ordered from Sadie. I'd found three different stuffing recipes, corn bread, oyster, and what Jackie called "normal stuffing." I'd read every holiday-based cookbook I had in stock at the store, and ordered two more last week, just to make sure I wasn't forgetting something. I'd even found a fresh cranberry recipe but planned on buying a can of the clear jellied type just in case. Holidays were special. You never knew what missing one thing could do to ruin a dinner.

I'd talked to Greg about his holiday memories. Since it was now just him and Jim, I didn't want to forget the one dish that would cause the day to miss the mark. Greg thought I was obsessing, but I also knew he thought it was better than me worrying about Ted's murder. I wiped down the kitchen counter and turned off the lights. Letting

Emma in, I repeated my routine and double-checked the locks on the back door, then we jogged up the stairs to the bedroom. I'd snuck a soda in my jacket pocket and had a book or two on the bedside. Even if I couldn't sleep, I could get lost in a story.

Jackie had already opened the shop when I arrived the next morning. Piles of floor pillows lay stacked in corners and by the bookshelves. One big overstuffed chair sat over by the history section, a white fur rug on the floor in front of it. A table sat nearby with a bowl of candy canes. Santa's den was almost ready. I could just see Toby sitting in the chair, grinning at each child as they whispered their secret wish list to the big guy.

Jackie burst out of the back carrying two boxes. She nodded to the coffeemakers. "Might as well make yourself useful. The coffee isn't started yet."

I hurried to the sink and washed my hands, slipping an apron over my head. "What have you been doing? Coffee is always the first priority when you open."

Jackie dropped the boxes on the floor with a bang. "Not when you're playing hostess to thirty kids waiting for a miracle to happen, like having heat in their apartment this year. Or for some, even an apartment." She shook her head. "I can't believe you're so selfish when there are true innocents out there who need our help."

"Making coffee isn't selfish, it's survival. Those kids have parents coming into a confined situation with excited, screaming children. Without coffee to serve them, we could be looking at infanticide." I measured out the ground coffee, inhaling the deep, dark smell. In one pot, I made the sinfully chocolate blend that made the shop smell like a bakery even though all of our pastries were made off site. "I didn't expect you until later. And why all this today? I thought the party was next weekend."

"It is. I just want the shop to look festive and inviting. I thought I'd get more done last night, but Josh came in and we talked for a while." Jackie ripped open one of the boxes and put a copy of *The Night Before Christmas* on Santa's table next to the candy canes. In the chair, she put a poster with a picture of Santa and next Saturday's date listed. "We're giving away the books as part of our donation."

"How many books did you order?" Thank God the holidays only came once a year or the shop would go bankrupt with all of Jackie's giveaways.

She frowned at me. "One for each kid at the center and any of the regulars." She paused. "I had the printer make up coupons for one free book for the kids and drink coupons for the adults. That way, they have to come back to redeem their coupon and maybe they'll buy another book then."

I couldn't argue with her marketing logic. Although it occurred to me that several of the families might just come in for the free book and drink, because paying for the bus to get here would take up their disposable income for the week. I hated the thought that families had to choose between buying books for their kids and putting food on the table.

We worked side by side all morning. Our regulars threw their change into the donation jar and filled it so often, Jackie had to empty it three times. When she grabbed it again, I raised my eyebrows. "How much do you think we've raised so far?"

Jackie grinned. "I don't know, but I think we may be able to do more than just buy books for the kids. We can talk to the center's social worker about where the money might do the most good." She handed a customer his cup of to-go coffee in a holiday motif sleeve. "I'm looking forward to our party."

As I got ready to leave, I watched Jackie chat with Mary Simmons. The early Saturday rush had ended. Now we just had a few stragglers sitting and enjoying a quiet moment in the weekend rush. Toby still hadn't arrived, but Jackie had waved me off anyway. She could handle the shop, and if she got in trouble, she knew how to use a phone.

Mary rarely left the B&B she ran with Bill—mostly, in my opinion, because there was too much work to get done. Bill wasn't much for the hospitality scene. He spent most of his days in his den, working on a new historical tome on California history, although I'd heard his new project focused on Central America. The couple had closed up shop for two weeks in September to tour every country from California to Panama.

Mary had her digital camera out, showing Jackie some of their pictures from the trip. I watched as a look of longing crossed my aunt's face. I wondered if the business was doing well enough to give out bonuses. But no, even without looking, I knew I couldn't take that kind of hit, not this year. Maybe soon though.

"Jill," Regina called me over to the sofa where she sat reading with David. "Were you at the winery last night? I told David I thought I saw you, but then we lost sight of you."

I sat on the arm of the couch. "Yep, that was me. You two are great dancers. Do you take lessons?"

Regina's laughter bubbled through the café. "David's the dancer. He's been teaching me since we've been in town. I only learned the fox-trot and the waltz as a girl." She glanced at the man reading next to her and dropped her voice. "Tell me about that hunk you were with last night. I hear rumors you're dating the local sheriff? His eyes are amazing."

I felt my face heat. "Greg King's South Cove's detective, not a sheriff." I straightened a pile of books on the coffee table. "But he does have dreamy eyes."

"Next you two will be talking about his butt. What happened to women? All they want to talk about is the pieces of a man, not the essence." David laid his book on his lap and took a sip of his coffee. "Mark my words, a man who is caring and thoughtful is worth ten times the man so hooked up on his own looks to notice the gem he has on his arm."

This time it was Regina's turn to blush. "Now you know how women have felt all these years, being objects of lust rather than people. What's good for the goose is good for the gander, correct?"

David shrugged and lifted his book. "I'm not saying that's not true. Women have to be smarter than men. If they want to win the game, that is."

"What game?" Now he was confusing me.

Regina patted my hand. "David's convinced that the only path to true love is one of challenges and compromises. He believes soul mates have to struggle to find and stay with each other. He's always been a sucker for the fairy tales, even in high school."

"The easy catch isn't always the tastiest dinner," David muttered, then returned to his reading.

I felt bemused by David's old-fashioned mantras. However, he did have a point. Women needed to be looking for more in a man than just the surface design. Greg might be a terrific package, but he was also kind, intelligent, and loving, underneath the sexy, sandy hair and icy blue eyes. Not to mention his strong arms and tight abs.

As if my thoughts of him had drawn him in, Greg entered the shop, glancing around until he saw me. Wait, no, he was looking past me. He walked toward me with Toby and Tim on his heels. My heart dropped. This show of force could only mean one thing, they were here to arrest someone. And the only people between me and the wall of bookshelves were Regina and David.

Greg stood in front of the coffee table, shooting me an apologetic glance. "David Webber? Can you come with me to the station? We have some things to clear up."

Regina gasped. "This can't be happening."

I sat next to her, ready to hold her back if she tried anything stupid. "Look, Greg just wants to ask him a few questions, that's all." I prayed I wasn't lying, but as I watched the men leave my shop, I could feel my nose grow.

CHAPTER 17

Jackie waved the phone at me. I excused myself from the distraught Regina and walked over to the counter. I nodded to Regina. "Get her an espresso shot. She needs a jolt."

"She needs alcohol, not caffeine," Jackie muttered, holding the portable receiver toward me.

"Unfortunately, we don't have a liquor license, so coffee will have to do." I shooed her toward the back of the coffee bar and held the phone between my shoulder and my ear, stacking dishes as I answered. "This is Jill."

"About time. I'm a very busy man, Miss Gardner. I wish you'd respect my time." Mayor Baylor's high-pitched whine grated on my nerves. My hands stopped moving, curling into fists.

I swallowed down some of the anger I felt and forced a smile to my face. "What do you want?"

"One, you need to help Amy with the reporting for the work study people we have. Ted never said there was this much paperwork. Did you know we had to file time sheets? And get background checks on the owners of each store where they're assigned?" The mayor sighed. "No wonder no one wants to help. You always wind up being sorry later."

"Ted didn't mention time sheets to me, either. I take it Candy stopped by for a visit today?" I glanced over at Sasha, who was help-ing a customer choose a dessert to go with their coffee. She'd come in just after all the commotion and seemed to take an on-site arrest in stride. I wondered what trouble she'd observed in her life that made this afternoon's activities run of the mill. Regina, on the other hand, was close to tears.

"The woman is a paper Nazi. She brought in a box of forms that each work site owner needs to complete and have back by Monday or the project will be cancelled." The mayor cleared his throat. "Al-though maybe that wouldn't be the worst idea."

"Hold on, I'm done here for the day. I'll meet with Amy and see what we can get together. Then I'll call Candy and see if we can get an extension. If not, I'll just run them over late Monday. The shop's closed that day anyway." Any dream of having a quiet, relaxing day off had just gone out the window. My gaze stopped at Regina. She appeared to have gotten a hold of her emotions and was now on her cell. Her face was granite.

"I'll leave you to fix this problem then." The mayor paused. Again I could hear the shoe drop although this one sounded like a man's size fifteen work boot. "One more thing. You'll have to take over the festival planning. Tina's been called away on business."

Business, my butt. Tina Baylor hadn't worked a job since she mar-ried her politically driven husband. The woman was bailing and leav-ing me holding the bag. My mind raced, trying to come up with a solution that would let her save face and keep me sane. "I'm not sure I have the skills to replace someone like Tina. Maybe we should look for a candidate better suited for the job?"

"Whatever you think. Just make sure we're not over budget. The way she was spending, I'm not sure there's a dime left for a tree or even power to hook up the old lights."

I heard a second voice over the phone talking to him.

"Look, my next appointment's here. Time to get new publicity photos done before campaigning takes up all my time. Just take care of these little problems."

"I'll try, but I don't . . ." The phone clicked in my ear, and I real-ized I was talking to dead air. I hung up the phone and motioned Jackie over. "You okay waiting until Toby shows up?"

Jackie nodded. "He pulled me aside and said Greg had promised he'd be done in an hour or so. What a mess."

I followed her gaze and realized she was referencing Regina. "You think David could have killed Ted? I don't." I smiled when Jackie raised her eyebrows. "Okay, unless Ted was attacking Regina, then all bets are off. I swear, that man would do just about anything for that woman."

"Including kill," Jackie agreed.

Sasha stepped closer. "I got a call from Candy this morning, wondering how I was doing and how I liked the job." She studied our faces carefully. "You two didn't complain about me, did you? I mean, if I'm doing something wrong, you would tell me first, not the program, right?"

Concern washed over me. "No, you are doing an amazing job. I think you have quite a knack for this type of career." I put my hand on her arm and she visibly relaxed. "Why? Did Candy say we weren't happy with your performance?"

Sasha sighed. "Thank the Lord and pass the peanut butter. I was worried that you'd let me go as soon as I walked in the door."

"Seriously, what did she say to get you this upset?" I glanced at the clock. The mayor's project could wait. I needed to know if Candy was a concerned partner or a judgmental, spiteful woman taking out her anger toward a dead man on our work participants.

Sasha leaned over, her forearms flat on the counter. She took in the almost empty shop before she spoke in hushed tones. "She said that people had been talking about the employers taking advantage of people in the program. Like the games Ted used to play on people. I swear, Matt was going to deck him the next time he pulled a stunt like that, but then Ted wound up dead. So there's not a problem now."

I wondered if that was true, along with my concern about how deep Matt's anger lay. "So you told her you were doing great, right?"

Sasha nodded. "I told her what I've told everyone since I started working here a couple of weeks ago. I love working here. I just wish there was a real job waiting for me."

"Keep doing this good of a job and we'll be hard-pressed to lose you. And you know what happens when we get comfortable around someone." I smiled at Jackie.

Her eyebrows furrowed, but she didn't respond.

Sasha, on the other hand, seemed to get the joke, and a small smile crept on her lips. "You find you can't live without them?" she asked, hopefully.

"Something like that." I nodded to Jackie. "I've got to get down to City Hall. I guess Candy's been causing trouble all over town."

Something froze in Sasha's expression.

"Hey, don't worry about it. All you have to do is keep working as hard as you do and we'll figure something out. For now, I've got to get busy on some paperwork Ted forgot to tell us about." I walked to the back room to grab my purse. Instead of leaving out the front door, I slipped out the back into the warm, sunny day. Something moved at the top of the building next door: Josh going into his apartment. Not wanting to get stuck in a discussion about Jackie, I skirted around the edge of the building onto a brick walkway that ran on the other side of Antiques by Thomas and headed down Main Street toward City Hall.

Amy was digging through a box of papers when I arrived. She stood and gave me a quick hug. "Thank God you're here. The mayor said he was calling in help, but I hadn't dared to hope it would be you. I figured he'd call Tina. Then she could tell me how to do the work rather than helping."

I laughed. "She does have a specific way she wants things done." I took off my light jacket. "Where do you want me to start?"

We decided to haul everything into the conference room, then set up ten piles, one for each work site. That way we could make sure all the packets were the same and had every form that needed signed in the same order. It would make explaining the process easier, as we'd always be saying the same thing. If we had more time, I would have called an evening meeting at Coffee, Books, and More and we would have done this as a group. As it was, we would have to hand-deliver the packets to each business, hoping they'd trust us and just sign the pages we put in front of them with little explanation.

A girl can be optimistic, sometimes. By the time we had the packets together with a short script of what we would say, it was four. We divided up the list and I tucked my five assignments into my tote bag. One would be easy, that was mine. The other four would be a little harder. I had the B&B, the Winery, The Glass Slipper, and Antiques by Thomas. As soon as I finished, I was going to track down Greg and find out what, if anything, he'd tell me about David. My thoughts were on Regina and her indisposed driver when I left City Hall.

As I opened the door to the outside, a band of suited gentlemen jogged through the glass doors, surrounding me. I gasped in spite of myself. A man in an even more expensive suit than the six who had tried to run me over, chuckled. His dark hair was cut short, but it still showed a smattering of gray. His eyes, a deep brown, were focused directly on me.

"Sorry, they can be a bit driven when they are on assignment." He dropped his gaze up and down my body. "You okay?"

"No one ran into me or stomped me into the ground. I guess I'll live." I turned away, stepping down a flight of steps before his voice stopped me.

"Anyway, I can take you to dinner tonight to make it up to you?"

When I turned, I saw he stood at the top of the stairs, his hand on the railing. He stared at me, a wide, sexy smile on his face. He'd taken off his sunglasses and I could see crinkles around his eyes. Laugh lines, my mom had always called them.

"Seriously, there's not a problem here. No scratches, no bruises, no broken bones. Your friends didn't hurt me." I smiled, trying to wave off his concern. "No need for an apology."

His smile grew even wider. "What if the apology is just a tricky way to get you to say yes to our first date?"

I shook my head slowly. "We are not having a first, third, or last date. Sorry, I'm kind of involved."

"Married?" He pressed. "I don't see a ring."

"Just because you're not married doesn't mean you're not involved." I leaned against the rail, the packets in my tote feeling like I was carrying concrete rather than paper. "Look, I'm sure you're perfectly nice. But I'm not interested in dinner or a relationship. It was very nice to meet you."

A laugh stopped my descent. "We didn't meet, not officially. I'm Dean Johnson." He leaned closer, offering his hand in greeting.

"Jill Gardner. And I'm late. Sorry." When I shook his hand, the warmth surprised me. *Strong grip*, I thought as I pulled away. This time I did step down the rest of the stairs. As I hit the sidewalk and started power walking to make up time, a voice followed me.

"Don't think I'll stop at just a handshake. I'm going to find you," Dean called after me. "And I mean that in a totally uncreepy, I'm-not-a-stalker way."

I should have called back that my boyfriend wouldn't like it, but then I felt like I was living out some Beach Party Bimbo movie from the sixties. Besides, I was laughing too hard to talk.

By the time I reached Antiques by Thomas, I'd calmed down.

Josh sat outside on a wooden bench, watching me walk toward him. He looked like hell. His eyes were sunken more than usual, and his skin, pale. When I got within earshot, he muttered, "What do you want?"

"Why do you think I want something?" I slipped onto the bench next to him and took a packet out of my bag.

"You're talking to me and no one is around to see. I don't have the energy for your games. Those cats keep waking me up at all hours of the night. Yet, when I went into the other apartment this morning, they were gone." Josh peered at the pile of papers. "What's that?"

I shrugged, trying to look uninterested. "Oh, just the paperwork for the intern you have working for you. How's Kyle working out?" I glanced behind me and saw the young man cleaning off a table. He waved, then returned to his work. "He seems like a hard worker."

"When I'm watching him." Josh snorted. "Sometimes I think he finds a place to hide and takes a nap."

A short laugh escaped my lips before I realized Josh wasn't kidding. "I'm sure he's not sleeping on the job. He seems to love antiques. You must be a terrific mentor for someone like him."

Josh shrugged, but I could see in his face the compliment had taken hold. The man could be nice. Jackie had found some redeeming qualities, so I guess I could, too. I tapped on the paperwork. "You were right, I do need something." I held out a pen. "The new program director wants to complete all the paper files for the crew by Monday. She sure is a stickler for rules."

Josh squinted at the papers. "I don't sign anything I haven't read."

I moved the pen closer. "Honestly, I've gone over all the documents. Jackie told you I used to practice law, right?" I waited for his almost imperceptible nod, then pushed on. "There's nothing here you have to worry about. Just legal stuff about keeping insurance on the business, just in case. And that you won't use Kyle for illegal activities, like the sale of hot merchandise."

Josh's lips tightened, and his face turned redder than usual. "I do not sell stolen goods. I'm an upstanding member of the community."

Crap, he'd taken my joke seriously. "Sorry, Josh, I was joking. I know you're a reputable antique dealer. In fact, I was going to ask you to help me decide what to do with some of Miss Emily's furniture and china. You have such a knack for these things."

I hadn't been going to Josh for help. I'd wanted to keep our relationship as professional as possible, considering he was dating my aunt. And probably eating Thanksgiving dinner with me. But I needed him to sign these papers sooner than later, so if I had to sweeten the pot with Miss Emily's antiques, I would let him sell the lot.

His eyes narrowed, but I had his attention. "When do you need the forms back?"

I sighed. This wasn't going as well as I'd hoped. "Sunday night. I'm driving them over to the center in Bakerstown first thing Monday morning."

He held out his hand.

I stared at it, not knowing what he wanted.

"Miss Gardner, give me the paperwork. You can pick it up at the shop at five on Sunday, right before I close."

I handed over the packet, pointing toward the stickers. "I've marked the places you need to sign. I appreciate you doing this so quickly. I know that this has been kind of a mess from the day Ted and the mayor made their back-room handshake agreement."

Josh harrumphed. "The mayor tends to align himself with the wrong sort often. He needs to be more circumspect about the friends he keeps."

Preaching to the choir. "Anyway, I do appreciate your help in getting all this cleaned up." I stood. "If we don't get it in on time, Candy might shut the program down early. I know Jackie would hate to lose Sasha as much as you'd hate to lose Kyle."

A look of dread filled Josh's face, and I knew it was more about displeasing my aunt than losing his own intern. "Be here promptly at five. I like to go into the city for a nice dinner on Sunday evenings." I nodded. "See you then." I stood, checking for cars before I crossed the street. I almost felt bad for the guy. But not bad enough not to use my aunt's name to get something I needed. I would probably have all the forms but his back in an envelope this afternoon. Josh always had to do things his own way. Be the stick in the cogs of a well-oiled plan.

The front door to Marie's shop was locked and no one answered when I knocked on the apartment door. Great. My luck was holding steady: all bad. I scribbled out a note and slipped it under her apartment door. I'd stop again on the way back from the winery.

My steps had turned from determined optimism to slower, drudging along Main Street. By the time I'd reached the South Cove B&B, I was ready for more bad news. Mary was in the living room, quilting when I entered.

"Hey, Jill, don't you look like someone just ran over your favorite potted plant? Come sit for a spell. Do you want a glass of iced tea?" Mary's concern almost brought tears to my eyes, but I swiped them away like a buzzing fly.

"No, I'm fine. But I need you to do something for me." I went on to explain the paperwork and why it hadn't gotten done before and that we hadn't even known about it. When I finally came up for air, Mary was already standing and digging through a drawer in her desk near the corner of the room.

"Here we go." She popped her head up and held aloft a pen. "Where do I sign?"

Five minutes later, I was back on the road, walking toward the winery. One out of four wasn't great odds, but at least I had one done, a promise of one, and two more to finish. Three black SUVs sped past me and turned onto the winery road. *Tourists.* Always in a hurry to get somewhere. I daydreamed as I walked and hoped Amy's progress had been better than my own.

When I arrived at the winery, the SUVs were sitting empty in the parking lot. I opened the door to the tasting room, and glanced around, looking for Darla.

"Jill, come on over. Join the celebration." Regina grabbed my arm and led me to the table filled with men in designer suits, David, and one more. Dean turned and smiled at me, standing as I approached the group. "Everyone, this is Jill. She runs the coffee shop/bookstore I've been raving about."

"Hi, Jill." A chorus of male voices responded to Regina's introduction.

David seemed subdued but no worse for wear. "You doing okay? I can't believe the way Greg took you into the station." I'd been a little miffed at my boyfriend's picking the guy up, especially in my shop. And, since he'd been released, probably over nothing. A little voice inside tried to defend Greg, listing off not overreacting as one of his strongest character traits.

David shook his head. "Detective King did what he needed to do. I never should have given her that gun."

Dean slapped David on the back, stopping his next words. "What you did and what they can prove are two different things, my friend. No way was the family going to let you get railroaded over this one mistake in judgment." Dean nodded at one of the guys sitting next to David. "Go with Harold. He'll run you back down to your room, where you can freshen up and be in a better mood for your victory party. Take a shower, or a nap, whatever you need. Don't hurry back, we'll still be here."

David nodded, but as he walked by me, he shot me a look, pleading for understanding. And for some strange reason, he reminded me of a convicted criminal walking into death row.

CHAPTER 18

Regina took a sip of her wine. "Jill, have you met my brother, Dean?"

So that's why this man was in town, on my heels like a tax collector on April 16th. I nodded. "We ran into each other at City Hall."

Dean chuckled. "Well, the boys ran into her. I just tried to make things better." He leaned closer to me. "How are you feeling? Any ill effects from the incident I should know about?"

"No. Like I told you, I'm fine. Still fine. No worries." I held my hands up in the air and spun around once.

"You sure are," he said in a voice so low I wasn't sure I'd imagined his words.

Regina's laughter tinkled through the room. "Now, Dean, you need to leave Jill alone. She's dating the local lawman."

His lips curved into a smile. "Is that so? Well, I guess what he doesn't know won't hurt me, right?"

Regina raised her eyebrows. She patted the seat next to her. "Sit with us. I promise I'll keep my brother on a leash."

I glanced around the room, finally seeing Darla. "Sorry, I'm kind of on a mission here. I'll see you in the shop later."

Regina sighed. "After this incident, I may have to cut my visit short. I worry about David."

Dean broke in again, his face red from anger or fear, I couldn't tell. "Look, we just need to let things die down. All idle gossip does is get in the way of the investigation. You have to trust that the local law presence will do the right thing."

"Greg wouldn't have taken him in for questioning if he didn't think that it was the right thing." Now I was defending Greg's actions. What was with me bouncing back and forth on this issue?

From the surprised look on Dean's face, he'd noticed the inconsistencies, too. "All I'm saying is we need to mind our own business. David's a good man. Good men don't go to jail for things they didn't do."

What world do you live in? I wanted to ask, but instead, I let the comment roll off my back. "Nice to see you again, Regina. And you, too." I nodded toward Dean.

"Come back and have a drink with us when your business is completed," Regina offered, her gaze and attention wandering through the nearly empty wine room.

I took that as permission to leave and heard Dean's voice calling after me, "Come back soon."

The man, as attractive as he was, gave me the creeps. It wasn't anything I could put my finger on. And I was sure I wasn't imagining the overwhelming feeling. I almost sprinted toward Darla, who saw me coming and put up her hand.

"I know why you're here and I'm not going for it. I won't come in at the last moment and save Christmas." Darla didn't even look up from the glasses she was washing.

"Actually, that's not why I'm here." *Although I should be*, I added silently. One disaster at a time. I wasn't that strong of a woman.

This time Darla did look at me. "Is there a problem? Did Greg send you down to warn me?"

"What are you talking about?" I didn't wait for an answer. Darla was in rare form this afternoon.

Darla threw an anxious glance at the table I'd just left. "Them. They look and sound right out of a *Godfather* movie. Do you think they're the mob?"

"Calm down. Those are Regina's friends and family. They can be a bit overbearing, but they're human, believe me." I turned, catching Dean's stare. "Of course, you need to protect yourself from that one.

He's a bit of a flirt. Besides, they're from Boston. I don't think the *Godfather* movies were set there."

"It's the East Coast. No difference. I visited New York once and never again. I was almost killed getting out of my taxi." Darla finished with the last glass and focused on me. "So, why are you here?"

"I need you to sign some forms. I guess Ted was supposed to do all of this prior to the workers showing up. Now we're halfway through the session, and the new chief is screaming about pulling the whole project." I pulled the bundle of paperwork from my messenger bag, putting South Cove B&B's completed packet at the bottom. "I've reviewed it for issues, and it all looks pretty straightforward. Can you sign now and I'll give you copies next week?"

A cheer went up around the table, welcoming a new arrival. I expected to see David returning, but instead, Mayor Baylor waved at the crowd. Regina walked up to greet him, planting a kiss on his jowly cheek.

What the hell? How did these people even know each other? I watched as Dean pulled out a chair, then pulled the other man into a hug. I turned back to Darla. "You know what's going on over there?"

Her eyes narrowed as she watched the waitress approach the table. "I don't. Looks like they're pretty chummy with our mayor, though." She cast a sideways glance at me. "You sure they aren't mafia? I wouldn't put it past Mayor Baylor to be in with those types."

"I didn't think so." But as I turned back to focus on the paperwork, a nagging feeling kept me jumpy. Maybe Greg knew the skinny on this.

Darla read through the pages, focusing on one clause, then another. "Give me a pen. I'll sign and we can run to the office to get my copy." She waited on me to grab a pen out of the bottom of the bag. "That guy is sure fixated on you. Do you know him from somewhere?"

I gave an exaggerated sigh as I handed her the pen. "No. He approached me outside City Hall, asked me out for dinner, and I turned him down. End of story."

Darla flipped through the marked pages, signing where the stickers were set. As she finished, she stood the pages on end and straightened them, her gaze now back out to the dining room. "Well, I don't think it's 'end of story' for him. Maybe Greg needs to make his move and put a ring on it before this new one turns your head."

"I do have a choice in the matter, you know." I followed Darla out of the tasting room and into her small office. I'd never been in there before and the décor surprised me. She had black-and-white photos all around the room, mostly of South Cove. The desktop was clean and polished and looked like no one worked there. A small professional copier sat near another door. I thought of my office at the shop. My desk looked like a disaster had hit most days of the week. Even the small office I'd set up at home had more paper floating around than Darla's entire room.

She made a copy and handed me the originals, clipping them together with a binder clip she pulled out of a drawer. "You never know when your heart will take over. I still think Greg needs to man up."

I chuckled, tucking the packet behind the one other set of completed forms. "Well, I'm not going to take Mr. Smooth out there up on his dinner offer just to make Greg jealous. I don't play those games."

Darla cocked her head and considered my words for a moment. Her next statement surprised me. "I thought every woman played games."

I wanted to ask her what she meant, but the clock struck five and I thought about Marie. Tonight's class was scheduled to start at five thirty. If I hurried, I could have all but Josh's papers done before I headed home for the night. Looking through the glass door by the copier, I realized that it exited into the main lobby, not the tasting room. I wouldn't have to worry about being cornered by Regina or Dean if I left that way. Calling out my good-bye, I scooted out the door and was back on the road, power walking, in less than a minute.

When I reached Marie's shop, the front door was open and Mindy was helping her prep for class. Mindy smiled as I entered; Marie, on the other hand, scowled.

"Hey, Jill. You taking tonight's class?" Mindy greeted me as Marie pretended not to notice my arrival.

I shook my head. "Sorry, I'd love to, but I'm busier than the chicken who crossed the road."

"Not the saying," Marie grumbled. Mindy shot her boss a surprised glance but then smiled.

"I'm sure Jill was just being clever," Mindy said, trying to smooth over a fight she didn't understand.

"Never mind. I need to talk to Marie. Do you mind giving us a minute?" I smiled, trying to look sweet.

Marie's eyes widened, finally showing interest in my arrival. "Mindy, go grab those new class schedules out of the car. You can stack the boxes in the back room."

She waited for her assistant to leave and then, without meeting my eyes, asked, "What?"

"Good evening to you, too." I wanted to call the words back when I saw her head jerk just a bit. I needed something from the woman. No need to make her angry over nothing. I hurried to speak before she could respond. "Look, I'm trying to get the work program paperwork that Ted was supposed to do done and in the new woman's hands before she shuts us down and cancels the project."

Finally, Marie looked up, but instead of looking at me, she glanced at the door leading to the back room. "He never could follow rules. What do I need to do?"

I hurried and pulled out the fourth set of papers. "Sign where I've indicated. I'll give you a copy after Work Today's director signs off on Monday."

Marie shook her head and pulled a pen out from behind her ear. "No need. You, I trust."

As I watched the woman flip through to the marked signature pages, I wondered about her statement. Had I done something that made her trust me? Or was it more basic? Like my position with the Business-to-Business meeting? Or, I thought ruefully, the fact that I'd strong-armed her into taking on an intern from a program run by her abusive ex-husband? Although, to my credit, neither Marie nor I had known that fact when this whole thing started.

She handed me back the completed pages. When I didn't immediately take them, she pushed the pile toward me. "Look, I'm busy here. Get out of my shop."

Mindy's gasp was our first indication that she had returned from her errand. When we turned and looked at her, the woman's face was white. I smiled, trying to ease her fears. "We're just kidding around. I've got to leave anyway."

The assistant looked toward her boss for confirmation. Marie smiled, her voice tender. "Jill and I have a history. She understands when I'm joking."

Mindy nodded, but I could tell she had felt the friction between the two of us. Hoping to appease her fears, I brightened and pointed to the coffee shop through the window. "Why don't the two of you head over and get a coffee on me after class? I'll leave word with Jackie and she'll take care of you."

"That would be amazing. I've been cutting down on buying coffee." Mindy slapped her hand over her mouth. "I'm sorry. I'm trying to save money for a down payment on a car. And, well, coffee can get a little pricey."

I shrugged. "I'm not the local pusher. You know where we are if you want a caffeine hit. Besides, I understand trying to save a little. When I first moved out here, I was watching every penny."

"We'll come by later. Thank you." Marie eased the uncomfortable conversation to an end.

As I left the shop, students were just starting to flow into the workroom, many with a cup from Coffee, Books, and More. Marie's evening classes had increased my walk-in traffic. And Jackie loved the variety of clientele. I crossed the street, enjoying the warm glow coming from the front windows. I could see Sasha at the counter, helping a couple purchasing a late-night treat. Jackie waved me in. She stood near the back, adjusting the Santa chair.

"What do you think?" She pointed to the chair sitting exactly where she'd placed it that morning before I left.

"Did you move it?"

"Seriously, you can't tell the difference?" Jackie stood next to me, staring at the setting. "I added a footstool and another table for a notebook."

I cocked my head. "Why does Santa need a notebook?"

"To write down what books the kids ask for? Then we can order them if they aren't in stock."

I had to admit, it was a perfect plan. Santa wrote down the child's first name and last initial, the book, and not only did we have a shopping list, but we could build a library for the center around the most popular books. "Smart." I nodded toward the window. "I told Marie and Mindy I'd treat them to coffee after the class. Can you make sure to comp whatever they order?"

Jackie nodded. "I've been thinking about the other businesses. The Glass Slipper brings us in a lot of business, especially now that they are having night classes. Maybe we should think about giving out holiday gift baskets to all the local businesses as a thank-you for the business they throw our way."

"What if they don't throw us business?" I was thinking about Josh and his antique shop. No way would that man refer anyone to the coffee shop unless he thought it could get him into Jackie's good graces.

"Then we'll guilt them into recommending us. I'll put together a proposal basket and a budget and you can approve it next week." Jackie waved at Mary, who'd just entered the shop. "I've got to go. Did you need anything else?"

"Nope. I'm heading home. I've got to check in with Amy, then do our own paperwork for Work Today. By six, I plan to be in jammies with a pint of ice cream." I waved at Sasha and headed out the door to walk the few blocks down Main Street toward home.

It was mid-November and still the streets were bare of any type of Christmas decorations. I guessed if Tina had really bailed and Darla was being pigheaded, the festival would fall on my shoulders. If that was true, I'd just assign the work to Jackie. She lived for this type of thing. Me, I didn't even decorate the house except for Christmas.

And that wouldn't happen until I got Thanksgiving done and in the books. The closer the day came, the more I wished I'd never offered to host this year. Lost in my thoughts, I power walked home in record time.

Opening the door, I realized I'd left Emma inside that morning. To pass the time, she'd decided to tear up not one but both of the throw pillows I'd purchased last month as my offering to the home décor gods. I shook a pile of fluff at her. "Bad Emma."

She ran to the back door and whined.

"Fine, but we will talk about this." I opened the back door and she bounded off the porch, chasing the birds out of the yard.

I opened the fridge and pulled out a soda. I glanced at the wine, but I hadn't eaten all day so regretfully I passed on the opportunity. I sank into a chair at the kitchen table to read the mail. Bill, bill, junk, another bill, and an envelope from the historical society. I ripped open the last envelope. I hadn't heard from Frank Gleason in months. But he'd warned me that the certification process was glacially slow. And he'd been optimistic.

I read the letter twice before I realized it was a *just checking in* letter. Nothing had been decided, but I was to rest assured that they were working diligently on my request for certification. If they'd worked the half hour on my certification rather than sending me this dumb letter, I would have been more assured.

Then I checked my e-mail. Two for two. The alumni representative had responded to my e-mail but had shut me down for information. Official requests were handled through the college press office.

I picked up the phone and called Elite Investigations again. This time my call was answered by a deep-voiced man. "Is Rachel there?"

"Sorry, there's no one here by that name." He put on his sales voice. "Can I help you with something?"

I took a deep breath and launched. "I'm trying to follow up on a client you had six years ago? He had you looking into a missing person case?"

The line was quiet. "If Rachel was the one handling his case, I'm sorry, her files would have left with her. We don't talk about clients or their requests over the phone."

"I don't know that Rachel was the investigator. I mean, I used to work with her, we were friends." I threw that out, just for a bit of sympathy.

The man laughed. "If you were truly friends, you would have known she was gone. Sorry I couldn't help you."

Then he hung up. Strike three for the day.

I glanced at the fridge. Maybe I still had some of Sadie's chocolate silk pie. Sounded like a perfect dinner to me. I'd almost caved when I heard a knock on the front door.

"Why isn't this locked? And what the heck happened in here?" Greg's voice boomed through the living room.

"I just got home and Emma's been busy," I called back. Sometimes having a police detective for a boyfriend was a royal pain. Like right now, I thought, sad to abandon the idea of pie for dinner. "I'm in the kitchen."

He walked in with a pizza box from Little Godfathers and a bag of bread sticks. I forgave him any transgression on the spot. "Hey, I took a drive this afternoon and decided to bring back dinner. You hungry?"

"I'm starving. What a day." I grabbed some plates from the cabinet and stopped at the fridge for a soda for Greg. Emma stood outside the door, looking in the screen and licking her lips. "You can just stay out there. I'm still mad at you."

Greg chuckled and opened the pizza box. The smell of thick pan crust and kitchen sink toppings filled the small kitchen. He served two slices onto each plate, then sank into a chair. Neither one of us said another word until we'd finished our first slice.

"Bread stick?" He held up the bag.

I nodded. One of the reasons we got along together as well as we did was that we both had a touch of the emotional eater in us. Tomorrow I'd run on the beach with Emma to burn off my calories. Greg would forgo his afternoon candy bar and be fine. I hated him sometimes.

As I dipped the bread stick into the marinara, I broached the subject. "Bad day?"

Greg groaned and pushed away his empty plate. "Well, since I thought we had a real lead with David until his team of lawyers swooped in to explain it all away, yeah, I'd say a bad day."

"I ran into them on the way out of City Hall. Literally." I thought about the celebration at the winery that was probably still going on. "I didn't know the mayor knew Regina's family."

"Apparently he and her brother were in the same fraternity. Different campuses, different states, miles apart, but frat blood runs deep. Even years later."

Well, that explained the mayor's arrival at the winery. I wondered if Greg knew that while he was driving around blowing off steam, the other group was celebrating. I wasn't going to be the one to mention it.

He threw a piece of pizza crust out on the porch for Emma and grabbed a trash bag out from under the sink. "You do the dishes, I'll clean up Emma's disaster, and then we'll go grab a beer."

"That little place down the coast with the deck?" I offered an alternative besides the winery.

"Perfect." He smiled and for a second, I felt bad not telling him about my day. But he didn't need more bad news, not yet.

We were in the truck when his phone rang.

"Hey, Esmeralda, I'm off the clock." He listened, and then instead of turning left out of town from my driveway, he turned right. "I'll be right there."

I groaned. "Problems?"

"There's been a fight at the winery. Regina is in tears and asking for you." He studied me. "Something you want to tell me?"

I shrugged. "I barely know the woman. Why would she ask for me?"

Greg focused on the road ahead. "That's the question, isn't it?"

CHAPTER 19

"You're not making this about me, are you?" Even though we'd just eaten, my grumpy mood hadn't passed. "I can't help it if people like to talk to me."

Greg snorted, his gaze focused on the road. He didn't even look my way.

"Seriously, this is not my fault." I crossed my arms and stared out the truck window, watching people leave Diamond Lille's, one of the few places on Main Street still open. Even the bookstore would be shutting down by nine. Saturday nights we stayed open a little later for the increased foot traffic.

"I never said this was your fault," he said. "It's just when things go bad, you're usually in the mix of things. That's one thing I can always count on, you being involved, somehow."

"I didn't kill Ted. I didn't start whatever fight is going on at the winery. I didn't even yell at our mayor today when he dumped another problem in my lap. I don't know what you're talking about." I listed off all the things I hadn't done today.

"Whatever. You know you tend to stick your nose in places it doesn't belong. And now, you and my murder suspect's boss are besties? What are the odds?" Greg turned off the engine and without saying another word, left the truck and headed to the winery tasting room.

I debated staying inside the truck until I wasn't so fired up, but I thought that might take all night. Besides, I was curious about why Regina needed to talk to me. Greg stopped at the winery door and turned to look at me, obviously waiting for me to join him. Unsnapping my seat belt, I had the sinking feeling that this discussion with him about my tendency to investigate issues wasn't over. Not by a long shot.

As I met him at the door, he leaned down and gave me a quick kiss. "Sorry. I've had a bad day and took it out on you."

His words almost drew tears to my eyes, but I tried to take the casual approach instead of breaking down into a sobbing mess, my typical reaction after a fight. "Same back at you."

He swung the door open and we walked in. The music had been turned off and instead of the festive atmosphere that had been running through the room when I left, now the entire area felt guarded and wary. Regina sat at the same table she'd been earlier that afternoon along with Dean and David. The other suits seemed to have left except maybe one or two who looked less like their attorney attaché and more like bodyguards based on their build.

Toby was standing talking to Darla and Matt over by the bar. I noticed Regina kept her gaze on Matt. I followed Greg over to Toby and the others.

"What's going on?" Greg looked at his deputy.

Toby held out a watch. "This is what started it all."

Greg raised his eyebrows. "I don't understand. Someone lost their watch?"

"That watch was a gift. And not from Ted. That woman's just freaking out," Matt babbled and tried to stand. Toby eased him back into his chair with one hand.

"Slow down, slugger. We're not accusing you of anything." Toby and Greg exchanged a glance over Matt's head. "Who gave you the watch?"

"That girl you met the other night, Becky. I gave her some money for food, and she gave me the watch. I didn't ask her to give it to me, she just did. She's pretty proud at times and stubborn when she doesn't want to be seen as a bother." Matt sighed. "I thought I was doing a good thing."

"Oh honey, you were. Don't let this upset you. I'm sure it's just a big mistake." Darla spat out the last words like she knew exactly whose mistake this had been and Greg better take care of the issue.

"Jill, Jill, come over here. I need to tell you something," Regina called to me from the middle of the room.

I glanced at Greg, who nodded. I didn't know if we were in the middle of a crime scene or what, so I wanted to follow his lead. "I'll be right back," I said to Darla, who glared at me, obviously thinking I was taking sides.

Regina took my arm as soon as I got close and pulled me into a chair next to her. "It's been such a trying day. I mean, with David and now with that horrible man. I seriously am going to need counseling after this vacation."

"I'm sorry things have been rough for you. But I don't understand. What did Matt do?" I peeked back at the group still surrounding Darla. Now the words flying were getting hotter and their voices were higher.

"That man had Ted's watch. The one I gave him for his thirtieth. I spent over five grand for that watch. No way would he give it away."

I considered her words. "Wait, you knew Ted?"

Regina put her hand on mine. "I know I should have told you, but you were being so nice. And I didn't want you to think of me differently."

Realization dawned on me. "You were trying to find out who killed Ted. Or were you trying to find out if I killed him?"

"No." Regina paused, then went on. "Well, maybe not after I'd met you. You're such a wonderful person, I knew after I talked to you the first time that you couldn't kill my boy."

Her words sank in. After all our speculation on why no one had come from the family, we'd been wrong. They had been here all along, just incognito. "You're Ted's mother." I didn't mean it as a question, but Regina nodded in response.

Dean broke into our conversation. "Regina, we're going to dinner now. You've been drinking all afternoon. You need some food."

"I couldn't eat. You guys go ahead without me." Regina stared over my shoulder at Matt.

I stood and pulled her to her feet. "Go eat. I'll find out what's going on."

Regina looked at me with tears in her eyes. "You'd do that for me? Even after I lied to you?"

"You didn't lie, you just didn't tell me everything. Right?" I traded places with Dean exchanging looks as we transferred his sister from me to him. Regina was three sheets to the wind for sure.

"I guess that's true. So you don't hate me?" Regina pulled me into a hug. "I love your little shop and our talks."

Dean pulled her away from me and started walking her toward the door. He glanced back at Greg. "I guess since the po-po are here, I can't ask you to dinner without getting arrested, right?"

"Greg wouldn't arrest you for asking me to dinner. And who over twenty calls the police the po-po?" I focused on Regina. "I'll see you later."

Dean leaned into me and whispered in my ear, "He would arrest me if he could read my mind right now."

I watched as the group left to find an open restaurant. Then I turned back to find Greg watching me. Great, now I had to explain Dean's attention. But first, I had to figure out what Matt knew about the watch that a mother had given her son. What had I said that morning? One disaster at a time?

"Interesting friends you have there," Greg drawled as I walked back to the group.

I rolled my eyes. "Not my friends, just people I know." I amended that statement, "Or, in some cases, people I just met today." I focused back on Matt. "So, this girl gave you the watch, just because?"

"What do you mean by that?" Darla growled. "You think Matt and this girl are dating or something?"

I put my hands up in front of me in a defensive stance. "Don't go all psycho on me. All I was trying to do was figure out how Matt got a hold of Ted's watch."

Matt shuffled in his seat. He put his hand on Darla's. "Darling, let it be. These two are trying to help. You don't bite the hand that's trying to feed you."

Darla harrumphed, clearly not impressed with the analogy. She turned and started stacking clean glasses.

Matt grinned as he watched her and for a second, I felt like I was interrupting a very intimate conversation. Then he turned the smile on me and I realized how charismatic this man could be at times. Maybe enough to convince a young girl to kill a potential rival? My blood ran cold at the thought. "Like I said, I took Becky some food one day. She'd approached me for money on my first trip into South Cove. I didn't realize she was even living here. I thought the family lawyer had set her up in a house in Oregon."

"Why? What did she have on Ted?"

His smile was sadder this time. "A child. Ted got his underage girlfriend pregnant, and the family sent her away with a ton of cash to give up the baby to the foster care system."

"And she didn't want to leave," I added.

"Sad, isn't it? Just think about what an effect that could have on a young girl's mind. I swear, Becky's gone over the edge. And I'm not sure she'll come back."

"You said the family sent her away. How do you know that?" I didn't believe Regina could be that cruel, even to protect a sleazebag son.

"Becky told me. She and I kind of got to know each other during the work program." He glanced at Darla, who had transitioned from stacking glasses to folding napkins. "We didn't date or anything, but we both smoked, so we had lots of time to talk. I worried when I saw Ted taking an interest in her. She didn't have family, lived with a distant relative, I don't know, a cousin or something who didn't care if she came home or not."

"So when Ted turned on the charm, she fell." I sighed.

"Like jumping off a cliff. She kept telling me he'd come for her. As soon as he could get one thing settled, he would be free to be with her." Matt shook his head. "I don't know what he thought he was doing, promising something like that."

My thoughts raced. Was the one thing he needed settled getting even with Marie? And had she known she was in danger? All lines of investigation kept running back to Marie, the vanished wife.

Toby finished his paperwork and had Matt sign the report. He put the watch into a baggie and handed it to Greg. "We'll be keeping this until we determine its rightful owner."

"Keep it forever. I don't care." Matt glanced over toward the table where Regina had sat. "Maybe, though, you should give it to his mom. She seems to need it more than I do."

Toby turned his attention to me. "Thanks for coming down and talking to the woman. She was getting a touch hysterical before you showed up."

"She's been trying to solve Ted's murder all on her own. That's why she's in town." I leaned into Greg. "I just wish she would have told someone. Well, besides David. She must have told him."

Stepping back, I narrowed my eyes at Greg. "What exactly did David tell you? Did he mention why they were here in town, that Regina was Ted's mother?"

"He didn't say a word about that." Greg shook his head. "He admitted he gave the gun to his niece right before she moved out to California. He'd hoped she'd be a little safer with the gun than without. Now, he's pretty sure she pawned it. I've got Esmeralda trying to track down where the gun was bought."

His words led me to believe there was more to the story about what David had said, but that he didn't want to talk here. I guess I couldn't blame him. Matt was as much of a possible suspect as David was. Matt had a possession of the deceased's. Whereas David had owned the weapon that killed him.

As Alice would say, things were looking "curiouser and curiouser."

When we'd returned to the truck and had turned off Main Street, passing by my house and onto the highway, Greg finally spoke. "Let's go get that beer now."

"Can you tell me what else David said?" I watched his face for any telltale signs. Greg could lie, but he didn't like to, so his face showed his distaste for the action when he did.

He slowed down for a school bus turned RV that was blocking the lane. He glanced around the slow vehicle and then sped around it, going over the posted speed limit. Not a normal action for the local police detective, but I'd noticed that when he was upset, his driving became a bit riskier. An old Heart song made into a ringtone sounded on his phone and he shook his head, hitting the Bluetooth in his ear. "What do you want now?"

I couldn't hear the other side of the conversation, except to know it was a female. And if I read Greg's mood right, it had to be Sherry. I tried to make eye contact, but he waved me away.

"No, I can't come over and talk about us. I'm busy." He rolled his eyes and reached over to grab my hand. "What am I doing? I'm on a date with my girlfriend. You know, you've met her, Jill. The one you tried to throw under the Mayor Baylor bus?"

Well, that was pretty direct. And honestly, it made me giggle, just a bit. My shoulders dropped and I watched the ocean view, trying to tune out the mini argument going on with Greg and Sherry.

"Stop calling me. If I need something from you, I know how to reach you." Greg clicked off the call. He squeezed my hand and sighed. "Sorry about that. She's been calling all day. Needing my help with one thing or the other."

"She wants to get back together?" I turned to watch him.

He nodded. "Something has triggered her need to own me again. I know it's not love. I've ridden that particular carnival ride too many times already. No way am I climbing back on board. I'd have Toby shoot me first."

"You sure there aren't feelings there?" I might be shooting myself in the foot if I didn't just stop talking.

Greg paused, slowing the truck to turn into the bar's parking lot. There was a line of cars coming the other way, so it took a few minutes to get off the road. When he found a spot big enough for the truck, he shut off the engine, pulled his keys, then turned toward me. "We were young. I thought it was love, I really did. The guys thought I'd won the lottery getting Sherry to say yes. Now, I'm not so sure. I know she didn't and doesn't love me. I just wonder if I ever loved her."

"I think if you have to ask, maybe the feeling isn't there." I thought about the way my toes still curled at times, when he threw me a look across the room. I had it bad for the hunky police detective sitting next to me.

"I think you're right. I don't want to talk about Sherry." He rubbed the top of my hand. "You are happy? I mean, with us."

I remembered the look Greg had given me when I'd come back from Regina's table. He was asking about Dean. Without asking about

Dean. "Before you hear it from some stranger, I'd better tell you that Regina's brother asked me to dinner today." I paused, then added, "Twice."

"You must have said no at least once," Greg pointed out.

I laughed. "See, you are a great detective. Take it one step further, though."

Now he was running a finger up my forearm. The simple action felt way too intimate. He watched the skin on my arm ripple as his finger rose and fell. "Well, there's the fact that we ate dinner before we left for the winery."

I slapped his hand. "That's not why I said no."

"And the fact that you're in my truck attacking me for no apparent reason. I think you like me. Next you'll be punching my arm and running, trying to get me to chase you."

"What, are we in grade school?"

He pulled me close and kissed me. "Not even close," he whispered. "Thanks for not being jealous."

"It's not like you've been visiting her during your time away from me." I laid my head on his shoulder. "No reason for me to worry. I'm sure you'd be the first to tell me if you had decided to go back to the barracuda."

"I would." He jiggled his keys.

I sat up and opened the truck door, turning a wicked smile on him. "Besides, if you didn't, we live in such a small town, I'd know before you could even pick up the phone."

The bar was dimly lit with beer brand signs on three of the walls, but the fourth was a wall of windows opening up onto a deck where several couples sat, watching the surfers ride the evening waves. Greg started toward the deck.

"Stopping at the ladies' room," I murmured.

He nodded, then pointed to the deck. "I'll be sitting out there with two cold ones."

As I walked toward the left where the restrooms were located, I noticed a tall man hunched over the bar, nursing a clear brown liquid over ice. Whiskey would be my guess. I never had been much of a hard alcohol drinker, but I'd dated guys who liked their spirits ninety-proof. Me, I'm more of a one-beer girl. I like the slight buzz without getting lost in the drink.

When I came out of the bathroom, my hair managed back into control from the windy ride, the man at the bar looked my way and I was surprised to recognize him. "David, what are you doing here?"

He shrugged as I walked up to the old wooden bar, stained with years of beer and, before the laws had changed, cigarette burns. The bar was famous for being one of James Dean's out-of-the-way hangouts where he loved to disappear in plain sight. I waved away the bartender who'd been watching a basketball game on the soundless television hung over the end of the bar.

"You want a drink?" David's words slurred a bit.

I shook my head. "Greg's out on the deck. We're having a nightcap. Do you want to join us?" Greg would kill me, but I couldn't leave David here alone, drinking away whatever problem he thought he had. Besides, maybe he'd do something stupid, like confess to Ted's murder. That train of thought made me wonder if a drunken confession would even be admissible in court.

David squinted toward the open sliding doors. "I heard you were dating the cop. Dean seems to have taken a shine to you. Watch out, he's a player."

I smiled and patted his arm. "No worries, I have no interest in dating Dean."

"Sometimes that doesn't matter with those types. They see what they want and they take it. Ted was just like his uncle. They're dogs." David grabbed my arm, raising his voice. "Don't let him turn you. You're a good girl, stay away."

"Calm down, David." I saw the bartender step toward us, worried about an escalation. But before he could reach us, I felt Greg push me aside. David lost his grip on my arm.

"I didn't expect to see you out tonight." Greg sounded cordial, even friendly. "At least, not without one of the Johnson lawyers or bodyguards."

David laughed. "They aren't that smart. I slipped out the back without anyone even noticing. I don't know why Regina puts up with that kind of treatment. She's an angel, you know."

"I bet she is," I said, wondering what I should do. Leave and go to the table, letting Greg handle the drunk was sounding like a winning idea, and sooner rather than later.

David focused his bloodshot eyes on me. "She was a good girl, too. Before he got his hooks in her, she was a very good girl."

CHAPTER 20

"Who are you talking about?" I held my breath for the answer, assuming he was reminiscing about Regina.

"I thought she needed it for protection. She was going to be all alone out here," David muttered.

I glanced at Greg, who shrugged. I thought about Regina's sadness about Ted's watch. Mothers did kill, mostly in a twisted attempt to save their children, but Regina's grief seemed real, not staged. Could she be that crazy? But how would she get the same gun that David had given away? None of this was making any sense.

Before I could ask another question, a hand clamped on David's shoulder. "There you are. Regina's been out of her mind with worry."

Dean Johnson stood next to David, with several men behind him. Now the bartender had given up any pretense of watching the basketball game and was standing next to the cash register, his hand on the phone waiting to call in the 911 when the fight broke out.

David finished his drink and stood up. He focused his bleary gaze on me, and in a loud whisper, said, "You listen to what I say and stay away. It's for your own good." He waited for me to nod before turning back to Dean. "Take me back to the gilded cage, warden."

The men behind Dean came around and, with one on each side,

led David out the door. Dean laid a hundred on the bar. "Will this cover his tab?"

The bartender dropped his hand off the phone and came around, all professional hospitality now. "I'll get your change."

Dean waved him off. "Take the rest for your trouble. David can get a little weepy when he drinks. He's never been a fun drunk." Now Dean looked at me. "He didn't say anything to you that upset you, did he?"

I shook my head. No way was I going down that road with the man in front of me. David's warning still echoed in my brain. Fortunately, Greg pulled me close and answered Dean simply, "He seemed like he had a hard day, that's all."

Dean glanced back and forth from me to Greg, considering his options. When he realized he wasn't getting anything else, he smiled. "That he has. Sorry for your inconvenience. Let's hope the rest of your date night is less chaotic."

The way he emphasized the word *date* made me want to argue, but we *were* on a date, right? Still, something in his tone felt challenging. Maybe that was one of the tricks David had warned me about. We walked back to the table and sank into the chairs, watching the darkening sky over the ocean.

"What a day, huh?" I finally broke the silence. I could tell Greg was running scenarios through his head.

He laughed. "Between the investigation, getting Mayor Baylor all up in my business for his buddy, then the scene at the winery, I thought we'd exhausted the drama for the day. But no, I get my hundredth call from Sherry on the way here, then David is drinking his troubles away at the bar."

"Add in the fact that I have to have all the paperwork Ted didn't do for the work project signed and delivered by Monday or your friend Candy is canceling the program, and you have my day." I took a big deep breath in. "Oh, and I forgot our mayor's wife backed out as the festival planner and now he wants me to take over that, too."

Greg chuckled. "Now that's your own fault."

My eyes widened, and I slapped his arm. "Mine? How is it my fault? I didn't ask her to butt in where she didn't belong."

"Hey, I'm not saying she didn't deserve it. Lord knows, that woman can be a thorn." Greg's eyebrows raised. "You and the rest of the business owners felt a loyalty to Darla. And when she was replaced, you didn't make Tina's job easy."

I sipped my beer, thinking about it. "No, Tina didn't make her job easy. Instead of coming in as part of the committee, she took over so she could tell everyone what to do. Then she doesn't understand when she gets pushback? So she disappears."

"Just saying you got what you asked for. Tina is no longer in charge." Greg drained his beer. "You want to stay longer or head home?"

"Let's go home. I bought some new movies we haven't watched." I finished off my own bottle and stood. I couldn't help it, I returned to the topic. "So you think we ran her off?"

He pulled me into a hug and whispered in my ear, "I *know* you ran her off."

When we got home, Emma whined and looked up at me with those big brown eyes, her way of saying, *Sorry I ate forty dollars' worth of throw pillows, but I love you.* I handed her a new chewy treat and she ran to her bed in the kitchen. Maybe I needed to get her out more. Even with the good weather, it was just hard in November to be excited about running, especially when all I wanted to think about was mashed potatoes and creamy soups.

When we settled onto the couch, I paused the DVR. "You never told me what all you know about the gun."

"I know." Greg took the remote from me and started the movie. Since we'd decided on a romantic comedy, it had been my turn to choose, I knew he was avoiding my question.

I paused the movie again. "So was it his gun that killed Ted?"

Greg closed his eyes. "Is the only reason you're dating me to be in on the investigations? Are you a true crime junkie?"

My eyes widened. "No. Do you really think that? I know I'm pushy sometimes, but you have to admit, I found Ted's body. This time, I have an emotional stake in finding his murderer."

"You always have a dog in the hunt." Greg pulled me close and took the remote from me. "Seriously, sometimes you just need to relax."

"But . . ."

He shushed me. "This is all I'm going to say. David's gun was used in the murder. According to him and his band of merry lawyers, he gave it to a family member a year ago when she moved from Boston out to LA for her big break. The kid thought she was going to be an actress."

He paused and I pushed my luck. "Have you been able to find the wannabe actress?"

"You know what happens to kids when they fall off the bus down in Hollywood. They fall off the grid. Apparently this girl was only sixteen, but her parents gave their blessing and sent her off. No one in David's family has heard from her since. I'm running a missing persons search now, but so far, *nada*. The theory that she pawned the gun is looking more plausible." He looked down at the remote. "So, now can we watch the movie? I seriously need some mental downtime."

I snuggled closer. "What are you waiting for?"

"Brat," I heard him mutter as he clicked back on the remote, setting it out of my reach. Emma brought her chewy into the living room and lay down between the couch and the coffee table. All was right in our little world, for at least the next two hours.

Greg's phone buzzed halfway through the movie. He glanced at the display and tucked it back into his pocket.

"Not work?" I asked, worried I'd cursed the perfect night with my high hopes.

He stroked my hair. "Not work."

But I noticed he didn't mention who had texted him so late on a Saturday night.

Amy arrived in the shop first thing Sunday morning. She piled her Laguna Beach tote onto the counter. "Coffee. Black." She glared at me. "And you owe me."

"Wait, how do I owe you?" I poured a large cup and set it in front of her. I felt great. I'd kept my promise to Emma that morning and ran on the beach before work. Now, an hour later, I'd had a protein bar for breakfast. Its mission was to keep me out of the dessert rack at least until after lunch. I wasn't sure the bar would work.

Instead of answering, she pulled out a stack of the packets for the Work Today program. "It took me all afternoon to run all these people down. Half of them I had to convince I wasn't taking ownership of their business with the signatures, the other half gave me a lecture on the evils of big government."

"You got them to sign, though, right?" I thought about my outstanding packet. Josh, who'd promised I'd have the paperwork at five today. If Amy had come through with her five, I'd be done before the sun set today. One worry off my list.

"Seriously? Who are you talking to? If I can get Mayor Baylor to support the Mission Wall project, even though it's on your land, and he hates you"—she grinned—"I can get a few conservatives to sign papers they're convinced are the downfall of civilization."

She sipped her coffee. "Mmmm, chocolate blend?"

"Best part, no additional calories." I always held back a few bags of the roast for my personal use during the year. The blend was so popular, we were going to be sold out of stock way before the holidays ended. Next year we could double our order and still sell out. I banded a large clip over the completed forms and took them to the back to stack on my desk with the other four. One more. All I had to do was trust Josh.

I was doomed.

When I came back to the front, Regina and David were browsing through the bookcases. I called over to them, "Hey, guys, can I get some drinks started?"

Regina turned toward me, wearing dark sunglasses. "Please." Her voice held a waver.

I looked at David and he nodded. He looked like the undead this morning. I supposed a night of knocking down whiskey meant to be sipped could do that to you. I felt for the guy. In the few weeks they'd been around South Cove, I'd come to enjoy their banter and company. Now, with Regina's relationship to Ted out in the open and the fact that David's gun had been attached to the murder investigation, I wondered how long they'd stay in town. And, as miserable as David looked, how long he'd still be Regina's driver.

Amy raised her eyebrows in a silent question, but I shook my head. "Later," I mouthed.

I worked on their drinks, then carried them out to them. "On the house. How are you?" I asked Regina.

She sat delicately on the sofa and took a sip of the coffee before she answered. "You know, when I found out Ted was gone, I didn't think I could deal with the pain. It overwhelmed me. But when I came here, I guess I started to heal. Now, it's all back." She pushed her glasses up on top of her head. "I shouldn't have come here. My husband told me to leave it alone, but I needed to know."

I sat down next to her. "I'm sorry for your loss."

Tears filled her eyes, and she glanced up at David, whose back was to us as he pretended to study the children's book section. "Thank you."

I wasn't sure what else to say. I knew that finding Ted's watch on another man's arm last night had reopened the wounds from his death, but I couldn't imagine what she was thinking about David. Could he have been involved? Ted was a piece of work, I knew that, but I didn't think David would have even considered killing the guy knowing how much Regina loved her son. The man worshiped the ground she walked on, and now, knowing that he in some way had hurt her this badly, it must have been killing him.

Luckily, the door chimed and I had a customer to attend to. "Let me know if you need anything," I said.

Darla was at the counter talking to Amy.

"Mocha?" I slipped behind the counter, interrupting a tirade about the mayor.

"Skim milk, sugar free, and double shot please." Darla's face was beet red. "Can you imagine he had the balls to talk to me yesterday about the festival? All 'you know how important this season is to South Cove', and threw in how it's my civic duty?" Darla climbed onto a bar stool. "I told him that he took the project from me and now that his wife has flaked on the town, he needed to find another patsy to do the work. Really."

Amy smiled. "I hear Tina's at a spa in Nevada recuperating from all of the stress she's been under."

Darla snorted. "If I know Tina, she's on a girls' weekend with her city friends gambling away her troubles. That woman never once listened to one thing I told her to do. Yet now, it's on my shoulders? No way."

I set the cup in front of her. "You need breakfast with that?"

"I ate some eggs before I walked down. I've been trying to diet again. Matt and I've been doing some weight lifting when we're slow.

He's a good trainer. I told him he should get a job at a local fitness club, but he just laughed." Darla beamed. "I'm down five pounds this week. Of course, the holidays are creeping up, so my weight will be, too."

"Sounds like you and Matt are spending a lot of time together." Amy took a sip of her coffee. "Where are his folks?"

Darla shot her a look that could curdle milk. "Nebraska. Why?"

Amy shrugged. "Just wondering where you might be spending Christmas."

I saw Darla's eyes widen in complete shock. "No, you don't understand. We're not a couple. He doesn't see me that way." She glanced down at her body, crammed into a velvet tracksuit, trying to convince herself of all the reasons Matt couldn't be interested.

"From the way I've seen him with you, he's interested." I poured myself a coffee. It was kind of nice, listening to others with relationship issues and worries. When I'd been a lawyer, I only saw the back end of a relationship, when they were breaking up and hated each other. Now, with my friends, I got to see the beginnings and the hope for something more.

Darla blushed. "It's not that way, guys."

"So, you wouldn't care if I asked him out?" Amy mused, tucking a strand of hair back behind her ears. "I need to have a boyfriend who would work out."

"You're dating Justin." Darla's voice came out a little too high, like a squeak. "Why would you want to date Matt?"

Amy grinned. "I don't. I just wanted to see your possessive side go up. Girl, you may not be in love yet, but you're well on your way. Get over yourself."

Darla threw a five at me for the drink, then climbed off the stool. She looked at the two of us with pain in her eyes. "I know what I know. Matt's not interested in me. Why would he pick me when that young girl keeps throwing herself at him? He'd be a fool."

She started to turn away, but I reached over and grabbed her arm. "Darla, he'd be a fool not to pick you. You're an amazing woman. You own your own business, you're funny, you're intelligent, and if he can't see what a catch you are, he doesn't deserve you."

She bit her lip. "But I'm . . ." She paused, not able to say the word.

"Physical attributes don't make you who you are. All that can change for the better or worse. You need someone who falls in love with your essence, not your body." Amy smiled. "Believe me, I've been with someone who only saw me as a hot body. Remember Hank?"

Darla giggled. "That man was a piece of work. I thought Jill was going to kill him or send you to a clinic to get un-brainwashed."

I was happy to see Darla laugh, but deep inside, I knew it would take more than some girl talk for her to be happy with herself. I hoped Matt didn't cause any more problems with her self-esteem than she already had.

I watched her walk out the door and greet Toby on his way in.

Amy sighed. "You think even some of that got through?"

I shook my head. "Let's hope Becky disappears and Matt is as good of a guy as we're hoping. Otherwise, Darla's going to hold a grudge for a long time."

Toby shoved some papers at me. "And thank you."

Confused, I glanced down at the packet. It was Josh's forms for Work Today. I checked my watch, eleven thirty. "How did you get these?"

Toby hung his coat up on the wall in the back room, holding the door open with his foot. "The guy ran me down as I was walking past his shop. I don't know what your aunt sees in him. Josh is a tad on the creepy side."

Doing a short happy dance since the paperwork was done, I grinned. "One, I didn't think Josh can run, but two, yay!"

Amy smiled. "So we're good?"

"We are. I'm going to Bakerstown tomorrow and dropping these off. You want to go with me?" I unfolded a crease in the top page.

"You forget most of the world works on Mondays. Not that we enjoy it." Amy hopped off the stool. "Since Toby's here, can we go grab lunch at Lille's? Your treat, of course."

I rolled my eyes. "Whatever, but yeah, we can." I headed to the back room to gather the rest of the packets, shove them in my tote, and grab my jacket. When I returned, Amy was checking her voice mail on her phone. I updated Toby on what had been done for prep work. "Thanks for bringing those with you. I wasn't looking forward to coming back into town this afternoon."

Toby shrugged. "Like I said, he tracked me down. He said he was closing early so he could get some sleep. Then I got a lecture about how we need an animal control unit for the police department."

"One thing about Josh, when he gets an idea in his head, he's relentless."

Toby filled a glass with water and drank about half in one gulp. "That's just the thing. He said the cats were keeping him awake at night. I think his interest is purely personal, rather than being a good idea for the town."

I thought about Josh's cat problem. I hadn't seen a loose feline in months. In the city, there was a small alley on my walk to work where someone had started feeding one cat, and now, it was filled with new residents. I was going to stop and chat on our way to the diner, but Antiques by Thomas was already shut down, a sign on the door saying they'd reopen on Wednesday. Josh spent his off days searching out flea markets and garage sales for pieces to add to his inventory. Jackie had been going with him on Mondays when the shop was closed, but now that they were on the outs, my aunt might be showing up on my doorstep more often.

I wanted to say the thought didn't make me sigh.

CHAPTER 21

Monday morning, I woke with the sun. Emma and I ran. I completed two loads of laundry and a shopping list for my trip to Bakerstown and made a quick omelet for breakfast. And yet it was still too early to take the drive. I curled up on the couch with a new memoir I'd been intrigued with when one of my customers ordered the book. I find a lot of my new favorite authors that way, by indirect referrals.

The week would be busy. Saturday was our Christmas Tales party for the center. Jackie had invited the entire town to celebrate the arrival of Santa in South Cove. Except no one had taken on the task of getting town ready for the festival. If I didn't find someone or talk Darla into putting aside her hurt feelings and taking it back over, I'd be stuck doing the entire thing by myself. And decorating was not my forte.

I ruefully glanced at the old pillows I'd pulled out of the office to replace the two that Emma had used as chew toys. I made a mental note to check out a couple stores for new pillows while I was in town.

An hour later, Emma barked and I heard a knock on my front door. I put a bookmark in the book and stood, stretching. I hadn't planned on reading quite that long, but the story of the country singer gone bad then redeemed had caught my attention and I'd just wanted one more chapter. And then another.

I swung open the door and there stood Esmeralda, with a basket. My thoughts went to the old fairy tale of the witch arriving with a poisoned apple. I pushed away the vision.

"Hey, Jill. I was on my way to work and thought I'd bring these over now. I baked all weekend." She reached over and uncovered baggies filled with cookies and candies. I picked one up, my stomach growling at the sight of the variety of treats in a Christmas-themed printed bag tied with a curled ribbon.

"These are great." I looked at her, confused. "What are they for?"

Esmeralda laughed. "I knew she would forget to tell you. Your aunt called and asked if I'd do treats for the party Saturday. Now, I know I was only supposed to do fifty bags, but I have a feeling you'll have more kids show up than that."

"A feeling or a premonition?" I asked, teasing as she passed the basket over to me.

My neighbor cocked her head at me and smiled. "Now, Jill, don't you know that there's no such thing as a premonition?"

"Says the town fortune teller."

She swished her skirts, brushing off some imaginary dust. "Only the true believers can hear my voice. When you're a skeptic, everything is suspect."

"So you're saying I'm a skeptic?" I was beginning to understand the woman. I didn't think we'd ever be good friends, but maybe good neighbors.

Emma nudged my leg, and I reached down and stroked her head.

The fortune teller smiled then. "Oh no, Jill. You're definitely a true believer. You just haven't found your faith yet. I'll tell Greg I saw you."

I watched as she wandered down the steps. Then as I turned back to the house, I heard her voice. "You'll see the problem today. She's hurting. You need to help her."

I turned back, but Esmeralda was out of the gate and down the road already. I could have imagined the words, but I saw Emma watching her, too. "Stranger and stranger," I whispered. I took the basket into the house and set it on the kitchen counter. No use letting Emma get cookie dreams into her head. I filled her water and food dishes and let her outside to the backyard for the time I'd be gone. I put the basket into the Jeep along with my tote filled with Work Today forms and my purse. Instead of heading out to the highway, I turned right toward town. I was surprised I didn't see Esmeralda. She must have hit a dead run to make it to City Hall before I passed her.

I parked in the back of the shop and grabbed the cookie basket. Unlocking the back door, I paused and listened. Josh's cats were yowling up a storm. No wonder he couldn't sleep at night. Maybe we did need to think about a South Cove humane society. Although where the funding would come from was another subject. Mayor Baylor claimed on a semiannual basis how poor the town was, even with the high taxes we paid on our property and sales in the shops. The cost of living in paradise, I thought every time I wrote the check to the tax assessor.

I set the basket on the table in the back and went up front to grab the mail out from under the door. Looking out the window, I saw Marie sweeping the sidewalk in front of The Glass Slipper. I waved and she turned away. Okay, so she was still mad at me. Why, I didn't even want to guess.

I double-checked the front door locks, and headed back the way I'd come, flipping through the envelopes and not finding much, unless you thought electric bills were exciting. I put the unopened bills on my desk and threw the junk mail into the trash can. I locked up the back door and within minutes I was driving down Highway 1, the tunes cranked up and the sea air flowing through the open car windows.

Before I knew it, I was in Bakerstown. First stop, Work Today. When I entered, Candy was sitting at the reception desk, looking through a stack of files. She frowned when I walked in. "There is no way I can grant an extension on paperwork that should have been done prior to the project starting, so there's no use asking."

I smiled and pulled out the stack of forms, slamming them down on the counter. They made a nice resounding clunk, if I did say so myself. "Why would I need an extension? The town of South Cove is happy to follow the rules, once we know what they are. You know Ted never even mentioned forms that were required. I'm sure if we'd asked your supervisors for an extension, they would have granted one."

Candy frowned. "They were also the ones who hired Ted in the first place. I tried to tell them he was trouble. All that good guy on the outside hid a monster underneath." She leaned forward. "If I didn't think it would hurt the center, I'd tell you tales about that guy that would turn your stomach."

"I think I've heard a few." I didn't want to sound like a Ted supporter, but she needed to know we weren't the problem. "Look, the paperwork is done. Sorry for the delay. But you need to lighten up. You could have given us more time."

Candy smiled, but the curl of her lips looked more evil than happy. "I could have, yes, but now I have one project cleaned up and I can work on the next. Thanks for jumping through the hoops so quickly for me."

Glad to be of assistance, I thought.

Next stop, Bakerstown Children's Center, and then my day off would be my own. I reminded myself I would have had to come into town for the center anyway. I guess Candy's scare tactics just got one more responsibility off my list. Seeing the kids would brighten the mood that Candy had just crushed. Her mother sure missed the mark naming the woman.

Baby names were always so full of hope and promise. You never met a child named Trouble or Sorrow. At least I never had. Maybe people should have their names examined after a few years of adulthood. That way we wouldn't be surprised when a woman wasn't as sweet as her name. Or, my other side said, you should watch the ones who looked on the outside too perfect. Like Candy. And Bambi.

I pulled the Jeep into the center's parking lot and banished the thought of the woman who'd killed my friend over some historic coins from my mind. Next time a Daisy or Wendy or Lily came into my life, I'd be on guard for their evil streak.

A four-year-old blond girl grabbed my legs as soon as I walked in the door. "I want my mommy," she screamed. Tears flowed from the child's eyes, and it was apparent she'd been crying for a while.

A young woman kneeled in front of me, removing the child's grip from me. "Come on, honey, it's storytime." The woman smiled. "It's Angel's first day at the center. It takes some adjustment."

"I can see that." I stared at the screaming child now being carried over to a ring of preschoolers watching the show with bored interest, ready for the drama to be over and the story to begin. I called after the lion tamer, "Is Diane in her office?"

"Go on back. She's working on the books." The woman sat at the top of the circle, the child held firmly in her lap and a book in the other hand. In a calm voice, she started reading aloud.

I traced my steps through the large building from my last visit. When I came up on Diane's office, she saw me through the window and waved me in. "Hey, I'm just finishing up the plans for Saturday. You can't believe how excited the kids and parents are."

"Santa visits are magical." I slipped into one of two cheap vinyl chairs in front of Diane's desk.

"Well, yes, there's the fact that Santa will be there. But we're so excited about your book program for the parents. You must have gotten a lot of donations to be able to give away a book for the kids and one for the parents."

I tried not to show surprise. One more marketing maven idea Jackie hadn't bothered to run by me. I'd call her on the way home. My impression had been we were giving away a drink coupon, not two books. And putting on a party. I saw the hole in this month's profit margin growing larger. I put on a fake smile. "We have a very generous clientele."

"I'm thinking you and your aunt are the generous ones." Diane's smile was real, not fake like my own. "Anyway, we're on schedule to be there right at eleven. We're taking the center's bus. Most of our families don't have a reliable vehicle."

"We're looking forward to Saturday." I tried to remember the number of families Jackie had thrown out the last time we'd talked. "How many do you expect to come?"

Diane grinned. "Hold on, let me get my list." She fumbled through the files on her desk, and opening one, she ran her finger down the list. "Thirty-seven families have RSVP'd. Now, some of them have two kids in the center, so I'd say we'll be close to fifty by the time you add up all the staff and kids."

Esmeralda's cookie count made sense now. I nodded and wondered if we had enough staff on Saturday to help. The last event we squeezed eighty adults into the shop. Hopefully kids would take less room. Maybe I should hire a couple of the local teenagers to work a shift, just to help with the party. I realized Diane was watching me. "Well, then, we'll see you on Saturday."

"You okay? You seem kind of surprised at the size of the group. Do I need to cull it down? We could only have the kids who are starting to read and their parents attend."

"No!" I swallowed and then softened my tone. "The point of having the party at the bookstore is to encourage reading. The more we get when they're young, the better. Besides, the parents are all future customers, right?"

Diane shook her head. "Honestly, I think several of them can't read themselves. It's amazing what doesn't happen in today's school system."

"Then we'll start slow. The party's going to be amazing." Diane's words had got me thinking about other ways I could help. Maybe this didn't have to be only a holiday act of goodwill. One more thing to add to my to-do list. "So we'll see you then."

Diane stood and reached over to shake my hand. "Thank you for doing this. Of all the holiday generosity, I believe this act of kindness may just change some lives."

As I left the office, I compared my two stops. One woman lived for the rules and the program. The other, for making a difference in her community. Both on the surface seemed to be part of the social service net and yet, if I, a community partner, could feel the difference, I wondered how people like Kyle and Mindy got through the system without giving up. Or going crazy.

I headed to the local department store to replace the throw pillows as well as pick up more dog food and treats. Then to the grocery store and home.

It was just past noon when I left Bakerstown, a bag of fast food sitting next to me, open so I could snack on French fries as I drove. I'd splurged and bought a vanilla milk shake, too. I was in a food coma as I drove.

As I came close to town, I saw Becky pushing a shopping cart stuffed with a blanket. She must be out scrounging for food. I parked the Jeep by the side of the road and got out, pulling my jacket close to my body. The wind had picked up and the temperature had dropped since my run that morning.

"Hey, Becky," I called as I walked toward her. She froze and, glancing at the cart, reached down to cover something with a blanket. She pushed the cart to the side of the road and then left it to come meet me.

"What do you want?" Her eyes were hard.

Not quite the greeting I'd expected, but after my experience that morning, I was willing to give her a little leeway. I'd never walked in her shoes before. The closest thing to my being homeless had been the few hours after I signed the final papers selling the condo and before I bought the building in South Cove. "Just wondering if you were okay. Can I drop you somewhere?"

She shook her head. "I'm going down to the public beach to walk. I'm fine."

Her lie confused me, as the first entrance to the beach parking lot was a mile closer to town. She had two more miles to go before she'd reach another access.

"You sure? I don't mind." I thought about the mushroom and Swiss burger I had in the Jeep. My lunch. "You hungry? I bought too much food when I was in town and I'm going to have to throw it away."

"You have milk?" She appeared hopeful.

"No, a hamburger. But it has cheese. And I have a milk shake if you want it." I'd been saving the shake to savor with my burger at home.

Becky glanced back at the shopping cart she'd left next to the road. She watched a car until it had gone past the silver cart. "I guess that would be fine."

She waited for me to get the bag and cup out of the Jeep. When I held it out to her, she snatched it from my hands and started walking back to the cart. She turned back. "I don't need no ride. I'm fine."

I smiled and waved. "Okay, then. Stop by the shop next time you're in town and I'll give you that milk, my treat."

I returned to the Jeep and watched as Becky checked the contents of her shopping cart, then the bag I'd given her. Apparently both had passed muster because she started walking back toward town. As I passed her on the road, I waved, but she was looking straight ahead. "Stubborn to a tee," I muttered. Anyway, she was not my problem.

Yet still my heart ached for the lost little girl who Becky must have been once upon a time.

CHAPTER 22

My phone rang that Saturday morning, waking me up. Since my alarm went off at five, the caller had better have an emergency or they were going to be dead. Jackie and I had stayed up late at the house, making fifty felt stockings for Santa to give out, stuffed with candies. I'd campaigned for homemade stockings, and after finishing the first twenty had cursed my frugal nature. But by ten, they were done and stuffed in boxes in the back of my aunt's Escape. We'd unload as soon as I walked down to the shop.

Prep was done. Squinting at the clock, I had twenty minutes left to sleep. Once I told off the joker on the phone. "What?" I croaked.

"You pulled it off. I didn't think you could, but you did," a man's voice squeaked in my ear.

"Mayor?" I must be dreaming. The mayor never complimented anyone, much less me. This was just part of a crazy, worry-filled dream. And I knew I had one more holiday project to deal with before I could relax. Decorating the entire town of South Cove, thanks to the mayor's flaky wife.

"I told Tina you'd do it, but honestly, with your lack of social skills, I didn't think it was possible."

Yep, that was our mayor. Never let a chance for a good dig to go by. Emma nudged me with a wet nose. This wasn't a dream.

"What are you talking about?" I muttered, swinging my legs over the side of the bed. Now that Emma was awake, she wouldn't let me go back to sleep. Time to get the morning going, in her mind.

The mayor ignored my question. "I'll see you at the party."

The phone clicked in my ear, and I realized he was gone. "So what got into him?" I asked Emma, who translated my words into *Wanna go outside?* She ran to the bedroom door and waited for me.

"You're just like the rest of the people in my life, Emma," I said as we trudged down the stairs. I opened the door and she flew out to the porch, missing the steps and floating to the grass, where she charged to the back of the property, checking her domain. "You don't listen to me, either."

So far, my new throw pillows had stayed safe from Emma's attention. Then again, I hadn't left her alone in the house for the last week. I kept hoping she'd grow out of the chewing stage soon. I set the coffeemaker and curled up on one of the kitchen chairs, waiting for the brewing to finish. As I waited, I watched Emma out the window.

There would be no run today. Jackie wanted me and Toby at the shop as early as possible. My normal Saturday 7:00 a.m. opening shift would start at six, even though the kids weren't due until eleven. Toby had grudgingly agreed to be Santa. And the girl he was dating was coming in for the party with her daughter. I think he was more nervous about that than having fifty kids on his lap telling him what they wanted for Christmas.

I wondered about the mayor's call. Maybe he'd been talking about the party at the shop. Jackie had gotten a lot of press interest, and good press was one thing the mayor thrived on. In fact, a television crew was coming in to do a piece for their evening news segment called Good News Happenings. I hoped it gave the Bakerstown Children's Center a much-needed boost in donations and support. Diane deserved some good news.

I poured my coffee and checked the outside temperature before I went upstairs to get ready. The weather had warmed up after Monday's cold snap, and right now, it hovered in the midfifties. My mind hadn't been far from Becky all week. Tuesday I'd called social services, where a patient social worker had explained that even if the girl was under eighteen, she wasn't a priority, not with so many homeless kids and no room at the shelters. I hadn't seen her around town again, so maybe she'd decided to return home, wherever that might be. I sent up a quick prayer for her safety and climbed the stairs to my room.

As I walked into town, my mind was focused on the mental to-do list that hopefully would make this party a success. I'd already passed Diamond Lille's when I noticed something different. I turned around in a circle. The holiday decorations were up all over. The lampposts dripped with garland and tinsel. The power poles held red, white, and green flags, proclaiming South Cove Santa's one-stop shopping town. The animated mechanical carolers Darla had blown last year's decorating budget on were singing in City Hall's front yard. White lights hung off every building, and in the shop windows, people were finishing their holiday scenes. Christmas had come to South Cove. I felt like I was on the last page of a popular Christmas story.

In the empty building next to City Hall, a huge Christmas present sat under a silver tree that changed color every few seconds. The tag on the box turned into a sign that read *Vintage Duds—Do Not Open Until After New Year's Day*. We had a new business coming into South Cove. Whoever was opening the store was plugged in enough to know about the holiday tradition of decorating for the holidays. Probably a townie. I'd check in with Amy to see who the new owner was and invite them to the next Business-to-Business meeting.

Christmas carols were being piped in through the town's speaker system. I'd argued against the cost when Darla had proposed the system a few years ago, but now I couldn't imagine the holidays without the sound. The front door was already unlocked, and Jackie was carrying in a box of the stockings to set next to Santa's chair.

"I would have brought those in," I chided her. "Are there still boxes in the car?"

Jackie set the box behind the chair. "Nope, all of them are tucked back here. I've got the copies of *A Night Before Christmas* all stuffed with the free coupons, and I set out the carafes we can fill with coffee and hot chocolate right before the party starts."

I took in the décor. The bookstore section had been turned into Santa's study, and the dining room area resembled more of Santa's workshop. All in all, we were smack-dab in the middle of the North Pole rather than the central California coastline. I loved it.

I poured a cup of coffee for my aunt and myself, and we sat in the middle of the room, enjoying the silence. "I can't believe you pulled this off." I had put up Christmas decorations in the window last year, but nothing to this extent.

"It was no problem at all." Jackie smiled. "I had a lot of extra time on my hands this year."

"Well, you're in charge of holiday decorating for the rest of time. I never imagined it looking this good." I sipped my coffee. "Maybe you should tackle the house next week before we have Thanksgiving. I was planning on doing a floral centerpiece and calling it good."

Jackie frowned. "You're joking."

"About the centerpiece? No. I have way too much on my plate to decorate the house for one dinner. Besides, I never know whether to go all full-blown Christmas or actually go pilgrim Thanksgiving." I pushed aside worries about the dinner coming up next week. I would deal with it Monday when I went shopping for the turkey.

"Dear, I'll be over first thing tomorrow to plan out the decorations, and then by Monday night, you'll be ready." She frowned at me. "You have at least bought the dinner supplies, right?"

"I've ordered pies from Sadie. The rest is on my list for Monday. The books say I'm right on target."

A look of horror crossed my aunt's face. "The books are wrong."

Toby opened the front door with a weak, "Ho, ho, ho."

I was glad to see him, hoping his entrance would stop the Thanksgiving talk. I didn't want to know all the reasons I was behind the eight ball, again. At least Darla had come to her senses and handled the festival decorations. "You sound like an anemic Santa. Come on, put some *umph* into it."

Toby grinned. "Ho, ho, ho." The words came out stronger this time.

Jackie shook her head. "That will not do at all. Good thing I've already replaced you."

Toby and I exchanged glances. "Who's going to be Santa, then?" Jackie smiled.

Sasha and her daughter came into the shop. "Wow. South Cove gets into this Christmas thing, don't they?"

Her little girl ran over to the Christmas tree we'd set in the corner, a pile of fake presents positioned on top of a fake snow wrap. "Pretty," she murmured, watching the lights change color.

"Olivia, don't touch." Sasha focused on me. "Sorry, but the center wouldn't let her on the bus without a parent. Jackie asked me to come early. Is it okay that I brought her? I can sit her at a table and she'll play with her dolls."

"We're fine. It's a special day." I thought about Emma stuck at home. She would have loved seeing all the kids. Maybe next year, after she'd grown out of the puppy stage.

The morning flew by, and next thing I knew, it was minutes before the bus from the center was due to arrive. The Santa chair still sat empty. I dropped off the last two filled carafes and cornered my aunt, who was talking to Mary Simmons by the tree.

"Where's Santa?" I whispered, trying not to alert Olivia, who had been watching the chair for over an hour now.

Jackie smiled. "Stop fretting. Santa won't show before the kids. He's got lots to do, not just hang around here with us."

I saw Olivia's shoulders drop just a bit. I supposed she had been hoping for a little one-on-one time with the big guy before the busload of kids arrived. I pulled Jackie out of earshot of the little girl. "Toby agreed to be Santa, right?"

"Stop worrying." Jackie focused on a bus pulling up outside the shop. "Look, the kids are here."

Before I knew it, the shop was filled with jumping kids and their just-as-excited parents. I waved at Diane, who had brought one final child, whom I recognized as Angel, from the bus. I wove my way toward her.

"Sorry we're a little late. Angel's aunt dropped her off at the last minute, and I just couldn't say no." Diane laughed. "Yep, I'm all rules and regs until you push me. Then I'm just a softie."

"No worries, we're still waiting for the guest of honor." I pointed to Santa's empty chair. The door opened, and I saw Becky enter the shop, her eyes wide as she took in the crowd. *Welcome to my world*, I thought.

A few more people came in after Becky, but I'd started putting out trays of treats to keep the kids going on sugar while they waited. I saw Marie come in and sit next to the tree. Most of the town had arrived, along with the news crew. They were interviewing Mayor Baylor over by the empty Santa chair.

I raised my eyebrows at Jackie, but she waved me away with a universal don't-worry-about-it look. I returned to the counter and saw Becky standing behind the coffee bar, shoving something into her large tote bag. She caught my eye and shrugged. "I needed a napkin."

I turned my head out to the tables, checking to see if all the napkins had been used, but as I did, the front door opened.

"Ho, ho, ho," Santa's voice boomed through the noise of the party. As he passed through the crowd, little kids screamed in joy and surrounded him as he finally arrived at his chair. The news lady positioned herself next to his chair, pushing the mayor aside.

"Santa, what do you have to say to all of the kids watching you today?" She moved the microphone into Santa's face.

He gently pushed it down and answered her question. "Make sure you listen to your parents, brush your teeth, and be nice to those around you. And Santa's elves will make sure you are on the nice list." Santa held up the notebook next to his chair. "Now, if you'll excuse me, I've got some wishes to write down."

Toby escorted the mayor and the news crew away from Santa's chair, and the first child in line climbed on Santa's lap. Sasha had been given the honor of being Santa's helper, so Olivia was first in line. The little girl started listing off the gifts she wanted under her tree.

The next few minutes were a madhouse as the kids jostled for a place in line. Everyone was chatting and smiling. I saw Darla standing by the front window and waved.

When she reached me, I gave her a quick hug. "Thanks for taking over. I knew I could count on you."

"I'm not sure what you're talking about." Darla glanced around the room. "I didn't do any of this."

"No, I mean decorating South Cove. It looks wonderful." I watched as Santa gave Olivia her book and stocking. Something about the man looked familiar.

Darla held up her hands. "That wasn't me. I got the call last night just like everyone else."

I turned away from watching Santa and focused on Darla. "The call?"

"Mary Simmons got everyone in town out last night, and we worked until about nine getting everything done. She said the kids deserved the best day no matter what kind of problems we were having in town." Darla shrugged. "She was right. I was being a brat."

I found Mary in the crowd and smiled. "I would never have guessed she could rally the troops that way."

"She didn't call you or Jackie because she knew you had your hands full with this." Darla glanced around the room. "You did a great job. And Santa is amazing."

Marie and Becky huddled together near the door. Then they left together. Something in Marie's body language said she wasn't happy about leaving. My sixth sense for trouble started tingling. "Excuse me, I've got to check on something."

I motioned to Toby that I was heading out front and he nodded. At least someone would know I had left and when. Of course, Becky and Marie could be talking about the one thing they had in common: Ted. Somehow that didn't make me feel any better. By the time I'd reached the door, the street was empty. I stood listening to the Christmas music, but then I heard the cat yowling again. I wondered if I could find the animal this time. I went around the building and started up the stairs toward Josh's apartment. Maybe he could help me trap the cat. It had to be hungry.

When I got up to the landing, the empty apartment door was wide open. I heard raised voices and the cat still crying. I pushed open the door and saw Becky holding a baby in one arm and a knife pointed at Marie in the other. There was no cat. The sounds Josh and I had been hearing had been from a crying baby. Becky and Ted's baby. The one that, according to Matt, she'd given up in Oregon.

"Get out of here," Becky yelled at me. "You said I could have the milk."

Now I knew what she'd been after behind the counter. Milk for the baby. The baby couldn't be older than six months, but it looked so tiny wrapped in a dirty Disney blanket that had seen better days. I glanced at Marie, whose eyes were wide. "I know I did. I just wondered if you needed another hand. Taking care of a baby is hard work."

Becky's shoulders sagged. "That's why I told Ted we had to get married. A baby needs both parents to care for it." She jostled the child in her arms, and she cried harder at the motion. "All she does is cry. All the time. It's like she knows her daddy is dead."

Marie blurted, "You killed him, idiot. Of course he's dead. And the kid's probably better off."

"Don't say that." Becky stepped closer to Marie, and now I saw that the blade was actually pressing into Marie's chest. "He would have married me and been a terrific dad, but you kept getting in the way."

Marie swallowed hard, her voice less challenging now. "What are you talking about? I didn't want Ted. I moved across the country and faked my own death to get away from him. You could have had him with my blessing."

Tears filled Becky's eyes. "But he still wanted you. I wasn't pretty enough or good enough. I was just like Uncle David, in his eyes. You . . . you were his soul mate."

"Why don't we go down to the party and talk about this?" I raised my voice, hoping Josh would hear us. "We could have some coffee and you could feed the baby. She sounds hungry."

Becky narrowed her eyes at me. "So you can tell your boyfriend I killed Ted? I don't know why you haven't already told him. You saw me do it."

"What are you talking about? I didn't see anyone kill Ted." I glanced at Marie and saw that Becky had pulled the pressure on the knife back a little. Maybe if I rushed her she'd drop the knife trying to save the baby. And maybe not. I raised my voice even louder. "I found his body."

Becky shook her head. "I saw you walking down the street all Little Red Riding Hood with your basket of goodies. You looked right at me."

I thought about that day. Had I seen someone? I'd been so focused on trying to avoid talking to Ted, had I missed seeing Becky running away from the scene? "I didn't see you. And I didn't tell Greg. So why don't you just leave and we'll forget about this entire thing."

She laughed. "Right. And I don't understand why you're yelling.

That guy's down at the party with the rest of the town. You could scream your lungs out and no one would hear you right now." As if to illustrate her point, Becky tilted her head back and screamed. That was when I saw Marie jerk backward away from the knife and knew, it was now or never.

I bent my head down and aimed for Becky's middle, hoping I didn't hurt the baby. When I hit, I heard her grunt and the baby's cries escalate. They fell backward onto the floor. I followed. "Take the baby," I screamed at Marie, but I saw her run out the door. Turning my head back to Becky, I saw the glint of humor in her eyes.

"The girl's a runner. Always was, always will be. You've messed with me for the last time. Now you'll pay." I saw her hand with the knife move toward me, but the only move I had left was to protect the baby. I pushed the child away from me and the knife, then I heard Becky's cry.

Turning back, I saw a boot on her arm, holding back the hand with the knife. Toby's boot. I started breathing hard when I heard Greg's voice.

"Okay, tough guy, want to move so we can secure the scene?"

I scooted to the left and picked up the baby, holding her over my shoulder trying to comfort her. I watched as they pulled Becky up and, handcuffing her, led her out of the empty apartment.

"Do I want to ask why you're here?" Greg put his arm around me as we walked down the stairs.

The baby was starting to settle, but she smelled like she needed a diaper change along with a bath. I sighed. "I thought I heard a stray cat."

CHAPTER 23

The smell of turkey filled the house. I had people sitting on the porch talking, people in the living room chatting, and a few at the dining room table, helping with the last few touches before I'd host my first ever Thanksgiving dinner.

Greg came up behind me. "Let me know when it's time to carve the turkey. Jim and I are out back with Emma."

"Sure, leave all the heavy lifting to me." I kissed his cheek. "Sometimes I think you're avoiding me."

He shook his head. "Not funny. Especially after your run-in with Becky. I swear, Jill, sometimes I just want to lock you up in the house to try to keep you out of harm's way."

Jackie laughed. "Then harm would just come here. You have to realize our Jilly is a magnet for this kind of stuff by now."

"Thanks, guys, I appreciate your understanding." I took a sip of wine and smiled at the group. Amy was arranging olives and pickles into dishes at the table while Justin stood at her side, "helping." Helping in Justin terms seemed to mean tasting the contents of every jar he opened.

"Since you brought the subject up, what's going to happen to that poor baby?" Amy slapped Justin's hand away from a plate she'd just finished setting up.

Greg leaned against the fridge, a beer in hand. "The last I heard, Regina was taking the kid. She bought a house down the coast."

"Wait, she's staying in California?" I hadn't seen Regina since Saturday, when she dropped off a check for the children's center. When she'd realized the baby was her granddaughter, she'd taken off for Bakerstown and the hospital.

"I don't like spreading rumors, but since David told me this, I guess it's okay." Greg smiled. "Regina is divorcing the Boston husband, taking her Johnson money, and she and David are finally going to have that happily-ever-after."

"Wait, I thought the money was in the Hendricks family?" Jackie frowned. "Terrance never called me back. I'd forgotten about that. But I read that in one of the gossip magazines."

"Nope. Regina was the trust-fund baby. Apparently she grew tired of his women on the side and decided to give David a chance." Greg stared out the window. "Did you hear the other gossip that's going around?"

"Spill," I teased. Greg never gossiped, so I knew it had to be juicy.

"You know that new shop opening up next to City Hall?" He nodded toward the back porch.

"I don't understand. Jim's opening Vintage Duds?" I glanced out at his brother. Not a business I'd expected from the painter brother.

"Not Jim. He's just been hired to do the painting. The new owner wants a family discount." Greg sighed as dawning understanding filled my face. "Welcome to my nightmare."

Jackie contemplated the two of us. "I don't understand."

"I do." Amy giggled. At that moment, I hated my best friend. "Sherry is the new owner. She's moving back to South Cove."

Dinner was over and the first load of dishes was in the dishwasher when I finally crashed into a chair next to Greg. Jackie had left moments before with Josh, who'd been the shop's surprise Santa. She'd apparently forgiven him when she found out that Becky was the one she'd seen going up the stairs to the apartment level of Josh's building. And, of course, after she'd made him be Santa for the party.

I leaned into his chest and sighed. "Next time I get an idea like this, just shoot me."

He chuckled and took another bite of pumpkin pie. From my count, it was his third piece. "In my experiences with family dinners, it was a success. No one got hurt, no fires were set, and everyone left feeling the exact same way about everyone else as they did walking in the door."

"Jackie wants to set up a murder mystery dinner over at the winery with Darla in January. That makes me hate her just a bit more than I did this morning." I grabbed a fork and took a bite of Greg's pie.

"You love your aunt." Greg waved his fork around the room. "Besides, this is her element. Party planning."

I thought about Darla and the winery. It would be a perfect place to have a dinner and a mystery. We could bring in the drama club from the local high school.

"Jill?" Greg's voice broke through my thoughts. "Earth to Jill."

I blushed. "Busted. I guess I think it's a pretty good idea myself."

"Want to go watch some football?" He stood and held out a hand. And for the first time in my life, I didn't want to be anywhere else but right there, at home.

Love the Tourist Trap Mysteries?
Be sure to check out
GUIDEBOOK TO MURDER
and
MISSION TO MURDER
available now from eKensington

More Tourist Trap novels to come
in 2015!

Guidebook to Murder

When Jill Gardner's elderly friend, Miss Emily, calls in a fit of
pique, she already knows the city council is trying to force Emily to
sell her dilapidated old house. But Emily's gumption goes for
naught when she dies unexpectedly and leaves the house to Jill—
along with all of her problems . . . *and* her enemies. Convinced her
friend was murdered, Jill is finding the list of suspects longer than
the list of repairs needed on the house. But Jill is determined to
uncover the culprit—especially if it gets her closer to South Cove's
finest, Detective Greg King. Problem is, the killer knows she's on
the case—and is determined to close the book on Jill *permanently* . .
.

GUIDEBOOK TO
MURDER
A TOURIST TRAP MYSTERY
Dying for a visit...
LYNN CAHOON

Mission to Murder

Jill Gardner, proprietor of Coffee, Books, and More, has discovered that the old stone wall on her property might be a centuries-old mission worthy of being declared a landmark. But Craig Morgan, the obnoxious owner of South Cove's most popular tourist spot, The Castle, makes it his business to contest her claim. When Morgan is found murdered at The Castle shortly after a heated argument with Jill, even her detective boyfriend has to ask her for an alibi. Jill decides she must find the real murderer to clear her name. But when the killer comes for her, she'll need to jump from historic preservation to self-preservation . . .

MISSION TO MURDER

A TOURIST TRAP MYSTERY

Don't miss the
deadly landmark...

ANTIQUES ON THOMAS

CASTLE TOURS

LYNN CAHOON

Lynn Cahoon is a multi-published author. An Idaho native, her stories focus around the depth and experience of small town life and love. Lynn has been published in Chicken Soup anthologies, explored controversial stories for the confessional magazines, short stories in *Women's World*, and contemporary romantic fiction. Currently, she's living in a small historic town on the banks of the Mississippi River, where her imagination tends to wander. She lives with her husband and four fur babies.

Printed in the United States
by Baker & Taylor Publisher Services